LAST ONE IN

LAST ONE IN

NICHOLAS KULISH

AN ecco BOOK

HARPER PERENNIAL

NEW YORK • LONDON • TORONTO • SYDNEY

HARPER ● PERENNIAL

P.S.™ is a trademark of HarperCollins Publishers.

LAST ONE IN. Copyright © 2007 by Nicholas Kulish. All rights reserved. Printed in the United States of America. No part of this book may be used or reproduced in any manner whatsoever without written permission except in the case of brief quotations embodied in critical articles and reviews. For information address HarperCollins Publishers, 10 East 53rd Street, New York, NY 10022.

HarperCollins books may be purchased for educational, business, or sales promotional use. For information please write: Special Markets Department, HarperCollins Publishers, 10 East 53rd Street, New York, NY 10022.

FIRST EDITION

Designed by Daniel Lagin

Library of Congress Cataloging-in-Publication Data is available upon request.

ISBN: 978-0-06-118939-5
ISBN-10: 0-06-118939-1

07 08 09 10 11   DL/RRD   10 9 8 7 6 5 4 3 2 1

For my parents, Jon and Wilfrieda

LAST ONE IN

CHAPTER 1

A SMALL PART OF JIMMY WAS OFFENDED AT THE THOUGHT OF someone eating gold. It was a very small part, and shrinking dangerously fast. But it was still there.

"I ate gold," the young man shouted to anyone who cared to listen. "I ate gold." He was, Jimmy guessed, a prospective intern for one of the investment banks a five-minute cab ride down Greenwich Street. His face was flushed red from hours of drinking.

His group had been hard to miss when they entered, though Jimmy had been paying particular attention. He was seated alone and craned his neck with every cold gust of wind when the front door opened. Each time he searched the entrance for the couple who had kept him waiting for two hours. His disappointment grew, as did the glares from the white-capped sushi chef.

Jimmy's red snapper and spicy tuna rolls did not suffice as rent for this prime stool. Just as his inevitable ejection was nearing, he ordered a sorbet and with it a little more time. If it had not been late on a Monday night and the place already emptying out, they might have politely chucked him anyway.

The young men in suits were the loudest group in the dining area, tucked between the sawed-off trunks of real birch and ash trees and the angled two-by-fours posing as branches to complete the arboreal sculptures. There was an element of the theatrical at Nobu even when its most famous patrons were absent. The crowd played its part, and this particular group performed the chorus of boorish bankers admirably. The tasting menu—*omakase*—came for $80, $100, or $120 per person, with a sly "and up" tucked beside the last figure.

"What's 'and up'?" the one with the deep, resonating voice had asked. The waiter murmured something about resting safely in the chef's hands for the evening, but in practice "and up" resulted in tiny flakes of gold on your rock shrimp tempura.

"And up, bitch," the pale blond banker with the squeaky voice called out. "And up." There followed high fives and shots for all.

By the end of the meal, the young man seemed awestruck. His cheeks flamed a brighter red than the sake alone could generate. He appeared shocked to have ingested a precious metal. The kid would never see the check, which had probably run to several thousand dollars. It would come discreetly shrouded in a black cover, and a regular employee would dispatch it with an expense-account credit card, carried away before the heavy toll could cast a shadow over the boy's evening.

Jimmy reminded himself not to begrudge this kid his fun just because his own reasons for coming were more serious and his visit a complete disappointment. The restaurant was nine years old and predictable to regulars, but for a young man used to Bennigan's and Mom's meat loaf, entering this enchanted forest for a mix of Asian and Latino cuisines in Hollywood-on-Hudson glamour was still a heady trip. And Jimmy felt it was right, somehow, to shout when you ate gold. Things had really gone a step too far when that became mundane.

His own meager feast was the result of a formal warning he

had received about his often-royal expense account. That, combined with a spate of firings and rumblings about further layoffs, led Jimmy to pay for this excursion out of his own pocket. He felt like a fraud in his off-the-rack suit, ordering minuscule portions under the scrutiny of the fish swordsmen before him, with the high-rolling financial wizards at his back. Jimmy was only a few years older than the would-be intern and about the same age as the full-timers, clinging in fact to the final year of his twenties. But they wore bespoke suits and ordered without a care, and he sat in discount threads fretting over a seven-dollar sorbet.

Jimmy was there to observe and chronicle the romantic rendezvous of a C-list actress and a B-list actor. As was normal in such cases, the lesser's—that is, the C-lister's—publicist had tipped him off to the encounter. He might have been able to write it up without a personal appearance, but Jimmy took pride in his work. He wanted to confirm that it happened and fill out as many details as possible. If the newspaper gossip columns were to survive the Internet-delivered onslaught of rumors and anonymous reports, they would have to differentiate themselves through quality and consistency.

At that exact moment of pessimism—spoon clinking against the empty ceramic dish—Jimmy would have placed the odds of his career survival pretty low. He rose to perform his final and most demeaning stalling technique. Jimmy passed the wall of thousands of shiny black river rocks that shielded patrons' aesthetic experience from the intrusive reality of the waiters' station and headed for the bathroom.

It was unremarkable for a normal establishment, jarringly basic for a restaurant that seemed ready to host scenes from a Kurosawa movie. There were no bronze Buddhist basins, no waterfalls. All that set it apart was an audio loop of thunder-and-rain sound effects. The black door to one of the stalls was closed, and Jimmy was about to enter the vacant one when something in the gap between the stall door and the tile floor caught his eye.

They were cowboy boots of supple reddish leather. It was the kind of leather that somehow shone with class and expense even in a darkened bathroom stall, the way each slice of fish in the restaurant looked like it had a pedigree and the papers to prove it. Jimmy had a feeling about those boots even before he bent down slightly and saw small letters branded just below the ankle bone. The monogram read "KRB."

Jimmy had written about those boots when their owner received them. They were a gift from the director for playing the lead role in the cowboy movie *Ride Like the Lightning*. It was a blockbuster, like all of Kit's movies since, and the film where the actor met his future wife, Nora Escavel, who played the Mexican maid and love interest. It was nothing unusual to find Kit Burkins in a bathroom stall at Nobu. Jimmy had sat back to back with Denzel Washington the last time he was here. But between the sounds of rolling waves and crashing thunder he heard what he thought sounded like groans.

He crouched lower. Habit had inured him to the baser requirements of his profession. Pangs of conscience struck at night in bed, not in these moments of rising adrenaline. So much of Jimmy's work was orchestrated, an alternative form of publicity like the botched event that had brought him to Nobu that night. A genuine scoop was rare, as it was in any form of journalism. The kind that would be followed by every publication in the country short of *National Geographic*, selling out your own paper at every newsstand in the city, might happen just once in a career. When Jimmy saw a second pair of feet, these in high heels, descend into view that night, he knew he had stumbled across just such a coup.

Nora Escavel-Burkins had no dragon tattoo on her ankle, but one of the restaurant's fetching young hostesses did. Jimmy took the notebook and pen from the inside pocket of his jacket and began to scribble hurried observations. The stall started to shake, and so did his writing hand.

CHAPTER 2

JIMMY AND HIS BOSS, TIM SUSKIND, SAT UNDERNEATH THE LARGE plate-glass windows of Curt Ellison's office, shielded from view by dusty white venetian blinds. They could hear the *Daily Herald* managing editor's deep, muffled yelling from inside. Jimmy thought the glass was flexing outward from the force of each shout. It was hardly the celebration he had awaited that morning.

"Those little orphan bastards must be eating like kings, don't you think?" Tim asked. Jimmy didn't answer. "How far do you think a dollar goes in Botswana anyway?"

"Further than here," Jimmy said, trying not to engage his boss.

"Ten thousand dollars for a pair of boots," Tim resumed. He was agitated but feigning indifference. It was part of his new cool persona, which included the hip clear-framed glasses and Steve Madden business casual sneakers he insisted on wearing. The shoes and glasses weren't nearly as bad as the slim-fit suit and fauxhawk hairdo Tim had adopted after their "David Beckham: Style Icon" spread. What looked good on an English soccer star did not necessarily transfer well onto a forty-year-old with a taste for liquor and an aversion to exercise. "Who has ten grand for a pair of boots? Seriously, Jimmy, who?"

"I guess the guy in the stall at Nobu," Jimmy said. He wished Tim would just shut up and let him feel guilty in silence. Ellison would make them miserable enough shortly.

"He must love the orphans in Botswana," Tim said. "What a charitable fellow. It was also charitable of him not to sue us like Kit Burkins."

"Well, Tim, I suppose we technically didn't libel him, since his name wasn't in the paper."

"Funny, that, seeing as he was the one actually fucking the hostess in—" Ellison's secretary, Cheryl, cleared her throat sharply. She was the older, executive-assistant type with the steel-wool perm—not to be trifled with. Tim leaned toward Jimmy and whispered, "A simple search of the clips was all it took to find the Botswana Boys' Home charity auction."

"You're the one who couldn't wait," Jimmy shot back. "I asked you to hold it for a day, but you said it was 'too hot, burning hot.' The competition would get it if we waited."

"Don't go trying to confuse the matter," Tim said. "This was your scoop, and it's rotten. Now we're going to get fired."

"Keep your designer briefs on," Jimmy said, loudly enough that Cheryl couldn't restrain herself from looking over at them again. "We're not getting fired. We're in the woodshed for a quick lashing, and that's it."

"This lawsuit isn't going away. Kit Burkins's marriage is on the rocks, he's on an image makeover kick, and you claim he's fucking some waitress in New York—sorry, Cheryl—when he's on location in Prague. Ellison's going to fire us," Tim added quietly.

"He's not going to fire us," Jimmy said. "We get sued every other month."

"Did you miss the purge in Sports?" Tim asked. "Or was that during your trip to Jamaica?"

"No," Jimmy said. "I was here."

"We have to change the DNA of the paper to an integrated multiplatform hard-news environment," Tim recited from a recent corporate memo. "They didn't bring in a heavy hitter from the *Times* to spruce up the funnies. They brought Ellison in for a reason," Tim continued, in the patronizing tone he never used when he wanted free passes to movie screenings or his name on the guest list at a club when his wife and the girls were away. "Those of us who still have one foot in the real world have been forced to recognize certain changes that are going on beyond the velvet rope. Have you noticed the little flags in the corner of the television screen, or the ominous trumpet music that CNN uses to break for commercial?"

"No."

"Weapons of mass destruction? Clouds of poison gas? Impending war?"

"They haven't mentioned it on *E!*" Jimmy said, only half sarcastically.

"The pendulum is swinging back, and we're on the wrong side. The light stuff is on the Internet. Newspapers are all about news again. Why didn't I see it coming when there was still time to get back to the news side?" Tim asked himself.

"It'll be okay," Jimmy said.

"I'm not hard news," Tim said glumly, his anger wilting into resignation. "You aren't hard news," he added, looking over at Jimmy. "Neither of us is hard news. We're entertainment. We're soft features. I bet we were already on the chopping block, just like those guys in Sports, and you just gave him the excuse he needed."

"The *Daily Herald* is a tabloid, Tim," Jimmy said. "We need gossip. We need lifestyle. So they trimmed Sports back a little? We're their bread and butter. And you hated being on the Metro desk,"

Jimmy reminded him. "You said the hours were shit and the parties were terrible."

"That was before they hired Ellison. You pop up at the wrong time, and you get your head cut off." As he said this, Tim made a swift chopping motion with his right hand. "Maybe we could have found jobs at Page Six if you hadn't pulled the 'eats, shoots and leaves' with what's-her-name, the one with the tits," Tim said.

"Don't be crude about Isabel," Jimmy said. "She's a charming, intelligent, and, incidentally, well-built young lady. Things just didn't work out between us." He had not been thinking about his career or the possibility that he would be fired while he was seducing his competitor. He suspected that Tim would have, but Tim was older and savvier. Until now he had always seemed to land on his feet. Jimmy had none of Tim's career sense.

"Mr. Ellison will see you now," Cheryl told them. Jimmy nodded and stood up. He paused before grasping the handle, taking a breath before entering the office of the imperial new managing editor, this colossal bastard who had fired dozens of his colleagues and dominated the newsroom with his high-decibel tirades and desk-rattling fist thumps.

Ellison sat behind an imposing wood partner's desk, his wide bald head gleaming with sweat. "Suskind." He nodded toward Tim.

"Good to see you, Mr. Ellison," Tim mumbled.

"What an unfortunate way for us to meet, Mr. Stephens," he said, rising and offering Jimmy his hand.

"I hope it won't be the last time," Jimmy said. Ellison's grip was strong, but not flagrantly so.

"What Jimmy means . . . It's ridiculous. What he's tr-trying to say," Tim stammered, "is that he's afraid he might get fired over this."

"That was my plan, yes," Ellison said evenly.

"Plan like serious plan?" Tim asked. "Planned out? Imminent?"

"I don't care for your kind of journalism," Ellison said. "In my opinion, there's no place for it in a real newspaper, and that includes the revamped *Daily Herald*. But . . ." He cocked his head and stared hard at Jimmy, as if taking his rough measure. He seemed completely uninterested in Tim. "It's possible you could help me out of a tight spot, and I'd consider exchanging favors." His eyelids looked heavy with exhaustion and skepticism, as though he found it very unlikely indeed.

"I'm—I'm happy to help if I can." Jimmy's voice was a narrow whine. He didn't understand whether he was fired or not. Panic began to set in. Jimmy felt unsteady in his chair, even though it wasn't wobbling. He gripped the seat tightly with both hands.

"I wanted to talk to you about—mm—a trip," Ellison said.

"I've actually got a couple on my schedule right now," Jimmy said, trying to sound cool even as he felt the sweat seeping out of his pores. "There's the Oscars, Cancun for spring break. Then Cannes . . ."

"Those might have to wait," Ellison said. "This will be fun too. Warm weather. Sand."

"I like that," Jimmy said. "Hawaii?"

"A little more—mm—exotic."

"Fiji?" Jimmy offered.

"Kuwait," Ellison said. Jimmy was vaguely aware of Kuwait, but couldn't have located it on a map if asked, couldn't think of a single Kuwaiti celebrity. Brad Pitt was filming a Trojan War movie somewhere in the vicinity. "And Iraq."

"They're doing a whole 'war thing' over there, right?" Jimmy laughed, putting the "war thing" in quotes with his fingers. Then he had the unpleasant realization that neither of the other two men in the room was laughing with him. "They are, right?"

"We are expecting a war thing," Ellison said. "Yes."

"You need a fun angle on that or something? What to wear in the desert, maybe? But, I mean, there's no fashion with the, like, Army guys."

"Isn't there?" Ellison asked.

"You know," Jimmy said. "They all wear the same thing."

"Uniforms," Tim obliged.

"Of course. Uniforms," Jimmy agreed. It was a word he could come up with instantly to describe a de rigueur outfit at the soft opening of a club, somehow absent in context. "That doesn't sound like my kind of thing."

"You're right. You'd be a real journalist," Ellison said. "Covering real news."

"Why me?" Jimmy asked. "There are fifty guys out there whose wet dream must—pardon me, who would step on their grandmothers to call themselves war correspondents. They said I wasn't good enough to do Metro, and now you want me in a war? I've got to be somewhere behind your secretary on that list."

"If it's really weighing on you, I can assure you that you were far from my first choice," Ellison said. "The *Daily Herald* has a Baghdad correspondent stuck in Jordan without a visa." Jimmy must have appeared confused, because he added, "That is like having a Hollywood correspondent in Arizona. And we have a reporter on an aircraft carrier in the Gulf, from which vantage he will be able to watch planes take off and land. Dramatic stuff for our readers."

"No doubt," Jimmy agreed.

"We have a bright young reporter assigned to the 101st Airborne, a distinguished unit known for daring helicopter assaults and some of the most vicious, nasty fighting assignments the brass in Washington can devise." Ellison's face was beginning to change colors, the veins pressing outward. "Unless, like our correspondent, you have been assigned to their rearguard water purification unit."

"That seems pretty important for a desert war, though." Jimmy tried to console him. " 'Water, mother of life, nectar of the desert,' and so forth. 'Without it, our soldiers wither and die before the fight. With it—' "

"As your very presence in this office reminds me, we are not the *Times* or the *Washington Post*. Those organizations, what they call the serious outfits—though they somehow manage to include television in that—are the ones with the plum assignments. Not us. When your newspaper comes wrapped in a lottery advertisement"—he was huffing audibly, his bald pate turning a startling scarlet—"or features a close-up of a female celebrity's derriere on the front page," he continued, growing louder, "when your readers are torn between buying your newspaper or tossing that stray quarter to a homeless person, in these instances, the Pentagon planners give you one worthwhile vantage point from which to cover the invasion." As worried as Jimmy was about his job and his life, he wondered for a moment if Ellison might not be on the verge of a stroke. "Our sole embed with the United States Marine Corps is James E. Stephens's spot."

"Of course, the great man himself," Jimmy said. "Not very personable around the office, but the best we have, professionally speaking."

"James has covered eighteen armed conflicts on four continents with great distinction and come away more or less unscathed. This morning, however, Eighth Avenue proved somehow more dangerous—"

"Mugger?" Jimmy interrupted.

"Delivery truck," Ellison answered. "James was jaywalking. A tragic accident."

"Is he—" Jimmy began to ask uncomfortably.

"He's alive. With a broken pelvis. It will be months before he can walk again, by which time I expect American flags will be flying over Baghdad."

"I still don't see why you would want me to—" Jimmy started to say.

"The Pentagon, Mr. Stephens, is an inflexible organization. They are very rules-bound. So when they say 'no substitutions' once our list of embedded reporters is finalized, they mean 'no substitutions.'" The faraway look in Ellison's eyes and the snarling twist of his upper lip suggested to Jimmy that the managing editor was reliving a particularly unpleasant exchange with a Pentagon bureaucrat. "The *Daily Herald* cannot and will not miss this war." He regained his focus, fixing Jimmy with a fierce look that brooked no argument. "Therefore, I need a James Stephens." He paused and then asked, "You have a passport? And the name James Stephens is on that passport?"

"Yes," Jimmy said.

"Then it's within your power to save your job." He glanced over at Tim. "And his, too."

"It wouldn't be so bad," Tim chimed in, quietly, tentatively.

"Well," Jimmy said, "I would rather work on my résumé than die. I'm weird like that." He began to stand up but felt Tim grab his wrist.

"Jimmy," Tim hissed. "Come on. This could be great for your career." Jimmy jerked his arm away. Turning to Ellison, Tim added, "I hadn't heard about the tragedy on Eighth Avenue, but if I had, Jimmy would have been the first person I turned to. A tenacious newshound, the kind of—"

"If you don't accept the assignment," Ellison continued, without so much as a nod to Tim's sycophancy, "you can walk out of here in ten minutes with a cardboard box." He reached across the desk and handed Jimmy a British Airways envelope. He opened it.

The name on the ticket read James Stephens. The departure time was that evening. There was no ticket back to New York, just a notation that it was an open return. "The president could decide to start this war at any moment. Becky Hardin will be the *Daily Herald* photographer on assignment. She'll get you up to speed. Meet her at Newark Airport." Jimmy looked at him, trying to beseech him with his eyes to relent. Ellison stared back, head at a thoughtful tilt, looking him straight in the eye, and said, "Now get the fuck out of my office. Please."

Jimmy stood up. He hadn't agreed or refused to go, but walked out with the ticket in his hand. Tim followed close behind. They crossed the newsroom back toward their desks in Arts & Lifestyle. For such a large open space, almost one entire floor of their office building, it could feel powerfully claustrophobic, constricted by the tight mazelike arrangement of the desks and recent newspapers, pictures of fighter jets and battleships gracing the pages, maps with bold red arrows piercing tan terrain around them.

It seemed now as though the impending war Jimmy had successfully ignored was everywhere. The televisions bolted overhead were filled with shots from the previous conflict, tanks rolling across the desert and blurry green missile-cam explosions, all surrounded by the patriotic graphics, eagles in sharp-beaked profile and digital star-spangled banners undulating in virtual winds. The new batch of American soldiers, in their desert camouflage uniforms, waved hello to their mothers and showed off the gleaming gear they'd been polishing for months in anticipation. Jimmy couldn't see it, couldn't picture himself out there, too, standing among them, preparing for war.

"I mean it. No one gets laid like a war correspondent," Tim said for the third time. Jimmy had not spoken for a good fifteen minutes. Every time he began to say something, he realized it was going to sound cowardly and shut his mouth again. He touched his chest and tried to imagine a bullet piercing it, blood pouring out like vintage cabernet from an overturned bottle. Hadn't Saddam Hussein used reporters as shields to ward off missile attacks during the Gulf War? Jimmy pictured himself tied to a rooftop as bombs screamed down from the sky, his death assured. There were kidnappings to worry about, beheadings.

"Remind Ellison that you worked in Metro," Jimmy said at last. "He might give you your job back instead of shit-canning you along with me."

"Are you just afraid?" Tim asked. "Because the United States military is unstoppable. You're safer with them than you are crossing the street. Just look at what happened to James Stephens. Safer with them than you are right here."

"If it's so safe, you can go," Jimmy said. "I'll give you my passport."

"How are you going to make ends meet without this job?" Tim persisted.

"There are other jobs," Jimmy said. "I can wait tables, anything. As long as it doesn't involve getting shot at."

"I'm not just talking about your salary. You live on your expense account."

"I don't *live* on my expense account," Jimmy said. He considered the really sharp D&G velvet jacket he had purchased—for work events, of course—using the corporate credit card. Jimmy's vacations were all "work-related," and for each one he found an excuse to bump himself up to first class. Then there was his regular table at Elaine's.

"Three meals a day? Your cell phone? Your drinks? Your dry cleaning? What aren't we paying for?" Tim asked.

"Let me think," Jimmy said. "My rent?"

"Anything else?"

"Probably," he said after a long pause. "But nothing springs to mind."

"Then there are the lawyers," Tim said.

"What lawyers?" Jimmy asked.

"Million-dollar lawsuit?" Tim reminded him. "If you're fired, the *Herald* no longer indemnifies you against libel, damages … you could be singly and wholly responsible for whatever a jury might award to the maligned Mr. Kit Burkins. If there's anything left after the lawyers wring you dry."

"Your concern for my well-being is touching, Tim," Jimmy said, his patience exhausted and his temper rising. "Saving me from bankruptcy by getting me killed. What a pal."

"I just think you should consider—"

"Be honest, Tim," Jimmy said acidly. "This is about saving your job."

"Fine. I admit it," he said. "I might as well call Tanya now and tell her to pull the girls out of school."

"Out of school?" Jimmy asked.

"I can't afford Spence without this job," Tim said. "Maybe I can at least get a prorated refund."

"Let's not go overboard," Jimmy said. "Things'll work out."

"Things don't work themselves out," he answered. "I don't even know how I'll make my next mortgage payment." Tim looked down at his fancy shoes, trying to hide an utterly forlorn look, maybe even welling tears, with a hand at his brow.

For all Jimmy's righteous indignation over the guilt trip Tim had laid on him, Tim was, in fact, Jimmy's benefactor, had given him his second chance at the paper after Jimmy had been banished to the night shift, putting together late-edition box scores and stock charts and proofreading the paper until three in the morning. Dredging nightclubs for drunken actors and morally compromised debutantes seemed the pinnacle of excitement by comparison, and Jimmy had proved to have a talent for it. How did he repay Tim's kindness and confidence? He filed an erroneous story that got Tim fired.

"You'll find something," Jimmy said quietly. It felt so inadequate.

"Yeah, and even if I do..." Tim said, trailing off. They both knew that with the seismic shifts in print media and the slave wages at the snarky Web sites, Tim would pull down half of what he needed to support his family.

Somehow it was easier for Jimmy to lose his own job than to take the blame for someone else's firing. A feeling that rarely troubled Jimmy settled over him. It was shame. He was ashamed to have played a part in his boss's misery, ashamed that it was within his power to rescue Tim and he wouldn't. At his parents' house, they barely acknowledged what Jimmy did for a living. If he covered a war, they might be willing to read what he wrote, put an article up on the refrigerator, like the first few Metro pieces he had written before the incident so many years before. Maybe this was an opportunity to be a real reporter, the kind who interviewed the president or at least the mayor. Jimmy felt a surge of pride in anticipation of what he could become. "No one's losing his job today," he announced.

"Seriously?" Tim asked. Jimmy nodded, chin thrust out resolutely. "My golden boy," Tim said with a grateful smile. "My sweet and low-down columnist, to the rescue again." Jimmy opened up the British Airways envelope and checked the tiny letters stamped on the ticket. He had eight hours to get to Newark, with a detour through Brooklyn to pick up his stuff. It was more time than he wanted to mull it over.

CHAPTER 3

THE AIRPORT IN KUWAIT CITY WAS THE COLOR OF TAR-STAINED TEETH.
It must have been white at some point, probably in the 1970s from
the look of the decor, but since then the gaggles of chain-smoking
Arabs had cured it to a shade of yellow most people associate only
with disease. Soldiers in khaki and olive uniforms patrolled the
airport with machine guns slung over their shoulders but uninterested looks on their faces. They grew vigorous and attentive only
when they stopped to light fresh cigarettes and argue with local
civilians in red-checkered headdresses.

Jimmy waited in the passport-control line with Becky Hardin, the *Daily Herald* photographer who had met him twenty-four
hours and three connections earlier at Newark International Airport. Her first reaction upon seeing Jimmy had been to roll her
eyes. After looking him over again, in his Hugo Boss suit, holding
the flak jacket she had brought him, her verdict had been succinct:
"Disaster."

She was a tough little creature, hewn rather than molded,
jerky-like strips of muscle on her forearms poking out from under
her rolled-up sleeves. Her large camping pack was almost as tall as
she was and twice as wide, but he never doubted that she would

throw it over one shoulder with ease and move out. Not walk, but move out, like they said in the movies. She looked like a park ranger in her khaki cargoes and gray fleece jacket. Underneath the mean exterior she could have been pretty, if it had ranked as a priority. To Jimmy's eyes she wasn't making the effort. Her tan was harsh, a wind-bitten brown with none of the smoothness of the Meatpacking District girls' winter regimen of misting and phosphorus-coated fluorescent tubes.

"You should be excited," she told him. "Grateful. Most people never get to visit the Middle East. A lot never even get to go overseas. You're seeing the world on the *Herald*'s dime."

"I'll tell you something about foreign lands," Jimmy said. "I'm supposed to be in Cancun in two weeks. On the *Herald*'s dime. But with college girls, bikinis, body shots..." A trio of Muslim women shuffled by covered in head-to-toe black robes. "... the flexible inhibitions of Spring Break?"

"Peroxide, silicone, collagen, date rape," Becky shot back. It turned out she had strong opinions about Spring Break and female exploitation. Her lecture went uninterrupted right up to the moment the passport inspector in his little booth handed Jimmy's passport back to him.

"No," the inspector said.

"I'm sorry?" Jimmy asked.

"No visa. No Kuwait," the inspector answered. "Next," he said to Becky.

"You know, I'm not entirely dissatisfied with this turn of events," Jimmy confided in the inspector, who shook his head as if to say he did not understand.

"Invalid," the inspector continued despite the lack of resistance. "No entry."

"We'll see about that," Becky snapped, grabbing Jimmy's passport and marching toward a nearby office with a sign that read

"Visa and Immigration" in English. Jimmy followed reluctantly behind her.

The atmosphere in the office was far too civilized for a workplace. Seven men, each with a military-style uniform more ornate and decorated than the next, sipped tea out of clear cups with plastic handles. All were smoking, but only one blew exceptionally even smoke rings into the air at a leisurely pace. As he exhaled the remaining smoke through his nostrils, he glanced briefly in their direction. The man must have seen Becky and Jimmy standing at the counter awaiting help, but reloaded with another deep puff and returned to shaping his smoke rings.

They waited for several minutes as the visa officials sipped and chatted. Finally the junior one, with a mere seven ribbons on his chest, probably one for each person he had served since taking the job several years before, came over and examined Jimmy's passport. "Wrong number," he said, and without another word returned to his chair, his tea, and his cigarette.

"I would like to speak to your supervisor," Becky said. There was quite a wait for the next official, as there was for each one after him. Over the course of an hour, the seven men slowly stood and ambled over to the counter, one at a time, to tell them that Jimmy's visa was invalid.

"Wrong number," the one who had been blowing smoke rings said. He was the most decorated of the group, with sandwich boards on his shoulders and more medals and stars than an American general in a Hollywood movie, despite the fact that he was night-shift chief at the passport control office. He looked exasperated as he repeated, pointing first at Jimmy's papers and then at Jimmy himself, "This is wrong visa, wrong passport, cannot enter Kuwait."

Becky knew that, of course, because she had glued the piece of paper onto an empty page in Jimmy's passport herself at the

Newark Airport TGI Friday's. She even had admitted to lifting it out of the first Mr. Stephens's passport too. As good a job as she had done, the bluish color of the paper and the regular placement of tiny Kuwaiti seals—the outstretched wings of a bird supporting a body of water that in turn bore an offshore oil rig—made changing the passport number impossible on such short notice. Jimmy didn't doubt that she could have done it with enough time and the right equipment. Becky had hoped they wouldn't notice.

The facts did not appear to discourage her from arguing passionately on Jimmy's behalf. "Why the hell do you even care? He's going with the American military. Not your problem," she said. The senior official was as skeptical as she was zealous. But she and Jimmy appeared to be winning by attrition. Every few seconds the official would glance longingly back at the genial conversation his colleagues were having.

"Of course," he muttered.

"We paid your processing service a lot of money to prepare our documents," Becky lied. "You can call them and ask them about the mix-up if you have to, but this is not our fault. We were certified by the consul general in New York, personally." This argument appeared to sway the official far less than the small television produced by one of his colleagues, placed on a desk and switched on to a soccer match. "We're not leaving," Becky said firmly. "We are here on important business with the U.S. military. Should I call the ambassador? Do you want him coming down here tonight?"

"Please," the official said. "It is incorrect. There is nothing we can do."

"There must be something you can do," Becky said. The official turned and barked an order at what appeared to be his second in command, based on quantity of decoration. The man sifted through the loose papers in a desk drawer and shook his head. The supervisor asked him something else, and the second in command went back through the drawer again, more slowly this time, and finally produced a slip of paper. The boss handed Jimmy's passport over to him, and he pasted the sheet into it. He pounded it with two different stamps, then handed it over to Becky. She looked it over, nodding approvingly.

"Welcome to Kuwait," the official said, seemingly exhausted from the exertion of doing his job. "Please go now."

"Thank you for your assistance," she said. As they left the office, she handed Jimmy his passport back. "Congratulations," she said. "You're a Kuwaiti immigrant."

"What do you mean?" Jimmy asked.

"I guess it's all they had," Becky answered. "I have a one-month travel visa, but you, my friend, have a one-year residency permit."

"I can only hope it doesn't come in handy," Jimmy said. "I'd like to keep my stay as short as possible."

"Well, you're lucky you aren't spending the war in a Kuwaiti prison," she said as they headed for the customs line.

"That's a matter of opinion, isn't it?" Jimmy said.

"More a matter of law, really," Becky said.

"Would you feel bad if I went to jail for the fraud or, you know, forgery you actually committed?" Jimmy asked her.

"I think in that case I'd be celebrating my own close call," she said with a rueful laugh.

"All for one and one for all?" Jimmy asked as his suitcase went through the X-ray machine. He was glad he hadn't picked up the duty-free alcohol he'd considered trying to smuggle into the country.

"Welcome to the real world, Stephens," Becky answered as they cleared customs. They found the hotel car service, loaded their bags, and didn't speak all the way to the Kuwait Hilton. The orange streetlights and the curling concrete ramps could have been pieces of the puzzle that formed any suburban ring in America. Jimmy pretended they were.

With the door closed and the curtains drawn, it was almost dark in the room. Jimmy crawled out from under the white comforter. He stretched and sauntered over to the window. Pulling the curtains open, he was blinded for a moment by the bright midday light. Once his eyes adjusted, he saw a man cutting a lazy breaststroke in a blue pool. Beyond him was a full oceanfront view, complete with palm trees and a sand beach.

"Oh, thank God," Jimmy said. "Oh, thank God for Mexico." He had had a terrible dream. The air-conditioning made it slightly chilly in nothing but his silk boxers. He turned back toward the warm comforter, looking forward to several more hours of sleep before setting off for a cocktail in a quaint cabana. There, on the floor by the door to his room, was a complimentary newspaper. At the top, the masthead clearly said *Arab Times*.

Jimmy laughed a hysterical laugh, but felt more like crying. He exhaled, then sat down on the bed with his head in his hands. Then he stood up and walked to the mahogany door of the closet and opened it. Black rubber gloves, a gas mask, and his helmet and vest were laid out beside the hotel's ironing board. It was difficult to accept that this was his closet and these were actually his belongings, but there they were.

And yet he had to admit that trying on the bulletproof vest made him feel giddy. He undid the straps and slipped the tan vest over his head. Once it was fastened snugly around his torso he got a good look at the new, militarized version of Jimmy. He sucked in his gut, then checked in the mirror. His chest looked big and hard, his shoulders somehow broader. It reminded him of childhood soldier games, playing "Red Dawn" in the woods behind his house with his friends, hunting imaginary Communist invaders with sticks. There was another knock at the door.

"Occupied," he called to the maid as he flexed for the mirror. The knocking continued. "Privacy, please." There was muffled yelling through the door. Jimmy moved to send her on her way and hang the Do Not Disturb sign on the handle. Instead he found Becky waiting for him on the other side. "Oh. It's you."

She had a large bag at her feet, which she picked up when the door opened. "Good morning to you too, sunshine," she said, staring at his boxers-and-vest ensemble. "That's cute, really it is." She reached up with her free hand and knocked on the front plate of his vest, then slipped past into the room as he stood facing the hallway. He turned and followed her. "Listen, Rocky, there's a lot to do if you're going to be ready for the big fight." She looked him up and down, stopping to stare at the boxers. "Quite a lot to do."

"Maybe breakfast?" He walked to the closet and fished a T-shirt out of his bag.

"I already had mine, thanks," she said as he stripped off the vest, not bothering to avert her eyes as he changed. "You don't have time. If the war started tomorrow, you would be shit out of luck, you follow? So let's just take care of business."

"Is the war starting tomorrow?" Jimmy asked.

"Jimmy," she said. "You never know for sure when a war is going to start. One side usually—maybe not always, but usually—wants to surprise the other side. There are hints, clues, if you will: troops massing at the borders, cruise missiles screaming overhead."

"Yeah, but, I mean, are we leaving today?" Jimmy asked.

"They haven't told us, Jimmy. But everyone knows we need to be in Baghdad before it gets too hot. Beyond that, our job is to be ready whenever it starts. You need gear. You need a little training. And then you'll wait. Hurry up and wait is practically the military's motto."

"I thought it was 'To protect and serve.'"

"I'm pretty sure that's the police," Becky answered. As Jimmy slipped into a pair of pants, Becky finally averted her eyes and began unpacking the bag on Jimmy's desk. She called out the name of each object as she set it down—satellite phone, backup satellite phone, backup satellite phone software, laptop, connection cords and chargers. "Do you know what this is?" she said, holding up a silver box with red and black clips attached.

"Do you really have to ask?" he said.

"This is your inverter. See, there are no power outlets in war. You have to charge off a car battery, or in this case probably a Humvee." She stopped. Jimmy must have looked shocked. "Did you think there was going to be electricity and other fine amenities? Air-conditioning? Maybe mobile shower units to keep you fresh on the road to Baghdad? It's not that kind of war, pumpkin."

"Hold me," Jimmy said.

"I don't have time for your jokes," she said.

"I'm not kidding," he said.

She furrowed her brow, with a finger to her lips and a smile behind it. "Jimmy, ignoring the *Herald* for a second, my life—my war—would go much more smoothly if I just killed you right now and paid the maids to hide your body, got it?"

"Okay," he said. She seemed a hint too serious when she said it.

She walked toward him with a yellow piece of paper from a legal pad. "This is your shopping list." He glanced down at the list, learning that he needed batteries, foot powder, a sleeping bag, field bandages, and goggles, just for a start. The list filled the entire page. He looked back at Becky with incomprehension. "Yes, you need all of it, sweets."

"Maybe a drink first?" Jimmy asked.

"Most of the people running around this hotel, whether they look like it or not, know how to survive in a hostile environment. If they haven't covered wars already, and most of them have, they've been trained by former Navy SEALs, British SAS, you name it. What you have is a few days of my advice, my sage wisdom. That makes me the only thing standing between you and the realization of the death and dismemberment clause in your insurance contract."

"What's first on the agenda?" Jimmy asked.

Becky smiled even bigger and patted him on the cheek. "There we go. Now, we both know you shouldn't be here. It's, like, two in the morning in New York, and you should be having drinks at some lounge with some tart. I know. But you're here, so let's just do this. And put some shoes on, for God's sake." He didn't much like following orders, but he had no clue how to prepare for a war. In the end, he did exactly as she said, first the shoes and then the shopping. When the call came, he wanted to be ready. He was a war correspondent, after all. He had to be prepared for anything.

CHAPTER 4

"THEY WILL CUT OFF YOUR DICK AND EAT IT FOR LUNCH, THE fedayeen.

"If they catch you in the morning, maybe even for breakfast."

"What's a fedayeen?" Jimmy asked.

"They know you are American. If you aren't a soldier, they think you're CIA. They kill you the same."

"My vest says 'Press' on it," Jimmy said.

"In fucking Arabic?"

"No," he admitted.

Jimmy sat in a cloud of smoke in the farthest corner of the patio, eating pancakes with chocolate syrup as the three French photographers took him on a tour of what would happen to him in the desert at the hands of Iraqis. They were the first unilaterals he had met. That meant they were driving into the war without military escorts, in their own SUVs. A light truck was about the only piece of gear he hadn't bought at Becky's instruction the day before. As dangerous as it sounded the photographers' way, they predicted a significant amount of disaster for Jimmy even with the Marines.

"Get someone to write it for you."

"Yes. Big letters."

"But make sure to check. They may just write 'American pig.' "

"It's true. They might."

"That's what I would do."

They relished their descriptions of calamity so much that Jimmy felt this would have been their conversation whether he was there or not. The vehement participation of the young one, who was the fat one's assistant, suggested that the junior member of the team had been the most recent target. Helicopter decapitations, maiming from mines, and the sick whistling of incoming mortars sounded almost pleasant, cloaked in French accents and the exhaust of several Gitanes. One smoldered unattended, though each of the three photographers had one in hand.

It felt good to wake up early, do a few push-ups, and head out to the tennis courts for gas-mask training. The light breeze had tickled the palm trees as they practiced donning the masks in seven seconds. "Seven seconds or you . . . are . . . dead," the instructor had screamed, but it still felt like a game. Only when they had to wear the masks for a few minutes did Jimmy begin to feel the old nausea creeping in. His hair-trigger gag reflex had embarrassed him more times than he cared to remember. But then they pulled the masks off again, breathed the fresh air, and strolled into the restaurant for breakfast.

"Are you ready?"

"I don't know," Jimmy said. "How do I prepare?"

The fat one and his assistant held up their hands. The one with the curly gray hair concentrated more on his cigarette than the teasing. "There's nothing you can do," said the old one. "Just hope you don't get hit."

"I will call you Louis, like the king, because your head and body will go home separate," said the fat one, with a mouth full of veal bacon and a bright sheen of grease on his chubby fingers. It was all halal meat in Kuwait, even for the infidels.

"Which costs your newspaper double. They will be angry."

This provoked another convulsion of laughter at the table. The fat one slapped him on the back. Jimmy suspected he wasn't their first Louis, or even their first at this hotel. They were making good sport out of Jimmy's fear and inexperience, and he played along the best he could. It made him feel important to be at the table with hardened veterans of the press corps. It reminded Jimmy of sitting with independent filmmakers at an awards dinner. They spent the entire proceedings scoffing under their breath at the pawns of major studios, watching them accept awards they claimed never to want to win.

The Kuwait Hilton restaurant was packed with military personnel whose camouflage had the opposite of its intended effect. Correspondents flocked to them. Jimmy, on the other hand, avoided them, having no desire to put his ignorance on full display. "How do we know when it starts?" Jimmy asked. "I mean, are we just supposed to wait?"

"*Oui*, Louis. You wait for the military to snap"—he snapped his fat fingers right in Jimmy's face—"then you will jump like a trained bichon frise from your lacy little pillow and face the fire."

"You will shit yourself when the bullets start," his assistant added.

"Some of them wear diapers. Do you have diapers, Louis?"

"Don't get the baby ones. Get the ones for grown-ups." The fat one tittered daintily. "For the old people."

"So do you guys work together?" Jimmy asked to change the subject.

"There are seven of us now in total," the photographer answered. "It's been a good year. We have a show planned simultaneously in New York, London, Paris, and Tokyo for the second week of the war."

"The magic of technology," Jimmy said. He looked down at his watch. "Are you going to this seminar?" he asked.

"This what?"

"He means the stupid class on WMDs," the gray-haired one clarified.

"Oh, Louis, you aren't going to that, are you?"

"It sounded important," Jimmy said. "And you get the shots afterward."

"No, this shit anthrax vaccine is how you get the Gulf War syndrome," the young one said.

"Really?"

"You make it home and then you're a drooling idiot for the rest of your life."

"So I shouldn't get it?" Jimmy asked.

"Why are you trying to scare Louis for?" the fat one said to his assistant, tapping the table with his forefinger. "We all know he won't get out of there alive, so who gives a fuck about some fucking vaccine?" They all cackled again, the assistant looking especially relieved, as if he'd believed the tide was turning back and he was nearly the whipping boy again.

"Who wants to go to the Sultan Center for more cigarettes?" the quiet older one asked.

"I will," the assistant said.

"Let's go."

"Ah, Louis, you stay here so you can make your class on nerve gas," the fat one said. As the others began to walk away, he pulled out a small silver point-and-shoot digital camera. "Louis, it was a pleasure and a distinct honor to meet the war's first casualty. A quick snapshot that I can sell to the other papers when—I meant to say if—you are blown into the little pieces?"

"How could I refuse?" Jimmy said. He smiled demurely—a big grin seemed inappropriate for an obituary—and let the Frenchman snap the shot.

"You are as gracious in life as you will be dignified in death, *mon ami*." They shook hands and parted ways. Alone again, Jimmy wandered the first floor of the hotel, past the pricey boutiques selling sunglasses and cutlery. He watched the other reporters swarm the halls brandishing business cards and notebooks. There were hundreds of them, with next to nothing to do until the Pentagon decided to send them to join their units. They were being tight-lipped about the embarkation date.

Jimmy's good humor dissipated at the WMD lecture. The slide show drew from the playbook of drivers' education shock videos, with each picture grislier than the next. Blood and running sores, spray and blast patterns, were explained, even the effects of nuclear fallout. Some of the worst pictures were from the side effects of the smallpox vaccine itself. There were horribly scarred faces, including a woman with her disfigured eye permanently swollen shut, all caused by the inoculation they were expected to receive right after the lecture ended.

"Don't touch your arm, then touch your eye," the Marine said, clicking to a close-up of the previous slide. There were no photos of blister-agent burns available, but the lecturer explained rather vividly how one blister could grow on the skin of another, piggy-backing into a grotesque pyramid of pus. You could suffocate from scorched lungs if you inhaled a single breath, as the burns scarred the air passages. Jimmy learned that nerve gases like VX would make him flex his muscles and flop like a fish on dry land until he broke his back. "We call it the Funky Chicken," the Marine instructor said. The reporters laughed.

The Marine assured them that if they stabbed themselves in the thigh with spring-loaded injections, they would be fine. "But be careful with your injectors. I've seen the needle go straight through a Marine's thumbnail before." A familiar nauseated feeling tickled Jimmy's throat. He fought it. There couldn't be another puking incident. The other reporters in the room took copious notes and raised their hands to find out whether it was five minutes or ten before they died. Was the smell of gas more like almonds or freshly cut grass? They didn't smell alike, one reporter pointed out, but both were listed. "Well, most people don't get a chance to talk about it once they've had a whiff," the Marine said, laughing. Everyone else laughed too.

Jimmy couldn't understand it. This is going to happen to you, he thought, and you won't get to tell anyone if it smelled like almonds and you won't file an article on whether it took seven minutes or eight minutes to die because you'll be dead.

It wasn't nervous giggling. It was hearty belly laughter. "You don't want to see one of these coming at you," the instructor said to a slide of a Silkworm missile. "Ha-ha-ha" went the room. Saddam Hussein was going to rain certain death in the form of hideous chemicals and germs onto their bodies, and everyone was having a grand old time laughing about it. Jimmy wanted to raise his hand and say, "No, I don't want to see one of those coming. Do the rest of you?" He worried they might say, "Yes, closer to the news, you know."

Once the lecture ended, Jimmy strolled out with the other correspondents, smiling, even forcing a laugh at a knee-slapper about blister agent and jogging shoes. As the others began to line up for their shots, Jimmy looked down at his watch quite purposefully and then slapped his forehead as if he had forgotten something. He walked away from the line and, once out of sight, ran up the stairs toward his room.

"British Airways?" Jimmy asked, the hotel phone book open on his lap. He had already pulled out his suitcase while he waited on hold, listening to gentle, Chopinesque piano music. Things were looking up. He hadn't even left, and already life felt more civilized. The suitcase lay open on the bed beside him, his own clothes draped across it. He left the mask and the vest and all the things that a sane person on his way to Brooklyn wouldn't need. "I would like a ... uh ... first-class ticket to New York." If he was going to get fired, he might as well go out in style.

"Of course, sir," a calm English-accented voice replied. Jimmy loved the English, so genteel, so composed. "You will be flying out of—"

"Kuwait," Jimmy answered. The seesawing between fear and a respectable career had tilted completely toward self-preservation. Jimmy was not ready to die.

"Oh, I see," the voice answered. "That could be a problem."

"I suppose I would be willing to fly business class," Jimmy conceded.

"No, that's—" the man tried to interrupt.

"It's awfully far for coach," Jimmy told the sales representative. "I might fly standby if necessary. A day or two's layover in London wouldn't really—"

"We . . . well, terribly sorry," he almost stuttered. Jimmy chuckled. The British were always apologizing for even the smallest things. "It's just that, we are no longer serving Kuwait, that is, we've temporarily suspended—"

"What?" Jimmy yelled. "What does that mean, no longer serving Kuwait?"

"It's just that there's a war expected, and a decision, of ... of course on a corporate level—"

"I know there's a war. Why do you think I want to leave?" Jimmy was breathing hard and fast, like he was already dodging incoming rounds. "You limey bastards flew me here. You have to fly me out. This is ... this is malpractice. I'll sue." He knew the hotels were running evacuation drills because he had slept through one that very morning. The Kuwaitis expected missiles to curl toward them at terminal velocity, refusing to discriminate between guests and staff, foreign and local. He stared out at the beautiful beach-front, hardly listening to the voice on the other end of the line.

"I am really terribly, terribly sorry, sir," the sales rep continued. "To be trapped in a country, a country on the verge of war. I cannot apologize deeply enough, on behalf of British Airways, but also, if I might add, on a personal note—"

"That's all right," Jimmy said, remembering his manners. "I know it isn't your fault."

The war was about to start, and Jimmy was stuck in the little country where they were launching it. His options were limited. He couldn't wait out the war in the hotel. Once his editors knew he had dropped out, they would cut off his credit card and his direct deposits. Then he'd be in Kuwait with nothing and couldn't even afford to get back. He had no choice but to go along like all the mad journalists who were laughing about chemical weapons. In all likelihood Tim had been right. It would be safer with the military's overwhelming force than laying low on his own.

And, after all, he told himself, the victory was going to be an easy one. He had seen the Pentagon officials explaining it on CNN. After the initial but short-lived phase of poison gas and Scud attacks, they would move almost unhindered to Baghdad. Then Jimmy could catch a flight from the liberated airport and return to his cocktail parties and free screenings, his *Vanity Fair* and MTV events, probably within a month.

Without his job, he'd be off every guest list in the city. Now he could drink for free any night of the week. He owned his own tuxedo, with different cummerbund and bow tie combinations because he wore it so often. The thought of living in New York but leaving the effervescent party spaces to join the sad masses pressed up against the plate-glass windows seemed worse than the missiles and blister agents. Jimmy did not want to be on the outside looking in. He hung up on British Airways. He went downstairs. He joined the line.

CHAPTER 5

THE ONE PERSON WHO HAD MADE AN EFFORT TO TALK TO JIMMY
at the party had passed out. The gangly cameraman's splayed legs
had combined with a chair and the coffee table to form an obstacle
course in the living room. Shampoo containers, clear plastic water
bottles, canteens, and a brown bottle that said "photo fixer" sat on
the table. Becky had poured a drink from one of the canteens. She
shouted to someone she knew from a place called Mazar-e Sharif
and left Jimmy standing by the table.

He poured himself a quick shot from the shampoo bottle and
gagged at the aftertaste as he swallowed it. With his second sip
he found he could manage the tang of shampoo along with the
Scotch and downed the rest of the glass. He filled it once more
and, properly fortified, tried to sneak into a nearby conversation.
He found he had nothing to add to a raging debate about East
Timor.

The flow to and from the balcony, where everyone was smoking, forced him into the corner, where he stood alone. About forty
people were milling around, yelling instead of talking. There was
a dog-pound racket to the crowded party, the different breeds all
yapping in unison. Rough-looking men, most with beards, con-

gregated together. Others looked more like the intellectual types that inhabited magazine offices, skinny and bespectacled. Muscular guys with a bemused detachment turned out to be retired military personnel earning their keep now as scribblers with a certain expertise. They lacked the common background of college newspapers and internships in places like Albany and Birmingham that tightened the bonds of the fraternity.

While Jimmy had been in Kuwait a mere seven days, engaging in the military's "hurry up and wait" exercise, some of the reporters had spent six months in this dull and dry little emirate. Jimmy had adjusted quite nicely to the routine, long dinners at seaside restaurants with Becky telling him war stories. At night on the balcony they practiced sending e-mail using the laptop and a satellite-phone hookup. A few of them had discovered a Go-Kart racecourse and begun making regular visits to the track. Others were not so content. They were vehemently rooting for the war to begin. When the announcement came down that the embeds were going to join their military units the following day, parties were hastily arranged and hidden supplies of bootleg booze broken out. It was like Christmas Eve for correspondents.

Jimmy knew he wasn't part of the fraternity and wasn't sure how to proceed at this strange yet festive occasion. He felt exposed standing alone in a corner of the suite. He nudged his way back into the closest circle of reporters. It sounded like old men fondly reminiscing on a front porch, but about a complicated geography class they had all taken. Half the places they talked about were meaningless to Jimmy—Luanda, Khartoum, Kigali—but they were exotic and evoked images of rusted-out trucks and loose chickens scattering to avoid cross fire in tiny villages. As daunting as the tough guys were, it seemed easier to play along with them than it would have been among the analysts and prognosticators of the intellectual set. What indeed was to become of the Iraqi Chaldean minority, Jimmy wondered. And what, more to the point, was an Iraqi Chaldean?

"You sat close enough to the waterfall that you could feel the mist tickle your nose, but there was a leafy arbor overhead to give you shade. Fifty shrimp in a spicy red sauce and two pitchers of sangria with fruit straight from the trees, for one dollar, U.S." The man was a thickset bearded type, but his recollections were colored by more than a tinge of sadness. His stained shirt and thick belly spilled over the waist of his pants. Still, his well-kempt associates hung on his every word. He enthralled them with his anecdotes, despite his slovenly appearance and the fact that he was very drunk.

"I would say you win, McNulty," another said.

"What's the game?" a man who had just entered the circle and stood next to Jimmy asked. His pink shirt was crisply ironed, and his khaki blazer betrayed not a single wrinkle. Unlike McNulty's, his shoulders were wider than his waist.

"Best meal, anywhere in the world, a dollar or under," the other answered.

"If that one's already been decided, we could move on to cheapest whore," the newcomer in the pink shirt responded, laughing brightly, his eyes gleaming. A couple of the other men joined him, Jimmy included, though his own laughter was due to nerves. McNulty glared darkly at the recent arrival. "Oh, I'm sorry, McNulty. I meant the best value for an oppressed sexual entrepreneur. Forgive my indelicacy."

"Not at all, Garland. Please continue. We might have a shot at tracing that virulent case of herpes you shared with your personal assistant. In the spirit of inquiry to which we are all dedicated," McNulty said, looking Garland straight in the eyes.

"An excess of dedication is a problem in itself. The world would be a boring place if we were all humorless workaholics," Garland said. "How is the Sumatran rain forest, anyway? That poor orang-utan. I could barely get through your lead before I started crying."

"Whose heart did you borrow?" McNulty asked. "I hope you gave it back."

"Unfortunately I've never had a knack for recycling," the other man said with a smirk. "I'm surprised you showed up for this, McNulty. How did you tear yourself away from that lengthy series on the Bolivian peasants? Now, remind me. I once again didn't finish the whole series. The peasants are still poor, right?"

"Not that you would care, but yes," McNulty said. He sounded calm, but his chest was rising and falling rapidly and a blue vein drew a border down the middle of his forehead.

"I'll care a little if they start shooting each other," the man said. "I'll care even more if Americans join the shooting party. It's the Mog imperative. The skinnies can croak all they want, but it won't lead the news until we start dying."

"Generation Mog," McNulty muttered coldly. "Twisted thrill seekers."

"Well, you weren't in the Mog, were you, McNulty?"

"Listen closely," replied the correspondent with surprising vehemence, his eyes still and lifeless. He leaned in and said quietly, "The Mog wasn't shit." An odor emanated from him that was impossible for Jimmy to miss. It was like the stench New York generated on the summer's hottest days, where the ingredients were hidden but legion.

"All right," Jimmy said, meaning to help break the ice. "I give up. What's a Mog?" He had been expecting laughs and found silence instead. They all turned toward him with looks of plain disbelief. Then McNulty's dead eyes fell on him.

"The Mog is where all these pussies watched some skinny-ass Somalis shoot AK-47s," said McNulty. "It made them feel cool. It let them pretend their dicks were twice as big, a full four inches long after that. Rounding up."

"McNulty's just bitter because he missed the Mog, and most other conflicts people care about," said Garland. "He has a flair for the obscure."

"You mean like *Black Hawk Down*? Somalia?" Jimmy suspected that it might have been wiser to have kept his mouth shut, but he hated to see Garland tormenting the poor sad slob.

"Another genius joins the fold," McNulty said. "Yes, junior. Like *Black Hawk Down*. Of course. That's what we mean."

"Of course, of course. Apparent to one and all," Jimmy said, and as he looked around, he realized that it really had been apparent to everyone else standing there. He had intended to help them end their argument, now he was blushing with embarrassment. "The blind drunk leading the blind," he added.

"Are you making fun of me, you little prick?" McNulty slurred.

"That's the famed reporter's intuition, the investigative instinct I've heard so much about, isn't it?" Jimmy asked, drawing a laugh from the little group.

"Who do you think you are?" McNulty asked him.

He never meant to take Garland's side in this dispute. Jimmy had enjoyed hearing McNulty talk about empty bars in towns cleared out by fleeing villagers and ramshackle airplanes flying on propellers held together with duct tape and bubble gum. But his pride had been bruised so many times over the last week. "I couldn't tell at first without the fedora."

"You sarcastic fuck," McNulty said. Jimmy fell back a step. McNulty had shoved him. Any doubt that it was a playful push dissolved, yet declarations of "Whoa" or "Hold on" were all the help he received. The others just stared. Becky was out on the deck, her back to the scuffle.

"Hey, man," Jimmy said, pushing him away with his own hand.

"You want to be touching me, junior?" McNulty asked, his foul breath flooding Jimmy's nostrils. Jimmy wasn't sure, but he didn't want to back down.

"Yeah, back up," Jimmy said, giving him a shove of his own. McNulty brushed Jimmy's outstretched hand away with his left and presumably it was his right that connected with Jimmy's eye socket. It seemed to have come from nowhere, a blur, a dark spot in his vision that folded his knees and made him sit down on the floor before he felt any pain.

The party seemed to go silent for a moment, and then it roared with shouting. He couldn't tell if the dynamics were real or the effect of his brain rattling against the inside of his skull. As his senses stabilized, the gravity peculiar to playground fights pulled everyone in the room toward the two of them until Jimmy was caught in a confusion of khaki trousers and tan boots. Jimmy's cheek felt hot. He stood on shaky legs and headed toward the door. Over his shoulder he saw an enormous man, a bull on two legs with the wide skull and thick hands of a born defensive lineman, holding McNulty back.

Jimmy realized he would have been better off keeping his mouth shut. This party—this whole war really—was no place for someone who had learned that very day the difference between a Sunni and a Shiite. The less he said, the better. And the quicker he got back to his room, the safer he would be.

It was surprisingly cool at night in Kuwait. The breeze felt good on his cheek. He had to be intoxicated, or else he would have been more shaken by what had happened. He heard someone coming up behind him and turned with his fists raised. "Looking for a fair fight?" Becky asked with a grin. "I heard you met McNulty."

"That guy is a menace," Jimmy said.

"He's in bad shape these days," Becky said. They strolled across the hotel grounds. It was safe by the standards of the region. That meant there were armed guards and barricades at the entrance protecting against suicide bombers.

"I got the feeling it was an everyday sort of thing," Jimmy replied.

"Certain occupational hazards you might not be aware of. One of his best friends got killed in Chechnya. Number three in about six months."

"That would explain it. Enough to put anyone off showers or sobriety," Jimmy said.

"It's the interns and greenhorns who show up early looking fresh and clean," Becky said. "A Pulitzer winner like McNulty can leave his shirt untucked if he wants."

"You kidding me?" Jimmy asked. Becky shook her head. "Wow." They strolled past row after row of luxury cars and massive sport-utility vehicles. A Toyota Camry or Ford Taurus would have stood out more than a Bentley or a bulletproof Land Rover. By some strange alchemy the correspondents and Arab princes together had reached the exact balance of automobile muscle and immodesty that occurred naturally only in the garages of multi-platinum-selling rappers.

"Where exactly are we going?" Becky asked.

"It seems like the beach by default," he said. They were almost there. Oil tankers were docked at a long pier down the shore. The pool was closed, and none of the guests seemed to care for scenery. "I just wish we had some booze. I can't believe we're embedding tomorrow. This is actually going to happen. I could use another drink."

"Who takes care of you?" Becky asked, handing him a water bottle. He took a sip. It was pure gin. He thanked her. "I bet you haven't been in a fight since high school."

"No, you might be surprised how often that happens in my line of work," Jimmy answered. "I get punched pretty regularly. Couple times a year. It's normally more for show than to inflict pain, though. Like slapping a guy in the face with the glove in those old Errol Flynn movies or whatever."

"No shit," Becky said, taking another sip. "I thought you might want to steer clear of the people you slander."

"You'd be amazed what kinds of quotes you can get while someone is yelling at you," Jimmy said. "Let's say you write that a guy is cheating on his wife. You walk up to him at a club and he shoves you and yells something like, 'You son of a bitch. My wife is leaving me.' Well, right there you've got your next day's story. Wife walks out on cheating hubby. 'She's leaving me,' cries the heartbroken star."

"But you can't duck and run when the swinging starts?" Becky said, laughing. "Taking a punch like a man is okay. Dodging it's better."

"You should come out with me sometime," Jimmy said. "Urban combat among the beautiful people."

"You never know," she told him with a warm smile. He beamed. His cheeks felt warm, and not just where he had been punched.

"If we live long enough," Jimmy said. "All this talk about bullets and bombs and poison gas has got me scared out of my mind."

"You'll be fine," Becky said. "But you know . . ." She trailed off.

"What?" Jimmy asked. She didn't answer. "Seriously, what?"

"It's just . . . I don't know if you should tell anyone that you're a gossip columnist. I mean, Marines are pretty macho, and they might . . ." For a second he was angry, but he reminded himself that people had been judging him this way for a long time. "They might . . ."

"What?" Jimmy asked sullenly.

"Not take you seriously," Becky said.

"You mean the way you don't take me seriously?" Jimmy asked.

She sat silently for a moment, then exhaled loudly and abruptly stood up. "This isn't therapy time, sweetheart," she said. He hadn't noticed how friendly their conversations had become until she switched back to her professional voice, the one he'd heard at the airport when they first met. "The rest is yours," she said, handing him the plastic bottle. "See you in the morning."

"Yeah," Jimmy said. He couldn't hear the sound of her footsteps in the sand and didn't turn to watch her go. A week earlier he'd been Arts & Lifestyle editor Tim Suskind's beautiful, heartless gossip columnist. He had never really considered what that would mean here. He just packed a bag and used the plane ticket. Now he knew. Even with a bulletproof vest and a gas mask, he was still just a fluff celebrity stalker, and that was a tawdry thing to be among these people. He watched the Persian Gulf rise and fall, the surface troubled by a strong wind. The moon and stars were out, and their light shattered into countless glittering pieces on the rippled surface of the water. War seemed like a distant, incomprehensible exercise. He rose unsteadily and began to walk toward the hotel, finishing the rest of the gin on the way.

CHAPTER 6

JIMMY WONDERED IF HE HAD STUMBLED INTO THE WRONG WAR. HE was hung over from the party and would not have said that he was paying close attention to the introductory briefing in the hotel conference room, but the discussion seemed to be devoted to Vietnam rather than Iraq. He gamely tried to follow along, mostly because the thick-gutted, hoarse-voiced older officer giving the lecture, Captain Childress, yelled very loudly and intimidated him more than a little. "We lost fifty-eight thousand men in Vietnam," Childress barked. "That is a tragic figure, and we honor every one of them. But the Vietnamese . . . the Vietnamese lost three-point-two million. If the Vietnam War had been a football game, that would be a final score of a hundred and ten to two. Fourteen touchdowns and four field goals compared to one safety. One freak accident of a safety. That is all they got."

There was a younger press officer seated next to a slide machine, but it appeared that Childress was ad-libbing. The junior staffer, with his blond hair shaved down to a fuzzy buzz cut and his large Adam's apple protruding above the collar of his desert camouflage fatigues, never hit a single button on the projector. He sat at attention throughout, thumb on the remote control, just in case. "You know, people talk about how important the last shot is," Childress continued. "Let me tell you something. And remember this. The last shot only matters if the game is tied. The last shot only matters if it's close." He repeated this as though it were a significant revelation. Jimmy assumed he had come up with it himself and been highly pleased with the insight.

"Vietnam was a lower point for the press than for the armed forces. The American military was not defeated. The American military did not lose a single battle of any consequence. It was an unprecedented tactical performance. Did we leave? Of course. We weren't going to make it a state. We already had Hawaii." Captain Childress paused in such a way that Jimmy assumed this was intended as a laugh line. The exhausted reporters did not oblige him.

Then Childress zeroed in on Jimmy, possibly, the reporter thought, because of the bright blue shiner from McNulty's punch. "We are proud of all of you for being out here. You guys are really redeeming yourselves for all those years. For all the garbage you wrote." Jimmy looked around. The captain was indeed speaking directly at him. Jimmy nodded and gave a tentative thumbs-up sign. The officer continued the lecture.

"But I'm happy to see the country getting better," Childress said without a hint of a smile. "September eleventh was a tragedy, but in many ways it brought us back to the core values that made America great. It is good to see people caring again. Civilians were getting soft." The sound of pens scraping on paper slowed to a halt as the assembled reporters looked around at one another to confirm that Childress had really said what they thought he said about the bright side of 9/11. Jimmy wasn't taking notes, but he hoped the officer would move along to an explanation of the war they were preparing to start, the one he was going to be participating in, even if it was only as a spectator.

"The mainstream media," Childress shouted, provoking a series of groans from the audience. He glared out at them until the groans ceased. "The mainstream media," he began again, "are practitioners of half-truths and manipulations, as we saw in Vietnam. It is our fervent hope that by putting your asses on the line, alongside the best that our country has to offer, you will be able to escape your warped worldview and depict faithfully the events on the battlefield." Here, Jimmy believed, was a little common ground. "Yet we do not expect that, however much we may wish for it. Still, the opportunity lies before you. Seize it if you dare. Godspeed, gentlemen. And ladies." He smiled broadly, hands behind him, shoulders back. A frown settled on his lips as he realized there was something he had to add. "Any questions?" he asked.

"When do we leave for Iraq?" Jimmy asked.

"Are you going to Iraq?" Childress asked back, with visible distaste.

"Aren't we ... aren't we going to Iraq?" Jimmy said again.

"Maybe you'll go to Seoul. Maybe Ramstein. Take a tour of Gitmo. There are U.S. forces stationed all over the world," Childress said. Jimmy recognized the strange vacancy of official lying. It was as clear when Childress did it as when a celebrity publicist denied a client's indiscretion in the face of clear photographic evidence.

"I thought we were here to invade Iraq," Jimmy said. There was quiet laughter among the other reporters.

"I had you pegged," Childress said more quietly, leaning toward Jimmy. "Had you pegged the goddamned second you walked in here." To the assembled group he stated, "No determination has been made. We have UN-sanctioned ongoing operations here. We have been in Kuwait since the First Gulf War. Should the commander in chief decide that military action is necessary, we will follow our orders faithfully as we always have."

"But . . ." Jimmy said before remembering that he intended to talk as little as possible. He closed his mouth and tried to scrunch down in his chair. Childress had heard him.

"But what?" Childress asked him. He wasn't ready to let it go.

"Well, it's just that . . . you said 'First Gulf War,' and that sort of implies that there'll be a Second Gulf War, doesn't it?" Jimmy pointed out.

"You are dismissed," Childress said through gritted teeth. "Buses load up at oh-eight-thirty local time." The reporters rose and began heading for the door. Several slapped Jimmy on the shoulder and thanked him for "showing that blowhard." Jimmy was completely bewildered. All he wanted was some basic information about the war. He sat in the chair, wondering how his questions had inflamed the captain so severely. At last he realized he was all alone with the slide operator, who was boxing up the machine he had never used.

"Hey, I'm Jimmy Stephens," Jimmy said, offering his hand. In his line of work he often chatted up the waiters and busboys, doormen and bellhops. This young man, with his thick glasses and stooped shoulders, looked like just the person from whom to finesse a little information.

"Hey," the slide operator answered, winding the cord neatly and carefully. "Specialist Almgren. Nice to meet you."

"What's, uh, what's your specialty?" Jimmy asked. Almgren looked down at the slide machine with disappointment. "Gotcha," Jimmy said. "So what's this all about? Is there a war or not?"

"Man, I just handle the slides. You got Childress worked up pretty good. I don't need an ass-chewing today." He had a thick Upper Midwest accent and spoke slowly. Jimmy could picture this gawky young man still playing Dungeons & Dragons and owning a large collection of swords.

"But"—Jimmy stood up and walked over to him—"somebody has to tell me what's going on."

"You serious?" the projectionist asked. He looked around. "You aren't trying to fuck with me."

"Scout's honor," Jimmy said, holding up three fingers, hoping that was the right number. "I don't know what I'm doing around here. Why won't he say that we're invading Iraq?"

"Okay, so this is, like, off the record and shit, right?" Jimmy nodded. Almgren looked around, as though Childress was going to come tearing out of one of the conference-room closets at any second. He took a deep breath and began to explain. "So we're going to Iraq, right? I mean, we are fucking going to Iraq. But the president and the secretary of state, they're all up at the UN and over at NATO and where-the-fuck-ever doing their diplomacy business. It's, like, a puppet show, while we get ready backstage to gut the motherfucker. But as long as there are weapons inspectors in Iraq and we're technically negotiating with the UN, we can't go around saying 'The war in Iraq' this and 'The war in Iraq' that."

"So what happens next?" Jimmy asked. "Aren't we embedding today?"

"You're going to your unit, man. There you will chill and hang with the warriors of your realm, the U.S. of A., as they sharpen their weapons and prepare to kill." Jimmy decided he had been right about the sword collection. Almgren was getting into his telling, bopping his head and shoulders a bit as he found a rhythmic groove. "When the president gives the word, and only when the president gives the word, you will hold on to your ass while the U.S. military takes you on a wild fucking ride straight into the unknown of Iraq. Fuck yeah-uh. If you come back, you will be certified as having testicles the size of bowling balls. If not, we will ship your carcass home to Mama, probably free of charge but

I'm not really sure. They might make her pay something." There was an obsession with body transit, Jimmy thought, remembering the French photographers. "That would be awkward, though," Almgren added more softly. "You might ask someone in Support Services if you can prepay."

"How long do we have to wait once we're embedded?" Jimmy asked.

"Two days. Two weeks. I don't know," Specialist Almgren said, picking up his slide projector. "Ask Colin fucking Powell." He slouched toward the door, humming AC/DC's "Highway to Hell." Two days, two weeks, that felt like a big difference. Becky had said they would have to invade before it got too hot out. The temperature had already hit 80 degrees the day before. That suggested they would attack soon. He went back to his room to get his gear. It was almost time to go.

Out front, an assortment of rented touring buses had gathered in the resort complex. Final cups of Starbucks coffee from the Hilton's own franchise were everywhere. The correspondents had to brace themselves for Army instant blends for weeks if not months to come. The public-affairs officers shepherded the reporters to the right buses. One media cluster wore specially printed sweatshirts, with "Kuwait Tour" over a picture of a tank on the back, as though they were working a rock concert. Others had tailored uniforms that looked exactly like the military's camouflage, right down to the names stitched onto the breast pocket, but listing the news organization instead of the service branch: Army, Marines, and ABC News indistinguishable from afar. Becky was there waiting for Jimmy, her usual outfit understated among all the garish vests outdoing each other in pockets per square inch. She led him to the bus where he could stow his gear in the cargo bay below.

"Good luck, champ. I'm sure you'll do fine."

"Good luck? What's this good luck?" Jimmy asked.

"I've got to catch my bus," she said. "I can't hold your hand all day."

"You said our bus was right here." He pointed at a curtained window on the tall cruiser.

"No, your bus is right here," Becky said. She turned and pointed in the opposite direction. "Mine's over there."

"But I thought we were—"

"That's the way the cookie crumbled, my friend. Or the way the Pentagon, in its infinite wisdom, chose to crumble it. You'll be fine. I wrote down all the phone numbers you need on this note-book," she said, handing him a reporter's notebook with the spiral binding across the top. "Call in to New York regularly." Jimmy nodded. "You have extra socks?" He nodded again. "Always change your socks, or your feet will get infected. And wear the vest. It's heavy, tempting to take off, but you have to wear it." He didn't bother nodding again, prompting Becky to ask, "Okay?"

"Okay," he said.

"Good." She backed up one step and looked about to pivot away and leave him.

"But I really thought we were going together," he said.

"Jimmy, don't make a scene. You don't want the other war correspondents to think you're a baby, do you?" she asked with a sardonic smile. He smiled and shook his head. "That's a good boy. Write as much as you can." Jimmy cocked his head, confused. "Not to me. For the paper."

"Right. Of course," he said. In the time he'd been in Kuwait, he hadn't given much thought to the actual writing of articles about the war. Everything had been focused on physical preparation, blood tests, equipment, training, and such. Surviving seemed complicated enough without having to write stories at the same time.

"You sure your eye's okay?" she asked.

"Is it really noticeable?" he answered. When he'd last stared into the mirror, it was a puffy region of malignant red and sickening blue blotches, hideous in contrast, half-mooned around the socket. The soft tissue of his right cheek felt hot and prickly; the dull ache seemed to come from the crescent of bone underneath.

"Jimmy?"

"Yeah?"

"Take things seriously. Don't screw around. I mean it. Take everything they tell you seriously," she said.

"Of course I will," he answered.

"What I'm trying to say is people are going to die: soldiers, reporters. Even if the whole thing goes perfectly, with a three-day invasion and a parade through Baghdad, people are going to die. And I'm worried you aren't taking that seriously."

"Becky," Jimmy said, "you have no idea how seriously I take that." He wondered if he was actually hiding his fear that well. Jimmy was terrified. How could she not notice? He had filled out forms listing his next of kin explicitly "in the event of untimely death." The accounting department had sent him a FedEx with life-insurance papers to sign. If he died, they gave his parents half a million dollars. It sent the message clearly that the possibility of dying was real. The *Daily Herald* would not have paid the premiums otherwise.

"I guess you'll be fine then," Becky said. He understood the look she gave him. It questioned whether she shouldn't just tell him to skip it, wait for the planes to start flying again and go home. Or maybe he was just projecting his own wishes onto her concerned face. He was ready but scared. It was an opportunity, but what was an opportunity worth if you were dead?

"But ..." he said.

"Good-bye, Jimmy," Becky told him.

"Wait." He caught her as she turned to go. "Thanks for taking care of me, for, you know ..."

"Hey." She sighed and gave him a funny look. "You'll be okay. You're a good guy. Just keep your head down." He nodded. "Ciao, kiddo," she said, and stepped into the crowd. Jimmy looked down at his stack of gear, then watched her small figure slip between the bigger correspondents strapped into camping packs.

"I hope you don't mind, but I just had to film that. Would you talk about it on camera maybe? It's a very touching scene. Husband and wife go to war. It's incredible. I'm Nathaniel Woodbridge, with the NBC family, cable and network, MSNBC, CNBC. Spots for local affiliates. Original material for the Web, MSNBC-dot-MSN-dot-com. You can call me Woody. Everybody does. Off camera, anyway." He held out the hand that wasn't holding a digital camcorder. Jimmy shook it.

Woody had television hair and the khaki cargo vest typical of war correspondents from Hollywood central casting. His tan was suspiciously orange and his hair delicately highlighted, probably to hide the gray. But there was such a great quantity of that hair, in the generous puff that led one to wonder if the hair made the man or the television magic made the hair. He looked about fifty, but his features were stiff in a way that suggested upkeep under the surgeon's knife. Pointing to a thick, rough-looking guy trying to lift heavy plastic crates of equipment into the cargo holds of the bus, he said, "That's Doug. He's my crew."

"Nice to meet you, Doug," Jimmy said, recognizing the man who had held McNulty back. Doug winked at him and returned to the crates he was pushing under the bus.

"We're waiting for permission to get our own rig into the convoy," Woody said. "They're saying 'No way' right now, but I think we'll bring them around. So how about the interview? Sad goodbye with the wife?"

"She's just a coworker," Jimmy said.

"Not your wife?" Woody double-checked.

"No."

"You looked so . . . so close. You aren't that married couple with the *Washington Post*?" Jimmy could hear the disappointment in his voice.

"*New York Daily Herald*," Jimmy said.

"Damn," Woody said.

"Sorry."

"Not your fault. But if you see some young people in love saying good-bye, give me a holler, right? I've been looking for them all morning."

"Got it." Jimmy realized that most of the cameras in the loading area were switched on as journalists filmed other journalists getting ready to leave. He watched them zoom in on one another's preparations. Jimmy doubted that many people at home would be interested in footage of reporters' luggage, but he wasn't a TV producer and didn't presume to tell them how to do their jobs.

"Are you prepared to indulge in this great adventure?" Woody asked him in his booming television voice, even though the camera was off. Maybe he was just warming up, Jimmy thought. "This mythic exercise of combat?"

"No," Jimmy said.

"No?" Woody apparently wasn't expecting that answer. "Don't you just feel . . . connected? To the ancient Greeks? To the Vikings? Paratroopers over the Channel? This is our link in the chain of history."

"I don't really feel like a Viking, in fact—" Jimmy started to say.

"We were in Chechnya once," Woody continued, unimpeded by Jimmy's attempt to participate in the conversation. "It must have been 2000. The old Soviet Army had disintegrated fast in the new world order, like the fall of Rome—" The puff and hiss of air brakes announced their imminent departure.

"Looks like it's time to go," Jimmy said, interrupting.

"No worries. We can sit together," Woody said, smiling broadly. Once he was on the bus, Jimmy just wanted to sleep, to forget the whole thing. But true to his word, Woody plopped down beside him and picked up exactly where he had left off in the "mythic exercise of combat" speech. His seatmate seemed intent on listing every war since the time of the ancient Sumerians and constructing some kind of parallel to Iraq for each of them. Even to Jimmy's uneducated ear, a lot of them sounded tenuous, but he didn't know enough about, say, the Mongols to ask.

Just as the bus was preparing to pull out, someone began pounding on the door. The driver popped it open, and Matt McNulty struggled up the steps, pulling his gear behind him. McNulty's double chin, bare now, rippled as he jerked his camping pack over the last step. The tough correspondent looked like a shorn sheep without his beard. They had said in the training sessions that beards had to go because the gas masks couldn't seal properly with facial hair. Unless, that is, you coated it with petroleum jelly—a fate worse than shaving in the desert.

McNulty looked a lot less scary, but Jimmy was far from overjoyed to see him. The Iraqis would be bad enough, but now it looked like he was going to war with a grudge on his side of the wire too. Woody said something about the invasion of Normandy, and Jimmy smiled unhappily at the monologist beside him. They would be halfway to the Iraqi border before Jimmy had a moment of silence.

CHAPTER 7

AT CAMP TRIUMPH, THE BUS DROPPED THEM IN FRONT OF AN ALUMINUM-sided trailer that served as the infantry headquarters. There a Marine Corps press officer who had accompanied them from the Hilton announced that they were a mere ten miles from the Iraqi border, but that in articles and broadcasts they should refer to Camp Triumph as an undisclosed location "near the Iraqi border," still on the Kuwaiti side, Jimmy concluded. This was where they prepared for the invasion.

The press officer introduced them to Lieutenant Katzenbach, executive officer for the infantry company with which McNulty, the television crew, and Jimmy would be embedded. "This is First Lieutenant Katzenbach," the press officer explained, after giving them another set of photocopied handouts along with recruiting DVDs. "He will be your guide and escort. If you pay attention and do as he says, you will have a safe and pleasant journey, wherever your final destination may be."

"Gotcha, sir," Jimmy said, feeling rather in the know this time around. "We read you loud and clear."

"Good," the press officer said, stepping toward the door and back toward the waiting bus. Jimmy looked to the front of the

room again just as Lieutenant Katzenbach bounded enthusiastically but awkwardly to the small podium up front.

"Welcome to Camp Triumph," Katzenbach said. "The United
States Marine Corps is dedicated to your protection and well-
being. To protect you, however, will require a little cooperation on
your part." He smiled pleasantly at Jimmy. They were about the
same age. Katzenbach was a bit taller, but of an unwieldy, bulky
build, like an overgrown toddler. He looked better suited for moving merchandise at a Lowe's than firing an automatic rifle, but
Jimmy was hardly one to judge.

"There are many ways that you can inadvertently jeopardize
yourselves, my men, and me personally. That is what we most
wish to prevent. We are, from this point on, all in this together."
He smiled at them, then held up a sheaf of paper from the hand-
out. "You will read the ground rules and follow them. The release
of any information that could aid enemy personnel in assessing
our tactics, techniques, and procedures is prohibited," he said. "Do
you understand?" he asked Jimmy.

"I understand," Jimmy agreed. Katzenbach smiled again.

"Very good," he said.

After the presentation, they took turns talking to the lieutenant
one-on-one. Jimmy flipped through his copy of the ground rules,
waiting for his turn. It was difficult to understand, from vague expressions like "security issue" to downright unintelligible ones like
"strike package." The war from the embedded vantage, he learned,
could be broken down into "releasable" and "not releasable" information. Not releasable included the number and location of troops.
He couldn't discuss operations before they happened or the date,
time, or location of missions after they happened, except in general
terms. From a work standpoint, it looked to be an easy war. There
seemed to be little about which he could actually write.

Listening in on his colleagues, he observed how McNulty was

adept at preying on the lieutenant's apparent weakness for a tough exterior and displays of masculine stoniness. McNulty shook the lieutenant's hand roughly, with a grip that Jimmy could see defining the veins on the back of the correspondent's meaty hand. With daringly direct eye contact, the pugnacious reporter sketched a picture of his previous combat experience and inquired after several Marines he had worked with in the past whom he thought Katzenbach might have known.

Jimmy didn't know a single one of the names bandied back and forth, but his understanding of the science of name-dropping—even separate from the specifics of the field—told him that McNulty was an expert. It wasn't just his words. Everything about Matt McNulty had changed since the party at the Hilton. Gone were the filthy casual clothes he had worn as he soused himself toward oblivion. He was showered and neatly combed. His eyes were alert and only slightly bloodshot. He hurried off to meet his squad with a spring in his step that Jimmy never would have thought possible after their first meeting.

Woody stepped up to introduce himself next. His cameraman had exempted himself from the proceedings entirely by wandering off with a muttered excuse about checking on their equipment. Woody carefully knitted his curriculum vitae into a single sentence, announcing that this war would "make my work in the West Bank, Chechnya, and Somalia seem like child's play." Then he launched an offensive of flattery so effusive that the average target would have found it embarrassing, if not insulting. Katzenbach soaked it up with the greed of a freshly minted valedictorian, still in cap and gown. At last the company's executive officer turned to Jimmy.

"So where are you from?" he asked.

"I work for the *New York Daily Herald*," Jimmy answered. "But I'm from New Jersey."

"New Jersey, like the Boss," Katzenbach said, giving him a tiny nudge with his elbow. He stood a bit closer than made Jimmy altogether comfortable, but his was the friendliest face he had seen since boarding the plane at Newark.

"Sure," Jimmy agreed. "The Boss."

"Springsteen," Katzenbach added unnecessarily, still grinning. Jimmy found this goofy friendliness somewhat endearing after all the posturing he had witnessed.

"The one and only," Jimmy said. "So, um, where am I off to? Do I get to spend the war with you?"

"The only way to get to know the Marine Corps is through the enlisted men," Katzenbach said. "They're the heart and soul of the Corps. You'll be in Sergeant Harper's Humvee. That'll give you a good feel for things. He runs, well, a lot of errands. And a seat just opened up."

"Opened up?" Jimmy repeated.

"Very unfortunate," Katzenbach said. "One of his Marines accidentally stabbed himself."

"Stabbed?"

"It happens a little more often than you might think. Kids with knives. Horsing around. We try to remind them that if they mess up, they miss the war. But what can you do?"

"Take away their knives?" Jimmy said.

"From Marines?" Lieutenant Katzenbach made no effort to conceal his friendly chuckle at Jimmy's expense. Jimmy didn't mind. Finally here was a jovial guy amid all the seriousness. "Oh, that'd be a different way to fight," he said. "Yes, it would."

Jimmy waited alone in front of an unoccupied canvas tent that slapped against its wooden frame in the wind. He perched on a pile of sandbags, his suitcase, two duffel bags, and frame backpack, all purchased from the Sultan Center mega-store at Becky's behest, piled high beside him. At one point a gigantic bulldozer rolled by, wafting sand into Jimmy's eyes and down his throat. He coughed. The sound of a jet engine roared overhead from time to time. At one point a young Marine with a hint of a mustache asked him if he wanted to see a scorpion fight.

"With what?" Jimmy asked.

"Another scorpion," the Marine said, as if the matchup were self-evident somehow. Embarrassed, Jimmy declined.

He had stuck his head into the tent and found a level of disarray he had not expected. In movies, sergeants are always prowling around looking for unpolished shoes and unmade beds. That did not appear to be the norm in Kuwait. Maybe they were disheartened by the fact that you couldn't shine desert combat boots and had slipped into a lethargic depression over it. Clothes hung here and there from nails pounded at random into the tent frame. Piles of *Hustler* and *Penthouse* and *Club Confidential* sat on the only empty bed. It wasn't really a bed, just canvas stretched tight over a rectangular metal frame. Outside there was nothing to see but more tents beyond his row. He waited for over an hour.

The sun had set by the time a group of Marines, eight in all, walked straight toward him, laughing and chatting. They headed into the tent he was watching without acknowledgment. The sound of bunks being pushed around, booted feet clomping on the wooden floor, and more laughter came from inside. One of the Marines stuck his head out.

"Do you need something?" The Marine was tall, with a slight southern accent. He looked to be in his mid-thirties, with a bored, distant look that was different from the animated expressions of the other Marines.

"I'm just—I'm supposed to—"

"Are you our reporter?"

"Yeah," Jimmy said. "That's it."

"Predictable. Well, come on in," he said to Jimmy, who followed him into the tent. "That's a beauty," he said, looking over Jimmy's eye.

"Yeah," Jimmy agreed. "I took pictures for posterity." Inside, four of the Marines had started up a card game, one was reading magazines, and another was beginning to take a nap. Two were on the floor doing push-ups side by side. One was built like a bodybuilder, with a mustache thick enough to sweep the floor; the other was a stick of a kid struggling to keep up. None of the Marines looked exactly ripe for an interview, which was fine because Jimmy wasn't either.

"This is—" The Marine prompted him with a gesture.

"Jimmy."

"He's our reporter." There were groans and rolled eyes. "Sorry, man. We were hoping for one of the more female and, well, attractive reporters from Fox News. No offense."

"None taken," Jimmy answered.

"Oo-rah," he said, which Jimmy took to be Marine-grunt-speak for affirmative. "I'm Sergeant Harper. Over there are Johnson, Martinez, Jones." A couple of them nodded at Jimmy. Most ignored him. In their matching uniforms and haircuts, Jimmy could barely tell the difference between them. "Freeman there's trying to sleep. That's Lance Corporal Dabrowski," he said of the muscular one who had just finished his push-ups and stood up right in front of Jimmy. He did not offer him his hand to shake. "And he's Ramos," Harper said, gesturing toward the floor where the scrawny creature strained—arms quivering—to complete his set. No one paid attention to his effort, even though he seemed to be counting louder than would be strictly necessary for his own benefit. "Your rack is over there."

He gestured toward the cot covered with magazines, the only unoccupied one in the tent. Jimmy walked over and picked up the stack of a dozen or so pornos. No one reached for them, so he set them gently on the floor. "If the lights work, we stay up for a while. If not, we usually go to sleep. Breakfast starts at five-thirty. You'll get the hang of the rest whenever. We'll tell you if you fuck up."

"Thanks," Jimmy said, a little unsure.

"Don't mention it." Harper turned to go. "I'm in another tent with the sergeants. These guys will help you figure things out."

"Okay," Jimmy said as Harper left. Somehow Jimmy had expected his own accommodations. He couldn't picture sleeping in a room filled with other people. A summer share in the Hamptons five years earlier was the last time he'd divvied up living quarters with more than a woman with whom he was involved.

"Hey," Martinez said. In a room full of nineteen-year-olds, the Marine stood out as the oldest, older even than Jimmy or Sergeant Harper from the looks of it. Tattoos peeked out from under his rolled-up sleeves. He was short and thickset with dark skin and a broad nose like the newly arrived Mexican immigrants moving into Jimmy's Gowanus neighborhood, nothing like the light-skinned Latino actors who made it in Hollywood and into Jimmy's column. His age was sketched in lines across his forehead and around his mouth. "Don't take a water bottle from under anyone's rack, okay?" Martinez said.

"No, of course," Jimmy said. He guessed that Martinez was a father. It was something in the tone of his voice, the way he spoke slowly and nodded as he said "okay." This was a man who had watched *Sesame Street* and *Blue's Clues* recently. "I would never—"

"I don't mean stealing," the older Marine said carefully. "Those are piss bottles, got it?"

"Got it," Jimmy said.

"It's a long ways to the Port-o-Johns, so you might want to get a bottle yourself," he continued. His Spanish accent was so slight that it served only to draw attention to its absence.

"Got it." Jimmy was tempted to say "Oo-rah," but thought better of it. He would try to avoid the smart-ass label for a while.

"And don't forget to button the tent when you come in. If a sandstorm kicks up, it'll trash everything."

"Button the tent," Jimmy repeated.

"And don't be afraid of these guys." Martinez grinned. "They're really a bunch of pussies."

"Fuck you," someone said.

"You want some pussy, Martinez?" said another.

"Right. Button the tent," Jimmy said, ignoring the last remarks. He went and dragged his bags inside. He unrolled his bright green sleeping bag. There had been none available in the military drab, but now he wished he'd just bought one in blue or black. The toxic green looked even worse as a failed effort to fit in than a simple declaration of difference would have.

Jimmy lay on his side, studying a six-month-old copy of *Hustler*, until the bare lightbulb hanging in the center of the tent winked out. A brief effort was made to carry on the card game with flashlights. After that, a few left for an unknown but presumably better-lit location.

"No fag shit with the reporter, kids," came the farewell.

"Why would I fuck him when you got such a tight, sweet ass?" someone acknowledged.

"Manhole," squawked another.

"Nighty-night." After that it was quiet, and Jimmy was glad.

He lay on his back unable to sleep. The wind had kicked up, turning the gentle tapping of the tent canvas against the frame into an all-out percussion solo. The rolling snare of snoring Marines came from all around him. He stared at pure blackness and thought how Brooklyn never got that dark.

CHAPTER 8

THE PUPILS OF HIS EYES HAD DILATED AND HE COULD SEE THE outline of the seam where the tent flapped, unbuttoned. He had not gone in search of the Port-o-Johns, he remembered, had not left it unsecured. His eyelids sagged and began to close but opened again with every whack of the canvas. Meandering thoughts and the impression that his eyes had remained shut for more than a minute told him he was nearly asleep.

"Gas!" someone screamed, but it sounded muffled, far away.

"Gas!" another voice added.

"Gas! Gas! Gas!" Marines chanted in concert, deep and raspy like a football team revving itself up to take the field. He snuggled deeper into his bag and tried to think of something more pleasant. That was when he felt someone grab his foot.

Jimmy found himself surrounded by what he could faintly make out to be six faces decked in gas masks, peering down at him, shaking his sleeping bag, screaming. He looked all around, then pulled the top of the bag over his head. Undeterred, the Marines started dragging it off from the end.

"Get your mask!" someone yelled.

"Get your mask! Get your mask! Gas." They all joined in. The sleeping bag was gone, and it was just Jimmy in his underwear.

"I don't ... Where's my—"

Jimmy scrambled. He jerked at the bags under his rack. The Marines at the end pulled him away by his feet. For a moment, he had a good grip on the handle of his suitcase. Then his hand slipped and he slid toward the bottom of the bunk. A hand seized one calf. Another gripped his upper arm. He lost track of all the places where they grabbed him. They hoisted him into the air and carried him out of the tent headfirst.

"Gas drill! Gas drill!"

"Nine seconds to live! No mask means you ... are ... dead!"

"Bury the dead! Save the living."

"One ... two ... three."

He flew through the air. There was a steep drop, and it occurred to him that it might be his grave after all. When he hit the sand, he knew for sure that it was real and not a dream. He screamed.

The Marines howled with laughter. They were pulling off their masks, slapping each other on the back. The scrawny one, Ramos, rolled on the ground, breathless with hysteria. It wasn't hard to see what had happened. The ditch was just a couple feet deep. The sand was recently plowed and soft. Sergeant Harper reached down and offered a hand.

"It's not that funny," Jimmy said, letting the sergeant pull him out. The Marines laughed harder. They patted his back and held out their masks in case he wanted one. He smelled alcohol in the one pushed closest to his nose. "It's really not that funny," he insisted, heart pounding against his ribs. They returned to the tent, and eventually the laughter settled down, but Jimmy never fell back asleep.

"It's really, really not that funny," he said the next morning over breakfast, wiping his mouth with a paper napkin. They were sitting in the chow hall, a large tent with rows of tables and folding chairs. Everyone was eating creamed chipped beef on toast off flimsy plastic plates. One of the Marines was holding a camcorder on the view setting. Another leaned over his shoulder to watch. "You had to tape it, didn't you?" Jimmy said.

"It's a memento," the Marine said.

"I wasn't scared. You guys were—were laughing so hard anyone could tell you were playing around." The footage was green and grainy. Somehow they'd attached night-vision technology to a personal video camera for the mission, a combination of American tax dollars and off-duty Marine ingenuity. The short film began with the group laughing too hard to properly explain their objective. They then sneaked commando-style toward the tent where Jimmy was half asleep. Unlike the others, his favorite part of the movie was when two of his attackers tripped and fell into another ditch on their way over. But it couldn't compare to the drama of the moment when Jimmy clawed at the air as he fell.

"I like how he screams when we throw him in the hole."

"No, no. How he tries to hold on to his rack while we drag him out."

"That's the shit," the Marine with the camera said.

"Thought I was working with professionals," Jimmy muttered. "And they let you guys carry guns."

"That's most of the job," Harper said.

"Unbelievable." At first Jimmy had been angry about the prank, but he knew better than to complain too much about it. If he couldn't handle a practical joke, how could they expect him to handle the war? He would have to put up with a certain level of torment. Besides, they did seem to think it was funny rather than intentionally intimidating.

"Pride of the Corps. Number one," Ramos said, flexing one of his Grade-A-egg-sized biceps. The skinny little Marine looked like a child. If they didn't have to be eighteen to join the Corps, Jimmy would have guessed that it was a mere sixteen years since Ramos had kicked and wailed his way into the world. Jimmy hadn't seen so many teenagers since college.

"Yeah, everybody must be so proud," Jimmy answered.

"Hey, now, Jimmy, don't take it the wrong way," Sergeant Harper said.

"Yeah, we didn't want to hurt your feelings," Ramos said, expanding the last word into a high-pitched aria, laying out the abject femininity of possessing feelings at all. "Dear diary," Ramos said, pretending to scribble with his forefinger. "Everyone at camp is mean to me. The big kids pick on me all the time."

"Let's cut the new guy a little slack," Harper said, and they were silent. "Come on, Jimmy. Let's go." The sergeant led him out. They dumped their trays and ducked under the flaps and into the morning sun. Martinez followed a step behind them, whistling.

Harper pulled a can of Copenhagen dip out of his pocket and tucked the moist tobacco between his gums and lower lip. He hospitably extended it toward Jimmy, who declined with a curt shake of the head.

"What's next?" Jimmy asked.

"Back home, my idea of babysitting," Harper said, "is to send the kids upstairs and turn on the TV. You can find your own fun out here."

"Will you at least—you know—show me around a little?" Jimmy asked.

The sergeant swirled the tobacco juice around in his mouth a bit as he considered this vague request, then spat on the ground. It looked like a momentous decision because he pursed his lips and stared off into the distance. The distance adequately scrutinized, he finally asked, "PFC Martinez, could you give the reporter our world-famous tour?"

"Yes, Sergeant Harper," Martinez said. "The long version or the short version?"

"Give him the long version," Harper said.

"Thank you, sir," Jimmy said. He followed Martinez at a brisk clip a few hundred yards. They stopped in front of a tent. Though there were hundreds of identical ones, this particular tent seemed familiar.

"Here you find our lovely tent," Martinez told him. "First and last stop of the world-famous tour. I'm off to get some gear."

"But—"

"Tour's over. Do some civilian things. We have work to do," he said. Martinez left him there with only a grunting chuckle. It was even hotter in the tent than it was outside, trapping the heat like a parked car on a summer day. Jimmy began to sweat. He felt grit in his nostrils, behind his ears, just about everywhere. He stepped out the back flap and saw four of the younger Marines sitting in the shade, cutting battle plans into the sand with knives.

"See, this is Iraq." Ramos clutched a knife in his bony hand and drew an hourglass in the sand with the point. "There are defenses here"—he scratched out a pair of breasts, including dots for the nipples—"and here." A tiny *v* sufficed for the crotch. More detail would have been difficult, given the medium. Pointing his knife at the *v*, he said, "Baghdad." Everyone nodded, including Jimmy. "We are breaking through here." A phallus hovered just past the breasts. He drew a line from the head of the dick, bisecting the breasts through the cleavage. "We'll then push through and penetrate the final defenses around Baghdad. Boom." He carved an X through Baghdad, then wiped out the whole maneuver with his left hand as everyone laughed.

"That's very informative, Private," Lieutenant Katzenbach said, standing behind the little group. His arms were crossed, and he was glaring down at them, but with his gentle, doughy face he seemed less like an intimidating officer than a vexed child. "Maybe our reporter could put that in tomorrow's newspaper for us. Your mother could read about it over breakfast."

"We're just playing around, sir. Not for the—"

"Jimmy, a word if I could? I heard there was an incident last night. Marines got a little out of hand?" Katzenbach asked, genuine concern in his eyes.

"Out of hand?" Jimmy repeated.

"Sounds to me like you were assaulted. Would you like to report anything about the event? Not, I've got to tell you, what I like to hear about my company." Every head around Jimmy hung to the ground. He hadn't particularly enjoyed being dragged out of his rack and thrown in a sandpit, but he wasn't about to snitch on anyone. It felt as though Katzenbach was trying to protect him, but Jimmy didn't feel bullied. He would never make friends with the young Marines with Katzenbach playing nursemaid for him.

"We were, uh, practicing some drills?" Jimmy said. Ramos nodded, his wide young eyes easily conveying innocence, and the others followed suit. "Yeah. Doing drills."

"What kind of drills were those?" Katzenbach said, looking a bit doubtful.

"Gas drills," Jimmy said, picking up confidence. "I'm a little, you know, a little shaky on how a lot of that works. Really slow with the mask and . . . well, they offered to help me practice."

"Practice," Katzenbach said, the geniality draining from his face. "Jimmy, I watched the video. That didn't look like any drill I've ever seen."

"Well, we got to horsing around, and—" He stopped. The young Marines offered no help. They looked like high school athletes about to get suspended before the big game for toilet-papering someone's house. It was sad. Then inspiration struck. "Instructional video."

"What?"

"Not entirely serious, mind you, but we decided it would be fun to make an instructional video. For, for other reporters, or whoever. In preparedness. You know, duck and cover? Be prepared, isn't that the Marine motto? No, that's the Boy Scouts. But you know what I mean."

"Ah, Jimmy. Could I get a word more privately real fast? The rest of you can stay right there." His tone was sharper with the Marines, but the moment he turned away, Jimmy saw Ramos puff up his cheeks and furrow his brow in imitation of the chunky lieutenant's displeasure. "I feel like we should be able to have a friendly working relationship. We have a lot in common, we're both college men and everything. I've actually done a little writing before . . ."

"Really?" Jimmy asked.

"I guess that's beside the point. Right now I feel like you're almost, well, insulting my intelligence with this video stuff a little. I really do." He stared off down the row of tents, as if he didn't want to look Jimmy in the eye as he spoke. "I . . . I just don't find it funny." He paused for a moment, then asked almost optimistically, "Is someone threatening you?"

"Of course not," Jimmy said.

"Then maybe you should straighten up a little. Maybe this seems like a game, but it isn't. These are my Marines. I have to discipline them. Without a little discipline, some of them might get killed. In fact, some of them probably will get killed up north. If there are troublemakers, unprofessional fellows in this company, the captain and I should know about it."

"I'm sorry," Jimmy said. "There won't be any, you know, any more problems."

"We have a saying around here," the lieutenant said with a smile. He held his forefinger up. Jimmy could see the black crescent of dirt under the officer's fingernail. "Sorry is bullshit."

"It won't happen again," Jimmy said, a bit taken aback.

"You're right. It won't." He left Jimmy and walked over to the enlisted men. "The first sergeant would like to see all of you right now. Hop to it."

"He's going to bust our asses," Ramos said to Jimmy as the lieutenant headed off, his ample backside putting a slight waddle in his gait.

"Why?"

"Lieutenant Boob Job won't do shit 'cause you backed us up, but First Sergeant can put us through some fucking PT to kill you, hombre." Ramos shook his head. Their respect for the first sergeant made their contempt for Katzenbach all the more obvious. PT was physical training. It was worse in the desert, because of the heat and the sand. "Feel like you're in the pit back on Parris Island," Ramos said. He didn't look like he'd enjoyed the pit.

"We got to quit bitching and get over to company," Lance Corporal Dabrowski barked. He was probably twenty-one years old, but with his deep voice, broad shoulders, and bristly black mustache he seemed like the perfect, ageless Marine. He was the most intimidating member of the company Jimmy had seen, a born nightclub bouncer, and Jimmy knew his bouncers. "Later, reporter," Dabrowski said. They shuffled off toward the company command tent, buttoning shirts and straightening up the best they could. Five minutes later they were back, changing into shorts and

T-shirts. "You can come if you want. A little exercise?" Dabrowski asked.

"Thanks. I'll pass. Sorry, guys."

"You did your part, man. Later." Dabrowski and the others left him in the tent. He was alone again, but for a moment he felt like part of the team.

CHAPTER 9

THE MARINES SAT IN A CIRCLE ON THE SANDBAGS OUTSIDE THEIR tent. It was evening now, and they were passing around a Listerine bottle, taking turns drinking the mouthwash straight. Desperate measures were needed in a country without alcohol, Jimmy thought. He didn't think he could drink mouthwash, but they hadn't offered him any either.

Ramos took a drag on his cigarette, making the ember at the end brighten, bathing his young face in an orange glow. A smoker throughout college, Jimmy was tempted to bum one but resisted. It was a pleasant sight, more pleasant than watching some of them dribble tobacco juice into empty soda cans. Lance Corporal Dabrowski had a different reaction.

"Get you shot in the field," Dabrowski said to Ramos as he exhaled.

"Come on," Ramos said.

"In Chechnya, snipers killed the smokers first," Dabrowski said. "At night, when the Russians were resting and having a butt, the snipers would aim at the cherries—"

"This isn't the Recon exam, D-Boy, and we aren't in the field yet," Ramos said. Dabrowski was trying to join the elite Marine unit, Force Recon. He was already the strongest and fastest and, Ramos told Jimmy, meanest among them, but he had to train himself to be stronger, faster, and meaner still. Instead of reading paperbacks or magazines in his downtime, he read training manuals on guerrilla fighting tactics. "You can stand down for five minutes."

"Whatever, man." Dabrowski laughed. "Dip and live."

"You should consult your Marine Behavior Manual, Lance Corporal Dabrowski. I will write you up for actions unbecoming of a junior noncom," Ramos said in an unflattering imitation of Katzenbach. The other Marines began a chorus of meowing and mewling.

"Sorry, Lieutenant Pussy," Dabrowski said.

"Now take my bras to laundry, Lance Corporal, and don't forget the fabric softener," Ramos continued.

"Lieutenant Pussy," Dabrowski asked, continuing their impromptu skit, "if I may, sir, just one thing?"

"Yes, Lance Corporal?"

"Well, the boys have been in the desert a real long time. And there's no girls out here except the adjutant to the command company, who looks like a hog. And, well, would you show us your tits?" Dabrowski asked. The Marines burst into the harshest laughter Jimmy could ever remember hearing, punctuated with shouts of "Boob job!" and "Double-D!"

"What's that about?" Jimmy asked. Ramos cupped a pair of imaginary breasts in front of his chest.

"Man boobs. XO has some titties, baby," Ramos answered. As executive officer for the company, Katzenbach had the no-glory jobs like paperwork and discipline. He was, Jimmy surmised, the object of particular hatred for all of the Marines in the company. All the men knew that he had been passed over for a promotion to captain and command of his own company for the second time. They called him Tits Ahoy and Kitty Cat and Lieutenant Pussy. They speculated about his wife's faithfulness in a way Jimmy found truly unpleasant. With the nose for fear that prisoners use to sniff over new guards, they had Katzenbach pegged as weak.

Jimmy felt terrible for Katzenbach, but was hardly in a position to defend him. As the squad's reporter, he wasn't sure what his role was, exactly. He had tried to think of an article to write, but what would he say about waiting? While the first sergeant put the Marines through a grueling array of exercises in their gas masks, Jimmy found himself engaged in a chat with the head Marine chef about his crew of Pakistani sous-chefs. It wasn't much, but it might provide the raw material for a brief feature story.

"Here's Sergeant. You missed PT, Sergeant Harper."

"Boys," Harper said, as a low, unhurried greeting. "Made a run into town for batteries."

"For the NVGs?"

"Yeah."

"Oo-rah, Sergeant."

"Got us a little Kentucky Fried Chicken down in Kuwait City too," Martinez said.

"Damn," someone else said with envy.

"I'd kill fifty Iraqis for some KFC, man," Dabrowski said.

"PFC Martinez, give these men their chicken," Harper replied. Martinez produced three crumpled buckets of fried chicken from his knapsack. There were scattered grunts of approval and even more hands reaching out.

"No offense, Sergeant Harper," Dabrowski said, half of a drumstick lodged in his cheek. "But your breath smells like shit. You want some mouthwash?"

"Appreciate the honesty, Lance Corporal Dabrowski. Let me

try to fix that problem." Harper took a long swig from the mouth-wash bottle and passed it to Martinez, who did likewise. It rounded the circle to Ramos, who was sitting next to Jimmy.

"Permission to give some Listerine to the sissy-ass civilian reporter, Sergeant Harper."

"Only if he keeps it off the record, Private," Harper said.

"Off the record, Jimmy?" Ramos asked.

"Sure," Jimmy said, reaching for the bottle. He almost spat as he tasted it but managed to hold it in, some of the liquid channel-ing up into his sinuses, where it burned. There was only a hint of mint flavor. The rest was pure alcohol.

"Ethyl alcohol. Grain," Dabrowski said. "Stuff's a little harsh, but gets the job done." They chuckled. The grain alcohol was tinted with food coloring. It had been delivered inside a ziplock freezer bag with a toothbrush, toothpaste, and dental floss. The seal had been reheated for any suspicious Kuwaiti inspectors.

"That was some pretty stupid shit, covering for the boys against the XO like that, Jimmy," Harper said.

"Aw, Sergeant," Ramos began.

"Hold on, now. He's got a different job out here. How do you expect to get good intel for your stories if the XO hates your guts?"

"Why's he so important?" Jimmy asked. Harper was older and somehow more authoritative. Jimmy assumed he was much more important for his daily work than Katzenbach.

"He's second in command for a hundred and ninety men," Harper said. "And he's the guy assigned to keep an eye on you. Give you information."

"Isn't he younger than you are?" Jimmy asked.

"He's an officer, with a commission. I'm just an enlisted grunt. Doesn't matter how many stripes I have on my shoulder, I'm still lower than any second lieutenant fresh out of the Naval Academy,"

Harper said. "This must be your first time covering the military?"

"What? No. Of course not. I know that." Jimmy felt a tremor of anxiety. He remembered what Becky had said. He could not admit to being a clueless gossip columnist just as he was starting to fit in. "I've ... uh, been doing more terrorism lately," Jimmy said. Terrorism sounded tougher than *American Idol*.

Bits and pieces of news, combined with what he knew about cop reporting, built his fake résumé. Since September 11, it had been all terrorism all the time for the hard-boiled reporter. Before that, he had mostly bobbed and weaved from crime scene to crime scene, sparring with tough NYPD detectives, with some time clocked in among military units on special assignment. The *Daily Herald* had a Pentagon correspondent, of course, "but he's more of a desk guy." Jimmy let it sink in that he was more of a man of action himself. He wasn't sure how convincing his act was, but Harper dropped the subject. "I just think that the enlisted men are the heart and soul of the Corps. Not the college boys. I dropped out of college," Jimmy said proudly for the first time in his life.

"You and me both, members of a truly auspicious club," Harper answered.

Once the grain alcohol was gone, they vanished one by one into the tent. Jimmy knew right away he would fall asleep without incident unless there was more hazing to come. The liquor made him drowsy. Even his cot felt more comfortable. The fact that he had lied to the squad, reimagined his past exploits in a way that he could never hope to live up to, would wait until morning to gnaw at him. In Jimmy's pleasantly drifting mind it was Fashion Week in New York, and his two favorite models each held an arm as the three of them strolled through SoHo.

Alone in the tent, early in the day before it had gotten unbearably hot, Jimmy ventured into his e-mail for the first time since leaving

Kuwait City three days earlier. In the back of his mind he knew he should have been writing and filing stories, but he chose to avoid the matter by leaving the phone off and the laptop shut. Ellison couldn't get to him at a forward base in the northern Kuwaiti desert.

What was he supposed to write? The Marines threw their reporter in a ditch. The mess hall served London broil. Marines smoked. Marines spat. Marines did push-ups. But he knew he could put it off no longer. Still, it was worse than he had expected. Requests had come in at a rate of about two an hour since he'd embedded, all of them unanswered and until then unopened. Entreaties poured in from the *Daily Herald*'s other embeds, its Pentagon correspondent, and even its reporter in Baghdad. The poor fellow who was waiting in Jordan had received his visa and made it to the Iraqi capital. Now he had an understandable desire to learn more about the American assault aimed at his location.

The telecommunications reporter back in New York wanted to know about the pay phones and Internet options for the troops. The retail reporter wanted to know about the PX. The local reporters all wanted interviews with Marines from their suburbs or neighborhoods. An intern was trying to write a story about the mail service and was particularly petulant about Jimmy's refusal to answer. It seemed like every writer at the paper wanted a little piece of the war. Requests had even come from Ellison directly.

Overwhelming, Jimmy thought. The whole thing felt overwhelming. He didn't understand the first thing about what was going on. Anyone with a television tuned to CNN must have had a better idea of what was happening than he did. Since both going to war and losing his job would be counterproductive, Jimmy got to work. But he found he couldn't banish parallels to red carpet events from his thoughts. It was a big gathering with crowds of tense, excited people. "Guess what time it is? Invasion time. It's ten p.m., America; do you know where your Marine Corps is? Getting ready to kick some ass in the desert, that's where." He typed to get it out of his system.

"My Marines taking care of you there, Mr. Stephens?" Katzenbach appeared at the flap of the tent, peering in at him.

"Excuse me?" Jimmy said.

"Are the boys taking care of you?" Katzenbach asked. They hadn't spoken since the incident with the videotape. Jimmy had detected some frostiness there, but the lieutenant came into the tent and sat down on the bunk across from him. He was wearing the standard-issue exercise shorts and a T-shirt soaked completely through with sweat. His husky build was not, Jimmy determined, for lack of trying. Katzenbach was probably fighting a losing battle with his genes. Against his will Jimmy noted the soft flesh of Katzenbach's chest pressing against wet fabric, an irresistible target for the young Marines.

"Oh. Uh, yes, sir," Jimmy said, hoping he had not been staring. "Of course."

"You writing good stuff about how hard they're working out here? Working to protect our country?" Katzenbach asked.

"Of course, Lieutenant Katzenbach," Jimmy said.

"We're so glad to have you here, Jimmy. So very glad. Because you're here to tell the story of the Corps." He broke into his goofy smile. "So you haven't asked me about how our men are doing."

"As ... as I was about to," Jimmy said. "How are they doing?"

"Their morale is high. They're ready. They've been training for this for years. They can't wait to go." This was predictable and therefore unpublishable in Jimmy's eyes, but he took out a pen and began copying down Katzenbach's words, skipping many, but flashing the notebook toward the lieutenant so he could see certain ones, like "morale" and "ready" written large among squiggles and chicken scratch.

"What are they doing, in particular, to be more ready for this, you know, versus another war? For this war, I mean. How are— how are they specifically preparing?"

"They're always ready," Katzenbach replied.

"But—"

"They're always ready," Katzenbach said, as if he couldn't understand the question or was stuck on a loop, "because they're Marines. Marines are ready to fight any time. At a moment's notice."

"I saw the wrong end of that at a bar in Boston once," Jimmy said, chuckling alone. The lieutenant stared and didn't react, glancing down at the notebook. "Anyway." Jimmy scribbled "at a moment's notice" extra large, tipped the notebook toward the lieutenant, then loudly flipped to the next page. "Perfect," Jimmy said. "That's great. Everything I needed." Katzenbach nodded eagerly. Jimmy waited for him to leave, but he remained seated and smiling.

"Remind me again where you went to college," Katzenbach said.

"NYU," Jimmy answered. Katzenbach seemed to cling to this common experience. The officers—lieutenants, captains, majors, and up—were almost entirely college graduates, from what in the old days might have been called the upper classes. Harper and Katzenbach were on completely different tracks, parallel ladders. Katzenbach was trying to make the step to captain, to end his time as the paper-pushing vice principal and command his own company. As high as Harper climbed, he would never become a captain, instead making first sergeant or sergeant major, with greater responsibility and higher pay, but always below the officers in the chain of command.

"I went to New York once." The lieutenant nodded enthusiastically. "Times Square. Dazzling. It's wild up there. How do you manage to live there all the time?"

"Well, coming from Jersey, just about everybody's parents

work in the city, you went a lot weekends." Jimmy had work to do, but more important, he didn't feel like pursuing this idle chit-chat with Katzenbach. He felt bad for the guy, but found it hard to be friends with people he pitied. The more ingratiating someone was, the more pathetic he could seem. "Sorry, I've really—"

"You need to work?" Katzenbach asked him. "I understand."

"Yeah, it's just ..." Jimmy began. He felt terrible. "You know how deadlines are."

"Absolutely," the lieutenant agreed. He stood up and walked toward the tent flap again. "But if you need anything," he said, "just ask."

Jimmy began to compose an article out of snippets of what he saw and heard around the camp, as well as his brief interview with Katzenbach. It was little more than a collection of sights and sounds, the bustle of activity around the camp, structured around bland quotes from the executive officer. It would, Jimmy hoped, never see the light of day in the paper.

His smallpox vaccination had given him a fever. On the bright side, the pamphlet with the American flag on the cover and the photos of hideously disfigured people on the inside reported that it was completely normal to run a fever and develop a bubbling sore on your shoulder. The downside was that the heat was already sweating every drop of liquid from Jimmy's body. He had developed a cough the Marines called "the crud," which they said was a result of his lungs getting used to an unpleasant coating of sand. He felt completely enervated and easily confused.

It did not help matters that for the fourth time he went through the unsettling experience of filling out a next-of-kin form. He suffered through his second gas-mask training session as well as his third lecture about threading a dog tag through one of his boot-laces. That way, in the event that his head and body disappeared, he could still be identified without too much effort, the lieutenant explained to him. He could see with ever-greater clarity what a mistake it had been to join the Marines for this invasion. So he expected at least a little understanding as he packed his belongings for the third time. He got none.

"Let's go. This is it. We're moving up," Harper said.

"This is it?" Jimmy asked, dropping the pamphlet. "We're invading?"

"No," Harper said. "We're moving to the assembly point."

"Aren't we assembled already?" Jimmy asked.

"We need to assemble," Harper said very slowly. "After that we can move ahead to the staging area."

"I thought this was a staging area. This isn't a staging area?" Jimmy asked the sergeant.

"This is a prestaging area," Harper said.

"Is there a poststaging area?" Jimmy asked.

"Iraq," Harper said.

"I mean between the two, between the staging area and Iraq," Jimmy said.

"There's the LD," Harper said. "Line of departure."

"Is that a location or a state of mind?" Jimmy asked.

"A little of both," Harper said. "You almost ready?"

"Almost," Jimmy said, zipping up his backpack. He heard Harper's footsteps moving away on the plywood floor and quickly gathered his belongings to follow. He hoisted the frame pack onto his shoulders, raised the handle on his suitcase with one hand, and grabbed both duffel bags with the other. The wheels of the suitcase were useless on the unpaved path. It dug a wide canal behind him in the sand. It was all he could do to keep Harper in sight. At last the sergeant stopped at a line of Humvees.

"I told you we were gonna get a chick," Ramos said.

"Play nice, Devil Dog," Martinez said, using one of the Corps nicknames for its troops.

"He's packed like a bitch, all I'm saying."

"What's wrong?" Jimmy asked.

"You can't bring anything to the staging area that you aren't bringing across the berm," Harper said.

"Okay," Jimmy said, moving toward the Humvee to load his luggage. Harper stepped in front of him. The bulge of tobacco in the sergeant's lower lip made him look even more square-jawed and tough.

"Jimmy, that's more than we can fit in this Humvee. For all of us." Harper loosed a string of brown spit on the ground, a foot from Jimmy's bags.

"Sergeant Harper, we could leave all our weapons behind, Sergeant. To make room for the reporter's panties," Ramos said.

"Private, no speaking for the rest of the day. At all," Harper said. "Jimmy, we got to repack you here."

"Um, this one's my computer and phones and stuff." He lifted up the heavier of the two duffels. "I got to take it with me. And, uh, this one has my clothes and shoes—I mean, boots—and stuff, in it. Kind of need that. Let's see. Chem gear over here. Toiletries. It's all on the list."

"What list?" Harper asked.

"The embed packing list."

"Do you have a copy of this list that maybe I could look at?"

"Sure, right here," Jimmy said. Harper took the pages from him and began to read.

"Six pairs of underwear?" Harper read out loud.

"That's what it says."

"Gore-Tex pants," Harper said, blinking and looking up from the paper at Jimmy.

"For the rain," the reporter explained.

"Sergeant Harper, we're supposed to—" Ramos began.

"Private, the not-talking? That was an order," Harper barked.

"Sergeant Harper," Martinez said. "I think what he wants to say is that we've got five minutes before we roll."

"You can have the backpack and one duffel," Harper told Jimmy.

"One?" Jimmy asked.

"One," Harper confirmed. "You have five minutes."

"Four," Ramos said. Harper didn't chastise him this time. The diesel fumes heightened Jimmy's nausea as he bent over to empty the pack.

CHAPTER 10

NO ONE COULD TELL HIM EXACTLY WHERE IRAQ BEGAN. THE STAG-ing area was closer, but it was still at an "undisclosed location near the Iraqi border" for publication purposes. Physically they were moving, but rhetorically they were stranded. There was constant talk of the berm and the need to breach it. Jimmy gathered this was like a man-made sand dune along the border. Whether they were going over it, through it, or under it no one had apprised him. But there was no hill within eyeshot, raising the possibility of another move toward the border.

Jimmy went for a walk. He said he needed to find Lieutenant Katzenbach, but the truth was that the Marines were working, and he had nothing to do. This process of inching toward Iraq while moving slowly away from civilization hardly lent itself to great feature stories. And Katzenbach had told him that moving forward was an operational detail that could not be published. He said it might give away the timing of the invasion. Rather than sit and watch the Marines work, he strolled aimlessly around the position. For the first time, Jimmy wished they would just invade and get it over with. It was like easing into a cold swimming pool, prolonging the discomfort.

When he returned from his walk, he found that each of the Marines in his squad had his own individual-size hole in the ground. He had watched other Marines digging as he wandered the encampment, but had not asked himself to what end. Digging seemed like the kind of thing Marines needed to do to stay busy. "What are those?" Jimmy asked.

"Fighting holes," said Harper.

"Is that like a foxhole?" Jimmy suggested.

"Foxes hide in holes. Marines fight in theirs," Harper recited, as if this were an old saw for Marines to repeat. The sergeant even had a secondary hole beside his to collect dip juice. It looked like a miniature tar pit for catching tiny dinosaurs. "But yeah. A lot like that."

"Where's mine?" he asked.

"You can borrow my entrenching tool," Martinez said, and tossed a two-foot-long shovel at his feet.

"You mean the shovel?" Jimmy asked.

"I mean the entrenching tool," Martinez answered.

"Of course you guys couldn't call it a shovel," Jimmy said. "How foolish of me." They had a more complicated name for the simplest of things. By the end of the war, toilet paper would be called rectal sanitary equipment, and they'd use the acronym RSE for an extra layer of obfuscation. He picked up the shovel and stared at the sand, unsure where to begin.

"Pretend you're looking for oil," Harper suggested.

"Isn't there someone who, you know," Jimmy said, looking at the shovel distastefully, "does this for us?"

"Who? The concierge?" Harper asked.

"I'll do it for fifty bucks," Ramos said. Martinez laughed, and Harper rolled his eyes.

Jimmy simply said, "Twenty-five?"

"No way," Ramos answered.

"Well, you can't do it after you're dead," Martinez said.

"As is true for pretty much everything," Jimmy agreed, thinking that they looked far too much like graves for him to laugh.

"Never heard of Scuds?" Harper asked. "You think Saddam's just going to let us walk across the border?" Jimmy didn't say anything. He'd given very little thought to Saddam Hussein's plans. "We might just get our hair mussed before this thing is out."

"Missiles are coming. Dig deep," Martinez said.

"You're trying to scare me," Jimmy said. "We've played this game before."

"Yeah, every Marine in the desert spent half an hour digging a hole just to play a joke on you," Harper said.

"I wouldn't put it past you guys," Jimmy said, "honestly."

"If you want to be the only man out here without a hole, be my guest." Harper swept out his arm at the flat expanse, inviting Jimmy to sit where he pleased.

"Shrapnel, Jimmy," Martinez said. "Chunks of metal five times bigger than a bullet. Think about it."

Jimmy picked up the shovel and dinged the front end into the sand. "It's hard."

"Fairly, yeah," Harper said.

"No, really hard," Jimmy said.

"If it was easy," Harper said, "Private Ramos would have done it for twenty-five." Ramos saluted Jimmy from inside his own hole, then held out his hand as if he fully expected the fifty dollars. When it didn't appear, he returned to cleaning his rifle.

Jimmy got to work on his hole. He'd begun to take off the tan bulletproof vest he'd put on for the ride from Camp Triumph to the staging area, but the Marines cautioned him to keep it on. He did, at a cost of great discomfort. First to throb were his shoulders.

The weight of the vest dragged straight down on them. The pain migrated to his upper arms as he flung what looked like teaspoons of sand into a pile.

The job wasn't sped up any by the fact that every Marine in his squad felt it was his duty to give Jimmy a little push in the back as he passed, then hold up his hands in mock self-defense and point giggling at the writing on Jimmy's vest. "It said, 'Press.'" He stood up, palms against his lower back, and addressed Harper, who looked half asleep, but still managed a smirk at Jimmy's plight.

"Let me guess. We're going to pull forward two hundred feet just when I'm finished." Harper didn't answer. "Right?" Jimmy said louder.

"Jimmy," the sergeant said, "I'm not going to say no and then have the Corps make a liar out of me." Jimmy went back to his slow digging.

"In the real world," Lance Corporal Dabrowski said to Jimmy, legs dangling into Ramos's fighting hole as he sat on the side, "I'd beat your ass if I saw you in a bar."

"Come again?" Jimmy said. He was trying to train himself not to respond to the Marines' comments, but with little success so far.

"If you were in Pittsburgh, in my neighborhood, I'd take you apart," Dabrowski said. "But out here, it's like we're all brothers. Even you. I feel a bond with everyone breaching that fucking berm." Dabrowski bummed a cigarette from Ramos simply by snapping his fingers. Ramos looked annoyed but complied.

"Thanks?" Jimmy asked. He stopped and wiped the sweat from his forehead with the short sleeve of his T-shirt.

"Hell, yeah," Dabrowski answered.

"You faggots need some time alone?" Ramos asked.

Dabrowski's mustache twisted to one side as he pursed his lips and considered Ramos's comment. "Did the little private just try to fuck with me?" Dabrowski asked Jimmy.

"Honestly," Jimmy said, "I can't really tell anymore."

"Little faggot, you call me a faggot?" Dabrowski asked.

"If the dick fits," Ramos said.

"How would my K-bar fit in your ass?" Dabrowski said in a tone so practical it suggested he was actively considering using the knife on Ramos.

"Why don't you try to put it there and find out?" the scrawny Marine challenged.

"That doesn't seem—" Jimmy began.

"Bitch," Ramos added.

"Suit yourself," Jimmy said.

"See, if we were at Pendleton, I'd have beat the shit out of Private Pussy over there by now." Jimmy noticed that Dabrowski had put his cigarette down, carefully balancing it on the lip of the fighting hole. That should have been his cue to apologize, but Ramos ignored the ominous gesture. "But he's going north too. So we're brothers." Dabrowski pounced from the edge of the fighting hole and landed on top of Ramos, who he may have literally doubled in weight. He had the private's face in the sand in no time and was pounding him on the shoulders. "Uncle, uncle, uncle. Any time you're ready. This is what I do to my little brothers, Jimmy."

"Pussy bitch," Ramos said between mouthfuls of sand. Dabrowski punched him twice as hard. Jimmy crouched down to begin shoveling again. In spite of the pummeling, or maybe because of it, Jimmy knew Ramos and Dabrowski to be close friends. Martinez sauntered up and stood beside him, watching the beating.

"What's going on here?" Martinez asked.

"Homoeroticism disguised as homophobia," Jimmy said. He looked up to see if Dabrowski was going to jump him for his comment, but the lance corporal was busy.

"Boys will be boys." Martinez walked over to his fighting hole, which was right next to the action and lay down, setting his floppy tan hat over his eyes to nap. He struck Jimmy as far too old and far too serious to take part in their horsing around. Dabrowski was obsessive about his training and his recon aspirations, but in reality he was barely out of his teens. "If one grain of sand gets in this hole, they're going to be looking for you two for the rest of the war," Martinez said to the younger Marines, in his most paternal voice. "I'm not saying who's going to kill you exactly, Lance Corporal Dabrowski," he said, a reference to Dabrowski's higher rank, Jimmy inferred, "but I'll make Jimmy bury you." The killing wouldn't have bothered him at just that moment, but Jimmy winced at the thought of digging another hole.

At dusk the order went around to put on their MOPP chemical suits. The suits were vacuum-sealed in stiff bags that looked like plastic on the outside and aluminum foil inside. Unfolded, the suits were roomy. The jackets bunched up under their bulletproof vests, and the pants were big and baggy. It was like trying on an oversize hand-me-down snowsuit, an unfortunate parallel for a group of men expected to wear the long-sleeved garments in the desert.

The acronym stood for Mission-Oriented Protective Posture, which did close to nothing to explain what it was: a charcoal-lined suit with a hood that, when combined with rubber booties, gloves, and a gas mask, was supposed to seal the wearer off from fatal chemicals. Only the word "protective" seemed necessary, but Jimmy understood why the Marines wouldn't want to call them "pee suits." On the other hand, "protective posture" sounded awfully meek for the Marine Corps. Maybe "mission-oriented" was added to make it sound dynamic, boost morale.

Martinez stripped naked to put on his MOPP suit. Even in the dim light, his canvas was impressive. A dragon breathed fire off his right arm. Its talon perched on a bloody skull. The tail wrapped around a naked woman. There was a skeleton with a sword on the other arm. Homemade tattoos, faded to blue, speckled his body from his neck to his groin in smaller designs. They were overshadowed by the professional ones, hyperreal and coursing with potential energy. The woman's tensed muscles made her look ready to burst off his arm and wrestle a biker into submission.

The most violent was the crucified Christ splayed across his back. It must have taken weeks of sittings and would have cost well into the thousands of dollars. Rivulets of blood cascaded off the martyr's forehead. His look wasn't beatific, but a grimace of agony. Jesus' pumped-up arms strained hard, but the spikes through his palms held fast to the cross. The artist had captured the exact moment that the lance pierced his side. The cross itself was black and maroon with dried blood, angry. Unlike his meditative doppelgängers on the walls of middle-class homes in New Jersey, this Jesus had truly sacrificed for mankind.

"Nice suit," Harper said.

"What?" Jimmy asked.

"Your suit," Harper said. "One of a kind." Jimmy was so busy studying Martinez's artwork that he failed to notice that the Marines were wearing green suits, and he had the only desert-colored one in the bunch. One more chance to blend in had been ruined by whichever supply clerk mistakenly sent the Marines forest-camouflaged suits for the desert. "And that's bad news for you."

"Because everyone will know I'm a reporter, I know."

"No, because the Iraqi snipers will think you're a general and shoot you first." Jimmy scrunched down in his freshly dug hole and opened his laptop. At least he was better camouflaged. Maybe, he thought, it was really jealousy.

Jimmy thanked the first sergeant for directing him and stepped carefully around the warren of fighting holes until he found Lieutenant Katzenbach's. Most of the Marines were gathered in knots of three or more guys, shooting the breeze as they waited for their marching orders. Katzenbach sat alone, a small camping headlamp strapped to his forehead instead of a handheld flashlight. It was smart, practical, and a little kooky looking. He was studying maps, marking them with a grease pencil, when he noticed Jimmy standing over him. Jimmy was momentarily blinded as the light flashed in his eyes.

"Sorry about that," Katzenbach said, switching off the light on his brow. "What can I do you for?"

"Yeah, good question," Jimmy said, hesitating. He was a little afraid to ask. Putting on their MOPP suits had seemed like the first clear indication of impending conflict. He wanted to know why they were sitting in one foreign country preparing to invade its neighbor. He didn't entirely understand why people on both sides were about to die. In the rush of the first two weeks he hadn't given it much thought. Now that the moment was nearing, he felt he needed to know before he could get into the Humvee and cross the border. He couldn't ask his colleagues. It was something he should have known already. Harper would make fun of him. "I was just, well, we're invading pretty soon, and—"

"Remember, Jimmy, that's future operations," Katzenbach said. "Read your ground rules. You'll know when the time comes."

"No, it was more of a . . . I'm wondering why. Why here? Why now? Is it going to be worth it?"

"Off the record?" he asked. Jimmy nodded. "I'm glad you came to me, Jimmy. Is it worth it? What are we doing this for? If that's what you're asking yourself, we have the best answer in the whole world."

"Good," Jimmy said.

"Liberty," Katzenbach answered.

"Liberty?" Jimmy asked.

"In the great American tradition," Katzenbach said. "We both bring liberty, like a redemptive trial by fire for those to whom we give that gift, as well as guard the flame of liberty we have been charged to keep at home."

"Liberty," Jimmy repeated. It sounded worthy. Lieutenant Katzenbach made Jimmy feel better. They were there to right wrongs, he explained, to help the less fortunate, to deliver democracy to the oppressed people of Iraq. They knew, through dissidents and intelligence networks, that this was exactly what the Iraqis wanted. They didn't have the strength or the will to boot out the dictator by themselves, so America was lending a helping hand.

The amazing thing, and this was the part that Jimmy especially liked, was that there really wouldn't be much to do. The intelligence suggested that the entire Iraqi Army was lined up not to fight the Marines, but to surrender en masse and fight each other for a cozy spot behind good old-fashioned American barbed wire, where they would get their first square meal in weeks. Their wives, meanwhile, were preparing a barrage of bouquets to welcome the arriving liberators.

"We're not talking about desertion—or even surrender," Katzenbach explained. "We're talking about capitulation. Our Articles of Capitulation have been required reading in Iraq the last few days. When we drive through, you'll see Iraqi tank turrets turned away from us and toward Baghdad. Sort of like spontaneous democracy in the decision to lay down their arms and work with us for a better Iraq."

"Spontaneous democracy," Jimmy said, impressed.

That night Jimmy curled up to sleep with visions of France at the end of World War II in his head. His memory from high school history had been a little shaky, but Katzenbach had filled in the missing details. Streets lined with waving, cheering crowds, free wine and free kisses, little boys running alongside tanks, sometimes getting pulled up and allowed to ride on the big gun. Old Frenchmen still told PBS documentarians that those rides were the highlight of their lives, Katzenbach said. It grew colder than he expected after the sun went down, and Jimmy ended up glad to be wearing his MOPP suit for one night at least. It was surprisingly warm, Jimmy thought, a head-to-toe security blanket, courtesy of the U.S. government.

CHAPTER II

WHEN THE WAR MOVIE BEGINS, THE BOATS ARE ALWAYS BOBBING just off the coast of Normandy. There's time for a moment or two of anxiety and the Catholic boy to kiss his cross. Then the anticipated hell breaks loose right on schedule. But how many times had they loaded up the boats, had the invasion been postponed on account of weather, had they sat around trying to get built-up salt deposits out of their guns? Jimmy had no idea whether his company would inch up to the border step by step, new camp by new camp, or hop into their vehicles and rush headlong toward Baghdad five minutes later. No one seemed to know how or when they were going. They didn't even seem to care, content to sit and bullshit, trained and conditioned to wait for orders.

They had been sitting by the border for two days. Rumors that they were about to invade were rampant, but nothing happened. The president issued an ultimatum, giving Saddam and his sons forty-eight hours to leave Iraq, but the Marines stayed put. Jimmy heard on a shortwave radio that the United Nations weapons inspectors had left the country. But rather than charging ahead, they sat in the Humvee and waited. They had been in position for eight hours. They were, as Harper put it, in a combat-ready posture, but Jimmy suspected a true combat posture involved less slouching.

After his talk with Lieutenant Katzenbach, Jimmy was in relatively good spirits, assured now that the war was more symbolic than anything. Still, the waiting gave him ample time to think. The more he learned about the possibilities, the worse they seemed. There was a hierarchy of firepower in a war. Light and heavy machine-gun rounds came straight at you. Mortars and artillery fire dropped from above. Surface-to-air missiles soared even higher in the sky before plunging toward their fatal detonation. Layers of deadly iron sought victims on the battlefield. Even the coward faced mines and barbed wire if he decided to run away from the fighting. It was a good thing they weren't really going to have to fight the Iraqis. It sounded horrific.

"Now I'm more worried about land mines than anything. Never see them coming. Just—boom! And that's it." Martinez had sat behind the wheel handicapping his relative fear of ways to die for close to an hour. He'd left out slipping in the shower, getting trampled by a herd of moose, and being run over by a delivery truck, but that was about it, Jimmy thought. He noticed that across the board Martinez was much more afraid of explosives than plain old gunfire. It seemed appropriate for their driver to be most concerned about mines.

"True," Harper said. He rode shotgun, with the best view and his hand on the radio. Jimmy and Ramos, meanwhile, would be stuck in the back like kids on a family vacation. The four of them shared one Humvee. Lance Corporal Dabrowski rode behind them with his own three-man crew. The chain of command divided and subdivided the 20,000 Marines waiting to break into Iraq. In all, Harper commanded a rifle squad of eleven men, down from the usual twelve due to their knife-play casualty. His job was to keep track of those men, keep them safe, and execute the orders he was given. It was not his job to think broadly about the invasion, or even the company, just his men and his orders.

"Bullets are bad too, right?" Jimmy asked.

"We have more bullets than them," Martinez said.

"Way more," Harper agreed.

"I'm not afraid of any Iraqi pussies," Ramos said. "They run before. They run again. I just hope they don't run before I get some." Get some meant get some action and kill some Iraqis. Ramos fused Marine bravado with hip-hop bravado into an alloy of violent slang. "But I'll tell my homeboys what. If I got to sneak across a border, I'm glad we got a Mexican behind the wheel."

"Sergeant Harper, if you could tell him to shut his hole," Martinez said.

"Just saying you the man for the job, baby," Ramos said. "He's got real-world training. You swim the Rio Grande, Martinez? Remind me."

"Yeah, Ramos. Your mom toweled me off, kept me warm when I got across." Martinez turned back toward Jimmy and said, "One minute he's all blood-in, blood-out Latino gangster, the next he's this punk-ass Mexican-hating bitch."

"Damn," Ramos said. "These wetbacks is sensitive and shit. I respect my Latin brothers from all over. I'm just talking about your résumé, sangrón. You know how to jump a border." Jimmy had never seen Ramos as happy as he looked making fun of Martinez. "It's a positive. A life skill."

"Aren't you—" Jimmy started to say.

"Fuck no," Ramos said, jabbing a finger at Jimmy. "You are not about to say that we all look alike. Do not insult the rainbow of people from the Andes to Havana by lumping us all in with those fucking border-jumping Mexicans."

"Private," Harper began.

"I will shut up, Sergeant," Ramos said.

Outside, the sky was smudged dark with streaks of oil smoke. Even where they sat in their Humvee on the ground, it seemed hazy. "We knew he was going to light them up." Harper pulled the clip out of his M16, blew into it, then locked it back in place.

"Light what up?" Jimmy asked. "Oh, the oil fields." Jimmy tried not to let the ominous darkness ruin his improved mood. The liberation centers hadn't been set up yet. Until the war officially began, Jimmy reflected, the Iraqi Army would have to follow orders.

"We've been waiting for two months. I'm ready to go," Ramos said. His voice cracked in regular conversation at times, so it was hard to say how scared he really was. Jimmy wanted to reassure him, but it was not a civilian's place to comfort a Marine.

"Game day," Harper said.

"Oo-rah," the other two Marines barked.

"I'm going to be pissed if I don't get shot at," Ramos said.

"Our little barbarian." Martinez was behind the wheel but reached back like he was going to pinch Ramos's cheek. The teenager slapped at his hand.

"Private, you are one dumb motherfucker," Harper said.

"We've been waiting for this shit, Sergeant. It's the old guys who ain't down. I ain't worried. I just want to kill motherfuckers."

"Come on, Devil Dog," Martinez said.

"Huh," was all Jimmy could say.

"We'll all get ours," Harper said. "You can be ready without looking forward to it."

"For all we know, they're coming for us right now," Martinez said. "They know where we are. They know what we're doing." Jimmy began to feel woozy again. He assumed it was the smallpox.

"They can't surprise us," Ramos said. "We have satellites. Helicopters. EP-3s."

"Unless everything's gummed up with oil smoke," Harper said. "Can you see through that? Last time they attacked us at night." Jimmy decided that Harper and Martinez were having a little fun with Ramos, but it still made him nervous. Iraqi attacks were not in keeping with the victory parade from Basra to Baghdad.

"They attacked us at night?" Ramos asked.

"They didn't understand night-vision technology," Harper said. "That we could still see them. And they couldn't find us."

A chorus of "Whoa," "Damn," and "Look at that" jumped from their mouths and could be heard rippling through the neighboring vehicles. Bursts of light scratched the dark sky, like a glimpse of fireworks in a neighboring town.

"It's … it's starting," Jimmy said, his delicate armor of confidence falling away, piece by piece, as the fear returned. Jimmy told himself to stay calm. This was a parade to Baghdad, nothing more.

Martinez bent his head and mumbled, praying to himself. "You religious, Martinez?" Jimmy asked. It was a good time to be religious, waiting for a cloud of nerve gas or a rain of blister agent to settle over them, with nothing but snowsuits filled with ground-up charcoal briquettes to protect them. The fear felt like a wind-up alarm clock ringing in his stomach. He couldn't turn it off; it just kept pounding and screaming its shrill metal scream in his gut. When it wound all the way down and the gears ground to a halt, he didn't know if he would feel normal again or if that was when his body, tense and exhausted from its adrenaline loop, would simply give out. Finality, reality, inevitability, it didn't matter what name you gave it. It had you, and you didn't doubt it. If the others felt it, they masked it well. Jimmy thought something in his head might burst right there as the fear trembled inside him and made him tremble on the outside. "Parade," he said to himself quietly. "Parade."

"Born once to my mother and again in Christ our Lord," Martinez answered.

"What's that?" Jimmy asked him. Martinez held a small book.

"Free Bible," Martinez said, handing it back to Jimmy. It had a tan, brown, and olive desert-camouflage cover. It was like a travel dictionary, small enough to fit in the palm of his hand, with wispy pages that felt like they would tear as he turned them. "They were handing them out back at Camp Triumph."

"Gideon," Jimmy read out loud. Harper ripped a snort of a laugh. The Gideon dispersal team's global effectiveness was unmatched. "No Old Testament."

"We're sticking to Jesus in this Corps," Ramos said.

"Private, don't be ignorant," Harper said.

"There's an index," Jimmy said.

"Seriously?"

" 'Where to find help, when.' Let's see. Nothing under fear. Oh, 'Afraid.' First one. That's very convenient. They know their target audience. Matthew 10:28. Page 18. Hold on." He squinted at the tiny letters in the dimness. The others were actually silent, waiting for words of guidance and comfort. " 'And do not fear those who kill the body,' " he began, " 'but cannot kill the soul. But rather fear Him who is able to destroy' "—he paused again, but they were waiting for the conclusion—" 'both soul and body in Hell.' " They were all silent. Jimmy said finally, "I do not feel better."

"No, me neither," Harper added.

"Give me that. There's a better one." Martinez took the Bible from him. "Two Timothy. 'For God has not given us a spirit of fear, but of power and of love and of a sound mind.' "

"That's a little better," Harper said.

"If your standard is that it doesn't make you more scared," Jimmy said. "Like the other one."

"You're some pagan motherfuckers." Martinez put the Bible back in his MOPP suit.

Outside, chanting cascaded down the line. "Gas gas gas! Gas gas gas! Incoming."

"Shit," Harper said. They hopped out of the truck and made for their fighting holes, safer from shrapnel underground than in the truck. It was happening. Jimmy was in the middle of a missile attack, a chemical-weapons attack. He pulled at the flapping canvas bag that held his gas mask as he ran, tumbling by accident into Ramos's hole.

There was sand in his hair, in his ears. It took him twice as long to put on the mask as it did when he was calm. The straps twisted. The mask felt too small. He got the cup over his mouth but fumbled with the clasps to tighten it. His heart was pounding. He sneaked a breath before fixing the rubber seal running along the line of his jaw. His instructor had called it the fatal breath. "Seven seconds or you are dead," he had screamed. Here it had taken him a minute, at least. "Seven seconds or you are dead."

"Chill, man," Ramos said through his mask.

Jimmy hadn't died, so he kept working. He had a hard time fastening the rubber boots, his dirty, sticky hands catching on the rubber gloves. Checking for nerve-gas symptoms was impossible. His entire body was seizing and pulsing. He was supposed to think about dimming vision and excess salivation. Ramos reached over and helped him tie the hood's elastic cord under his chin. Jimmy yanked the Velcro strips around the cuffs at his wrists, but panicked and began trying to reseal them. There were too many things to do all at once. It was the mask. It felt like he was suffocating. What if there was no gas attack but he died in a blocked mask? He had to take it off.

"Just leave it," Ramos said. Jimmy breathed deep and fast, but couldn't catch his breath. "Hey, man. Not so hard. You're getting air. You just feel claustrophobia and shit. You're getting air. If you breathe too much, you might pass out." Jimmy nodded. There was no way to tell the Marine that passing out and missing the whole thing would have felt like a blessing. "Might be a false alarm."

Harper stuck his head over the side of their hole. "He's rocking the Scuds, probably. Don't know what's in them, but better safe than sorry."

"Okay," Jimmy said. "Okay."

"Listen to you," Ramos said. "Sound like Darth Vader, man." Jimmy nodded. "Nobody can hurt Darth Vader." Jimmy shut his eyes under the mask. "Right?" He felt a hand shake his shoulder. "Right?"

"Nobody can hurt Darth Vader," Jimmy recited.

"Well, except his kids," Ramos said. "His kids done fucked him up good."

Three more times they jumped out of the Humvee. After the third alarm, the vehicles started grinding forward in fits and starts. They were moving up, Jimmy realized. A blanket of fatalism settled over him. It had started, and it was real. At one point they hit thirty miles per hour, and the speed made him feel safer. But Martinez immediately jammed the brakes, and they remained stock-still for close to half an hour. The invasion barely had begun and there were breakdowns on the side of the road. There were smoke and barbed wire and low-flying Cobra helicopters, rotors beating the air in rhythm. Every little crest felt like the berm that was supposed to mark the border. Every second they expected guns to open fire on them. They could hear it up ahead.

CHAPTER 12

ELLISON FELT THE SATISFYING SENSATION OF FLESH YIELDING BE-
tween his teeth. He was hungrier than he had realized. The afternoon had slipped away as he swiveled between television set and
computer screen, phone receiver fixed to his ear, a tide of under-
lings washing in and out. Lunch had become an afterthought. The
arrival of this deli sandwich, warm through the paper wrapping
and fragrant upon opening, made his salivary glands water immediately. The hunger he had ignored surged to the fore, presenting
him with a hollow feeling in his throat and his gut that had to be
filled. What held him back, just for an instant, was the sandwich's
provenance.

Tim Suskind had carried the hot pastrami and Muenster
cheese like a sacrificial offering. Ellison might have rejected this
blatant ploy if it had not been so perfectly executed, down to the
brown mustard and sweet peppers, his favorite sandwich to his
exact specifications. He could not refuse. His brand of cream soda
to wash it down, Sioux City, was a flourish, but it also sent Ellison a
message from his subordinate. This was not an accident. This was
not subtle. Ellison admired directness, even in bribery.

"It's refreshing to have an editor with a real news background for a change," Suskind was saying. "If I might speak freely," he added, to which Ellison nodded, since he had an enormous hunk of kaiser roll and several layers of finely sliced pastrami in his mouth. "The place was going to the dogs. All fluff."

"Aren't you," Ellison said, mouth still half full, but moved to speak by a powerful combination of incredulity and disdain, "the *lifestyle* editor?"

"A job I accepted under duress," Tim explained, an edge of nervousness in his voice. Ellison liked that. "When you have a family, when you have mouths to feed, you make compromises. I cut my teeth on cops and courts," he said. Ellison was also pleased to note that his hair was no longer swept upward in that ridiculous rooster's comb, but was parted on the right side. "It feels safe to care for the first time in a long time. I mean to say," he rephrased in a slightly manlier fashion and, Ellison noted, a deeper voice, "maybe a newshound can work at the *Daily Herald* with a little pride again."

"That is the plan," Ellison said. He sucked a seed from between his teeth.

"I notice," Suskind ventured, having gained sufficient confidence to broach what must have been his real reason for worming his way into Ellison's office, "Jimmy isn't writing much." Ellison did not answer. He tore another big mouthful from his sandwich and looked through the window from his office out into the newsroom. It was early, but the office had twice the activity of a normal day at deadline time. Ringing phones overlapped, keyboards tapped, and stories wrapped. No one strolled or lagged. Clusters formed under television sets—to watch the rolling tanks and armored personnel carriers—instead of at the coffee machines. Only Jimmy Stephens seemed incapable of rising to the occasion.

"Stephens," Ellison said with genuine distaste, "isn't doing much of anything that I can tell."

"Jimmy's talented, but he's a little unfocused," Tim said. "And he doesn't really respond to the usual kinds of prodding. It makes him petulant. He needs stroking."

"Think you can get anything out of him?" Ellison asked, wondering if Suskind was really a newsman languishing in entertainment or a simple opportunist.

"Maybe not," Tim answered, to Ellison's surprise. He expected Tim to promise him the stars if he asked for them. "It's a very different situation. It's a war."

"Would you try if I told you to?" It did not matter what Suskind's motives were, he decided. Ellison desperately needed stories coaxed out of his hapless embed. He tried to seem strong, commanding, intimidating even, but his mission was in jeopardy. To turn the *Daily Herald* into a competitive newspaper required a launch pad, a big success to draw attention to the paper's new direction. James E. Stephens's war coverage was supposed to provide that boost. Without him their war reporting limped along. It emboldened the naysayers. Jealous editors, the ones who had been passed over for him, the outside candidate, tested Ellison's authority. He needed more out of Jimmy.

"I have a lot of work to do," Tim said. "The weekend section may be trashy, but it takes a lot of time to put out." He played hard to get like a woman, Ellison thought.

"Right. I'd really have to detail you to the war team as an editor to reapportion that workload, wouldn't I?" Ellison asked, leaning over the crinkled white sandwich paper, crumbs, and slivers of iceberg lettuce.

"You're the boss," Tim said cheerfully. "I'd have no choice but to say yes. Let me clean this up," Tim continued, bundling the sandwich wrappings carefully so neither seed nor crumb escaped. "I'll take care of this mess for you."

"I see that you will," Ellison said with some satisfaction. "I see you will."

CHAPTER 13

"DID WE INVADE OR JUST MOVE FORWARD?" MARTINEZ ASKED.

"Can't tell," Harper said. There were two radios in the front, and they both crackled with orders, voices overlapping.

"Well, are we in Iraq or not?" Jimmy said.

"I said, I can't tell. The GPS is on the fritz. But I don't think so."

"Wasn't that the berm back there?" Like Jimmy, Ramos had an obscured view in the back.

"Might've been a hill. I didn't see any barbed wire."

"Headline: 'Marines Think They Entered Iraq,' " Jimmy said.

"Fuck you."

"The greatest high-tech fighting force on the planet was fairly certain that it attacked a member of the Axis of Evil yesterday," Jimmy said as if composing a story out loud. "Marine sources reported that the glorious invasion had begun, unless they should have made a left at the gas station right past the church, in which case it hadn't."

"Fog of war," Harper said. "Get used to it." The sergeant reached back and handed a bag of instant coffee crystals to Jimmy. He grabbed a pinch and passed it on to Ramos. It helped them stay awake after a sleepless night.

At first the ride had been miserable and tense. In his gas mask, Jimmy had concentrated on not puking. Thinking about not puking made him think about puking, which made him feel like puking all the more. He had a morbid curiosity about what would happen if he puked in the mask, with its tight seal. The rubbing of the drinking tube against his lower lip didn't help, encouraging him to imagine models shoving fingers down their throats in restaurant bathrooms. He knew he would fill the mouth cup, but wondered if it would get up to the lenses and blind him. The mask might clog and become useless, and he didn't have a spare. They would be merciless if he puked. It seemed unfair to blame someone for something they couldn't control, like a gag reflex, but he knew from experience that they would anyway.

He was supposed to be thankful even to have a seat. Martinez had told him he could have been stuck in the rear of one of the covered pickup truck Humvees. Then he would be sitting on sandbags, getting sores on his butt made worse with every rut in the road. He was supposed to be glad that he had his own door in the event of an emergency. But it was soft, flexible, decidedly unbulletproof, and never closed right, a sieve for sand and wind and anything else smaller than a quarter that wanted to knock into Jimmy's head. Under his feet were empty soda cans, rucksacks, bullets, and grenades, making him nervous in reverse order. In the end he was just a civilian, crammed into the backseat of a Humvee, with a heavy machine gun lying across his lap making him feel very uncomfortable.

They were on a road in a long line of Humvees and amphibious assault vehicles designed for storming beaches. Right then, they were bumping along over fifty miles from the Persian Gulf, a few car lengths behind the vehicle in front of them. The gap stretched and narrowed with Martinez's concentration behind the wheel. It was morning on their watches, but the sandstorm lengthened the night. Martinez took his NVGs on and off, unsure if a little more light or a little better depth perception would stave off the accident he was expecting.

The tension had been broken when Dabrowski's Humvee tapped their bumper, rocking them all forward and causing the Marines to clutch at their rifles. It wasn't funny per se, but everyone burst out laughing. They were laughing at themselves, at their tension. They took off their masks to gulp air and rub their eyes. No decision was reached or order given, but the three of them didn't put their masks back on. Martinez hadn't been wearing his all night anyway so he could use his NVGs. The combination of sand blown by the wind and kicked up by the tires and exhaust mixed with oil smoke from the burning wells made it hard to see beyond the vehicle in front of them.

Harper leaned his head out the window to try to get a better view than the dirty windshield afforded him. Everyone but Jimmy had big goggles like skiers wore. Jimmy's were blue-tinted swimming goggles. He had bought them himself but didn't feel at fault. Becky's list hadn't been specific enough: "Goggles." He'd felt too silly to put them on, but Harper warned him that it wasn't just discomfort from the sand that he was fighting but serious eye infections. They also brightened the mood in the Humvee as the Marines took turns making fun of them.

"It sounds like the intro to a Nine Inch Nails CD out there," Jimmy remarked about the squeals, clangs, and pounding sounds all around them. Ramos leapt on the subject, a huge industrial, Goth, and heavy metal fan, as he'd explained. Any kind of masculine music seemed to suit him, Jimmy thought. The reporter couldn't bring himself to explain that he wasn't much of a fan himself. He simply had a weird thing from high school for little Goth girls who looked like vampires and wore fishnet stockings

with combat boots. It would have ruined any rapport he was beginning to build with the angry private.

That newborn rapport was slaughtered anyway, shortly after
Ramos began expounding on the virtues of Rage Against the Machine. With a crushing sound and a Hispanic front man, they were
Ramos's ideal band, even though they'd broken up. "It doesn't
bother you that they're Communists?" Jimmy said.

"The fuck they are," the private answered.

"What exactly do you think the Machine is, Ramos? It's the
capitalist machine. They're proud Marxists."

"Fuck you, Aquaman," Ramos said.

"Note all the songs about revolution," Jimmy said, annoyed.
He was feeling trapped and cranky.

"Sergeant," Ramos had appealed.

"Private," Harper snapped. He looked back at Jimmy. "Sub-
mariner. I need you kids to stop fighting. And they are raging
fucking pinkos, Private. The sissy-ass civilian reporter is not just
pulling your dick."

"Could we stop calling me that?" Jimmy asked.

"No," Harper said. "We can't."

"This is bullshit," Ramos said.

"He's more fragile than you think," Harper said. "If you tell
him that Metallica is full of homos, he may kill himself."

"Country music is for homos," Ramos said.

"Touché," Harper answered. Martinez hit the brakes, jerking
them all forward in their seats. "Wonder how much you'd have
to pay Geico to insure a Humvee for the war. I mean, what kind
of rates?" Harper asked. "Five times, ten times what we pay at
home?" The sergeant began holding forth on the topic of escalating car insurance prices in San Diego. As they surged forward, one
vertebra in the military serpent winding its way into hostile ter-

ritory, Harper announced that he was considering switching to a higher deductible for lower rates.

"Sergeant Harper," Ramos said, "your truck was repossessed before we left."

"It's still my truck, Private. I just have to get it back."

"You're paying insurance on a repossessed truck?" Jimmy asked.

"Well, right now I am," Harper said. "My brother was supposed to get it out of hock for me. It hasn't quite, um, hasn't quite come together yet."

"But even if he got it back, you wouldn't be driving it," Martinez said.

"Those three years of college did you real good, Sergeant Harper," Ramos said.

"Not today, no." Harper responded to Martinez and ignored Ramos. "But insurance isn't just for those kinds of accidents. What if a tree fell on it? Or someone trashed it?"

"Like some major whose wife you fucked while he was in Okinawa, Sergeant?" Ramos asked. Harper turned all the way around to look at Ramos, as much surprised as angry. Jimmy had heard Dabrowski joke about this before. He had also heard it was a very serious but often overlooked offense. For once, Martinez joined Ramos in laughing at the sergeant. "Hypothetically, Sergeant Harper," Ramos added. Martinez started to say something, but Ramos cut him off. "Yeah, a real big word. My semester at community college done me good too, Tino."

They drove along in what was probably Iraq without a working GPS, through the intensifying sandstorm. "Was there a man dismayed?" Harper said. "Not though the soldier knew. Ours not to make reply. Ours not to reason why."

"Who's that?" Ramos asked, his voice tinged with disgust.

"Travis Tritt," Harper answered.

"Country music is bullshit," Ramos said. "Yo, I can't see anything."

"Me neither," Martinez said, his black-gloved hands gripping the steering wheel tightly.

"That," Harper said, "is a bigger problem, since you're driving." No one contradicted the sergeant on that point. The radio spat and hissed like eggs on a hot frying pan. Like the GPS, it was now broken too. "No word," Harper said.

"Should we stop?" Jimmy asked.

"We can't just stop," Martinez answered.

"But you're driving and you can't see," Jimmy said. "That's insane."

"Insane," Harper said, "is breaking out of your formation, making even a single move alone in enemy territory. What if we lost them? No radio, no GPS."

"Okay, I get it," Jimmy said. "Driving blind is the very height of sanity."

"Shit," Martinez said, and the Humvee lurched to a hard stop, throwing Jimmy into the back of Harper's seat. "That was close." As Jimmy pulled himself out of the foot room, he could see the back of an amphibious assault vehicle so near that the hatch could have opened onto the hood of the Humvee. "Guess we decided to stop after all."

It was impossible to see more than a foot through the sand. Harper opened his door and bent toward the ground. "Not on pavement," he announced.

"Or a mine, I guess," Martinez added.

"We don't need to go rocking the jeep to find out." But the wind didn't leave them any choice. The vehicle bounced and sagged on its shocks, leaning at times like it was going to roll over and begin flipping whichever direction the weather willed it.

"The only thing worse than driving through enemy territory

in a sandstorm?" Harper said. "Sitting in enemy territory in a sand-storm."

"Respectfully disagree, Sergeant Harper," Martinez said. "We were driving by the grace of God, 'cause I could not see shit."

Lieutenant Katzenbach and the first sergeant appeared at Harper's door. "Yes, sir?" Harper said.

"Lost contact with you there for a second, Sergeant," Katzen-bach said.

"Radio ate too much sand, sir," Harper said.

"The weather's dog shit. We have no choice but to sit tight and—what is the reporter wearing?" Katzenbach's gaze had wan-dered behind Harper and into the backseat. Even with the sand and the blue tint, Jimmy could see Katzenbach was pissed off.

"Uh." Harper coughed to cover his laughter. "Sorry. Sand." He finally brought himself under control enough to say, "Goggles, sir," without cracking up.

"You're wearing goggles, Sergeant. What is he wearing?"

"I—ahem—guess they're swimming goggles, sir."

"Is that supposed to be funny, Mr. Stephens?" Katzenbach asked.

"No, Lieutenant, I—"

"Sir, the Kuwaiti help at his hotel bought him the wrong gog-gles, sir," Martinez jumped in. "He wasn't going to wear them, but we apprised him of the dangers of severe eye infections, sir."

"I see." Katzenbach looked at Jimmy, shaking his head, giving him a very disappointed look.

"He doesn't think they're funny at all, sir. He was quite angry. At the Kuwaitis, I mean. Sir."

"How difficult it must have been for him. Thank you, PFC Martinez." Lieutenant Katzenbach looked back at Harper. "Ser-geant, we have to sit tight. Keep an eye out. There's barely any aerial surveillance right now. We're blind down here. Gentlemen."

Katzenbach turned and walked back toward the head of the convoy.

"Maybe we should have asked Lieutenant Katzenbach if we were in Iraq," Jimmy said. "Since we can't really—"

"Shut up, Jimmy," Martinez warned.

"Okay," the reporter said.

The day was orange. Not the sun, which wasn't visible, or the sky, which was beyond the few feet they could see outside the Humvee, but the air all around them. If they had not been in a combat zone, it might have held a strange beauty. If the sand had not been floating in the Humvee as well, invading their respiratory systems with each strangled breath, they might have been able to appreciate it for a moment. None of them, Harper included, had ever seen anything like it. They all had bandannas over their mouths and noses except for Jimmy, who had a scarf he had bought from the souk, the large open-air market in Kuwait City, on his shopping expedition.

"You look like you're in the PLO," Harper said. Jimmy was willing to trade looking like a terrorist for sand filtration just then. He could wrap it several times and really cover his nose and mouth. Ramos had a hacking cough that couldn't seem to clear the sand they were all swallowing. "The PLO swim team," Harper added.

"I think we already covered that" was all Jimmy would say. The flexible plastic band between the goggles was rubbing the bridge of his nose, a problem Jimmy remembered from swim team in high school. Then you could pull them off every time you hopped out of the pool. Now he had to leave it, rubbing a raw spot further irritated by the sand.

The gaps in conversation were torture, since there was no dearth of terrible scenarios the imagination could conjure. After several minutes of miserable silence, Jimmy announced, "You know, I've been here for a week, and I haven't seen one camel."

"Oh, who fucking cares?" Martinez said.

"Yeah, fuck your camel," Ramos added.

"Do you have any idea what's happening here?" Harper asked. "I'll take it nice and slow. We don't know where we are. We don't know where the Iraqis are. And our radio isn't working if someone else spots them."

"Don't patronize me," Jimmy said. All he'd wanted to do was to lighten the mood, not open himself up to more ridicule.

"There could be fedayeen standing in a circle around us, ten feet away, and we wouldn't know," Harper said. "There." He pointed out his window. "Or there." He pointed out Martinez's side.

"I said don't fucking patronize me," Jimmy said.

"We could be smack in the middle of an Iraqi artillery grid and die at any fucking second. And you want to talk about camels?"

"I may not know what an artillery grid is," Jimmy said, leaning forward so Harper could hear him clearly over the wind and through the scarf. "But I'm in this fucking Humvee. I was there for the gas drills. I noticed the fucking guns."

"Yo, chill out, Jimmy," Martinez said.

"Aquaman," Ramos muttered beside him.

"Tell sergeant-fucking-artillery-grid to chill out," Jimmy shouted, thinking as he did that Martinez was right. He needed to chill out, but once it started coming out, he found he couldn't stop it. "Every minute since you've met me, I've had one thing on my mind. Thinking, 'I'm going to fucking die. I'm going to fucking die.' But do I whine about it? No. Because—because it'd get pretty boring to have me screaming about dying in the backseat all the way to Baghdad. Don't you think?" Harper didn't answer. "Don't you think? So maybe I fucking want to talk about camels instead."

"Jimmy," Martinez said at last, very gingerly. "You haven't seen one camel?"

"No, man," Jimmy said with a laugh for the preposterously camel-free desert. "Not a goddamned one."

"I've seen a couple," Harper said.

"Me too," Martinez said. They were using the indulgent tones of orderlies in an asylum.

"One hump or two?" Jimmy asked.

"One, I think," Martinez said.

"Yeah, I think they were one," Harper said.

"Cool," Jimmy answered.

"Motherfucker," Ramos said.

"What now?" Harper responded.

"How come I'm the only Marine who hasn't seen a camel?"

"Everybody shut the fuck up," Harper said. "That's an order." The talking ban was surprisingly effective, lasting a full hour, probably because each was a little pissed off at the others. Harper kept leaning back like he was trying to sleep, but Jimmy found it impossible to get any rest with the fear, the bouncing of the jeep, and the sand caked against teeth, tongue, and nostrils. He took notes instead. When no one spoke, all they could hear was the groaning of the vehicle on its shocks and the static of tiny grains of sand pelting the canvas top. The sandstorm lasted longer than they could stand to listen to those sounds. It was Ramos who cracked.

"What you writing?" he asked Jimmy. "Saying we're lost? Don't write that shit."

"Not saying anything. And you can't tell me what to write anyway."

"C'mon, Jimmy," Martinez said. "Step up."

"Quit censoring the civilian, Private," Harper said.

"You saying we fucked up?" Ramos asked.

"I'm writing a letter to my mom," Jimmy said.

"What's it say?" the private continued to pry.

"You know what?" Jimmy told him. "It says we're lost. Says you fucked up. What do you think now?"

"You ..." Ramos began. "You tell her a real Marine said hello."

"Yeah. And tell her little Macho said hi too," Martinez added. Jimmy looked down at his paper and finished writing, blessedly undisturbed.

CHAPTER 14

THE MARINES CALLED IT THE BIG SANDBOX, AND IT WAS MORE THAN just another way to say desert. This wasn't the land of Lawrence of Arabia, with climbing dunes and oases and stunning sunsets. No shimmering majesty. Beyond the road was a flat, featureless expanse, pocked with bits of scrub. The sand was closer to dust in consistency than the granular stuff on the beaches in the Hamptons. The towers of a castle would never rise from the sculpting hands of a child. The color had overtones of gray rather than gold or yellow. It wasn't the desert of imagination. It was just a very large sandbox. Jimmy went out, like a cat, to try to find a spot to scratch in private. It was impossible. Beyond them was nothing but horizon. It was the world emptied out, two-dimensional.

Relieving one's bowels required a delicate balance both literally and figuratively. Literally, because the crew's toilet was an empty MRE box reinforced with duct tape. It was not there as a receptacle, but for stability and privacy at the moment of truth. With the entrenching tool, the person in need dug a small hole, placed the box over it, and used it as a seat for balance. From the loving, detailed conversations about shit that surrounded him, Jimmy doubted that the Marines would have minded watching each other take dumps. Indeed, he thought the whole process might include applause and scorecards, if not ticket sales.

For someone who had a hard time crapping in a crowd, the figurative balance came into play. Wandering too far from the group meant risking stepping on a mine. That was troubling. But the calls of encouragement that a lone civilian carrying a shit box elicited from Marines made the risk worthwhile. Jimmy accomplished his goal and was returning to the squad when the NBC empire cameraman, Doug, called out to him.

"MREs," Doug shouted. "Keep you regular. Shit like once a week."

"I'm ahead of schedule," Jimmy said.

"Started too late," Doug continued. "I was eating MREs back at Camp Triumph too, just to keep regular and perfect."

"If we could all be so lucky," he said.

"So how's your war going, Jimmy-boy?" Doug asked in his unmistakable Boston accent. He had told Jimmy at Triumph that his neighborhood sent more men into the Marines per capita than anywhere in the nation. His father was a retired Marine and his brother was active service, though he was stationed in Asia and, as Doug put it, "missing the war." Doug said he felt right at home, and he was acting it, his expression completely untroubled despite three days trapped in a vehicle, sucking sand.

"Oh, super," Jimmy said. "If I wanted to die in a car wreck I could have stayed in Jersey." At least he'd gotten what he thought was a decent story out of it. The so-called letter to his mother would go straight to New York as soon as he could get his phone set up. "Fog of War" explained the confusion, anxiety, and boredom of being a little piece in the larger puzzle, aimed at all the CNN watchers at home who, Jimmy presumed, actually knew what was going on. From an earlier e-mail he knew that Tim would be editing him, which was a welcome development workwise.

"Relax, man. Today is a beautiful day," Doug said. He was right. The sand was where it belonged, on the ground again, and the sky clear and bright. He leaned in close and said, with Christmas-morning delight, "And I got to shoot the fifty-cal."

"You shot the fifty-cal?" Jimmy asked, now sufficiently in the know to realize he was talking about the giant mounted gun on some of the vehicles.

"Just a few rounds. Man, that thing is killer," Doug said.

"Are we supposed to do that?"

"Oh, don't worry so much." Doug laughed and turned to leave. "This is supposed to be fun." Resuming his walk back to the Humvee, Jimmy wondered where Doug had heard that it was supposed to be fun. But he could not deny that surviving the initial phase of the invasion had been a bit of a buzz. He was less scared than before. Rather than worrying about dying, he thought about the stories he could tell back in New York, maybe even that summer.

Jimmy still had plenty of fear. He could see Marines sweeping for mines and lying in wait on their bellies, with guns pointed away from the convoy. But he also felt a cautious optimism that if he made it a little farther, he could earn a little respect. Plenty of people liked him, but before he got into the Humvee no one had respected him, as far as he knew.

He found the right cluster of fighting holes, easy to spot, since his own was a foot deep at best. If it looked like they were staying longer, he'd burrow a few more inches down. "All right, Jimmy. Took your first field shit. How'd it feel?" Harper said.

"Way to go, Jimmy," Martinez said.

"Thanks, man."

"You showed that turd who was boss, didn't you?"

"I guess I did," Jimmy said. "Here's your toilet back."

"It's a Marine's proudest day when his reporter takes his first shit by himself," Harper said.

"No more diapers," Martinez said. "No more waking up in the middle of the night." Martinez held the box by the sides and carried it to its storage place, tied outside on the back of the Humvee.

Jimmy studied the map at the rest stop. He couldn't read the key, but they had not gotten very far, according to the red dot that appeared to mark their location. Baghdad was five times farther up the long, squiggling line of the highway than they had traveled so far. The convoy had passed Bedouins and sheepherders. They saw a few children waving from behind the metal guardrails. Warning shots were fired at civilian vehicles driving down the other side of the highway. But as yet no Iraqis had fired at their part of the convoy in four days of stop-and-start driving.

Often the landscape seemed alien, if not like another planet, at least displaced in time. Then they would stumble on something like the rest stop and find the familiarity more jarring than the foreignness. Why shouldn't they have rest stops? The Iraqis had cars. They had children. They must have gone on trips to visit relatives for holidays. What did Iraqi families sing to pass the time? Jimmy wondered if the kids were any better behaved, or did they fight in the backseat as he always had with his older sister?

He went back to the concrete table with the plastic umbrella where his crew had broken out their shaving kits. The green and yellow stripes on the umbrella were straight out of the 1970s, but had faded over the years. It still provided plenty of shade. The unit's defensive posture was somewhat more relaxed than usual because the roof of the main building provided an excellent observation post for the team of recon Marines keeping watch. Tanks blocked the highway in both directions. And even the Marines seemed to recognize that one couldn't dig holes in concrete by hand.

Ramos had an electric razor out and was carefully buzzing a cheek where Jimmy saw no stubble. "Oh, you got to shave, Jimmy," Ramos told him as he worked the razor over his chin again. "XO came by and told us. He's going to check our asses later to make sure we wiped good."

"Private," Harper said.

"I'm on it," Jimmy said. He rummaged around in his frame pack and found his mirror. Looking into it, Jimmy was startled. His reflection looked like a meth addict's mug shot. His face was gaunt, his body shrinking barely a week away from the hotel buffet. He had a sore on his nose where the goggles had been rubbing the bridge. The bruise around his eye was now green. Small scrapes and scratches filled in the expanse of his forehead, and his eyes had a faraway, tired look.

"This war sure got a lot of sitting around," Martinez said.

"That's 'tactical pause' to you, Private First Class Martinez," Harper said.

"This war needs better food," Ramos said.

"This war needs cold water," Martinez said, after sipping from one of the warm plastic bottles.

"This war needs less whining," Jimmy said, face half covered with lather.

"Fuck you say?" Ramos asked.

"Old question on Corps exams," Harper said, waving at Ramos to calm down. "What do you do when a Marine stops bitching, Jimmy?"

"Throw a party?"

"Check his pulse."

"The food's still shit," Ramos said.

"Write a letter to Secretary Rumsfeld," Martinez said.

"Donald Rumsfeld can stick these MREs in his ass," Ramos said, looking into an unsavory pouch of food with disgust. Jimmy began to shave, a slow, painful process with a disposable razor and a metal cup of lukewarm water. As Jimmy scraped at his stubble, the NBC reporter embedded with the company wandered over for a professional consultation, or maybe just to commiserate.

"So we have breached the berm and entered the upside-down Wonderland of violence," Woody said, actually sounding serious.

"The what?" Jimmy said, half his face still lathered over.

"Scratch that." Woody waved Jimmy off, pressed a hand to his forehead, then snapped his fingers. "We've breached the berm and now forge ahead into the unknown danger?"

"Uh . . ."

"I know. That wasn't right either. And I've got a live shot in an hour," Woody said. "We've got to do something. We're getting hosed back here."

"Back where?" Jimmy asked.

"Back here," Woody said, looking over each shoulder, "pulling up the rear. You've seen the maps."

"The maps?" Jimmy asked.

"In the command tent," Woody said.

"Oh, those maps," Jimmy said, now wondering what the command tent was.

"Tip of the spear, they said. More like the shaft. So far back in the pack we're not going to get any action." There were thousands of Marines in a miles-long line on the road to Baghdad. In the front, according to the radio, there was light resistance. Not pitched battles, but skirmishes. Their company, the close to two hundred Marines who carried Jimmy, McNulty, and the NBC crew, were well back from finding trouble. Only a flanking attack by the Iraqis would hit them, but between the helicopters, airplanes, and satellites, it was unlikely they could pull off such a maneuver. Yet the Marines took no chances and strung out security perimeters everywhere they stopped.

"That's a relief," Jimmy said.

"Nothing to joke about, Jimmy. You made your name in Mogadishu. I know you're dying for a little action."

"Sure," Jimmy said. He did not want to explain that he was a gossip columnist and not the James Stephens of *Herald* lore. "A very little."

"I'm not making a dent in prime time," Woody said morosely. "I might as well be in New York." Here, Jimmy realized, was a grown man disappointed that no one was shooting at him. At least Ramos had youth as an excuse.

"I can sympathize," Jimmy agreed, wincing as the blade seemed to pull out the short mustache hairs under his nose rather than cut them.

"We need to distinguish ourselves with analysis, because a traffic jam without gunfire isn't getting you on the front page or me any face time with the anchor," Woody said. "I've been giving this a lot of thought, and I think it might be time to drop the q-word."

"The q-word?" Jimmy asked. Woody bit down thoughtfully on his upper lip and breathed in deeply. "Can't just go throwing hand grenades like that around willy-nilly," Jimmy ventured, wrinkling his face into his most serious expression. "Might as well use the h-word."

"The—" Woody paused. He seemed curious about the h-word, but unwilling to display such ignorance as to ask.

"But explain yourself," Jimmy said. "I interrupted. You must have your reasons."

"We've been stalled. Hardly moving. This was supposed to be"—he paused, the tip of his forefinger perched on his lower lip—"a lightning thrust," he said, finger leaping from his lip to point at Jimmy. "A lightning thrust into Baghdad, and here we sit, the most powerful military force on earth. Ever assembled."

"Ever?" Jimmy asked to humor him.

"Not in terms of sheer numbers, but ... that's not my point. We are"—he looked both ways before speaking—"bogged down."

"Yeah ...," Jimmy said, looking around.

"So?" Woody prompted. This question must, Jimmy knew, have had something to do with the q-word, with his conclusion. "Is it time?"

"It's a quandary," Jimmy said neutrally, probing. "I've reached my quota of ... patience. But I'm ..." He struggled. "I'm not a quitter, if that's what you're asking."

"Jimmy," Woody said with feeling. "I wouldn't imply—"

"Of course." Jimmy shook his head. Finished shaving, he set down the razor and cup. "It's like ... like quicksand?" Woody nodded energetically. "A quarrel?" Woody looked confused. "Quiche?" Jimmy shouted at last, out of guesses.

"Quiche?" Woody asked.

"New MRE," Jimmy said quickly, waving a hand dismissively. "Said to be poisonous. At least in flavor."

"Poison? This ... You're making fun of me," Woody said, a dark look in his eyes that suggested his confidence was easily broken.

"No, Woody," Jimmy insisted. "I'm trying to lighten the mood. It's a serious subject."

"It is that," Woody said warily, but seeming to accept Jimmy's answer. "Not undertaken lightly but ... I think I'm going to do it. We're in a quagmire."

"Quagmire," Jimmy shouted, snapping his fingers. This was a television pundit word, a Vietnam word. He was disappointed in himself for missing it. "Quagmire," he said again. It sounded smart.

"You agree?" Woody asked.

"I ..." Jimmy had not had a chance to think it over yet. "I can't say one way or another, but I can easily see where you're coming from."

"Yeah."

"Maybe just 'marshy,' " Jimmy suggested.

"What?"

"Nothing," Jimmy said.

"A question," Woody declared.

"Shoot," Jimmy told him.

"That's the answer."

"Shoot?" Jimmy asked.

"A question," Woody said.

"Are you fielding or pitching?" Jimmy said.

"The answer to the conundrum."

"The quagmire conundrum?" Jimmy asked.

"Exactly," Woody said. Jimmy must have looked confused, because Woody relented. "The answer is that I'll ask, in a question, whether we should begin to ask ourselves if we're in a quagmire."

"Like a sneak attack," Jimmy said.

"Zing." Woody pointed at him again. "What else can I do? There's nothing new to say, poetically speaking. They got it all in the last war," Woody said. "I mean, in imagery, evocative language. One NPR radio essay, and there isn't a metaphor left for the rest of us. But the pressure's still there. New York will take anything right now."

"Will they?" Jimmy said, feeling a touch guilty.

"You said it," Woody agreed. "And what little I've got, I need to keep in reserve. Like cauldron."

"Cauldron?" Jimmy asked, probing the razor nicks on his neck with his fingertips.

"It's a good word, but not one you can throw around all the time. You can't use it in back-to-back broadcasts, certainly. So if I declare Southern Iraq a cauldron, and then I get to Baghdad, and the only word, the only word that sums up the situation—"

"Cauldron?" Jimmy offered.

"—is cauldron—" Woody continued.

"Then you would be screwed," Jimmy concluded.

"Exactly. It's only going to get hotter as we get into spring. Much less summer."

"Summer?" Jimmy said, uncertain of the exact date but pretty sure they were still in March. "We're going to be here in the summer?"

"Right, keep your powder dry," Woody said. "Let things simmer. In the cauldron." Woody made a circle with both hands. They appeared now to have a sign for cauldron. "You ready for the actual thing? The fight itself?"

"I don't expect to do any fighting," Jimmy said.

"Ha-ha. Of course not. Well, what about the ducking? The running? Avoiding the cross fire?" Woody asked.

"Probably not. How can you be?"

"So true. Like the first time, every time. Boot camp, though, I thought, was excellent preparation."

"Were you a Marine?" Jimmy asked.

"No, no. The reporters' boot camp, I mean."

"We have that?" Jimmy said.

"Didn't think you needed it? Braver man than I, Mr. Stephens." Woody shook his head in apparent disbelief. "But you've been around the block before. From everything I hear, you were crazy in the Mog, and I say that with all due respect, admiration, and envy."

"Oh, yeah, the Mog," Jimmy said. "I guess I was."

"Never would have gone to some of those neighborhoods myself. Alone among the skinnies—I mean Somalis. Never in a million years. There's brave, and of course there's stupid."

"People tell me I'm stupid quite a bit," Jimmy said, with less self-deprecation than Woody seemed to infer.

"They're just jealous. I deal with jealousy a lot, too. My colleagues say I hog the good stories, but some people just aren't made for covering wildfires and parades. Some of us are made for action."

"Made for action," Jimmy halfheartedly agreed.

"Jimmy, thanks for talking. It's always a pleasure."

"Never a quagmire," Jimmy said. Woody laughed as he walked away, usually the sign of a successful conversation, but Jimmy could never tell whether Woody was sincere or playing the appropriate part for the moment. When he turned around, the Marines were looking right at him.

"Yo, man. You was in the Mog?" Ramos asked.

"I don't like to talk about it."

"Come on," Harper said. "Educate us."

"Oh, you know," Jimmy said. "I don't want to scare you guys with those stories." They didn't laugh when he said it. He thought for a moment about ratting himself out once and for all. But he couldn't bear the thought of their condescension and disparagement if they knew. He closed the topic with: "It's not the kind of thing that you talk about." The Marines nodded. They seemed to understand.

CHAPTER 15

THE TRAIN MOVED HALTINGLY FORWARD. RAMOS SERENADED THEM with high, sweet whining about the lack of action. An unspoken agreement to ignore him meant that he went uninterrupted for what felt like an hour. Traffic stalled at a bridge over a canal that Harper swore was an offshoot of the Euphrates River. Jimmy was the most patient of the group, having spent a good chunk of his teenage years on the George Washington Bridge trying to get into Manhattan.

There were two speeds, sitting with the engine off and sitting with the engine idling. The tactical pauses were growing so consistent that the tactical advances actually became more noteworthy. Ramos borrowed the map so he could be more specific about the action they were missing: Basra, Umm Qasr, the al-Faw Peninsula. He ran through the list of places where they could have gotten shot. It was a song filled with longing and regret.

Martinez's stout frame was bent over the steering wheel, tense with annoyance. Harper leaned all the way back, breathing loudly as if trying to calm himself with improvised yoga exercises. "Rush hour," Harper said through gritted teeth.

"This is bullshit," Martinez said.

"Too many Marines. Not enough highways."

Ramos was preoccupied with Jimmy's state of preparedness and ignored the traffic problem. "You really don't have a gun?"

"I'm a civilian," Jimmy said.

"So what? I don't do shit at home without a nine. I'm always strapped," Ramos said. He often spun wild tales of his Arizona exploits as the two of them sat in the backseat. These included, but were not limited to, simple drug deals, drug deals gone bad, breaking and entering, home invasion, animal torture, and improvised Satanic rituals. How the young Marine could find time for his criminal enterprise and still play his starring role on the high school football team didn't really add up. More likely it was exaggeration augmented with borrowings from gangster rap. But Jimmy was not about to call bullshit on an armed teenager who was at best a fantasist and at worst disturbed.

"Noncombatant," Jimmy clarified.

"They could still give you a gun, though. I can find you a gun. Over there." The side of the road was littered with discarded weapons, helmets, and uniforms due to the light combat at the front of the column. They heard about it on the radio, then passed the evidence an hour or two later.

Harper said that everything of consequence was happening in the air. The divisions they expected at each town's outskirts were evaporated victims of the high fliers. The Iraqi Army died unprepared, without heroism or bravery. There was no meet-your-maker philosophizing, no hand reaching out to touch a fallen comrade, just zap or boom. Everyone gone together, from a plane so high they'd probably never even heard it. The main resistance they encountered on the ground came in the form of ambushes where one or two Marines were picked off in a weak but sudden flurry, followed by a thousand American rounds sent downfield. The Iraqi shots punctured the dam, and they drowned themselves in the flood. A few Americans were wounded and sadly a handful in other units had died, along with many more Iraqis, but the wagon train kept moving.

"So why are we here, then?" Jimmy asked.

"Too boring for the people back home," Harper said. "We're like a made-for-TV movie."

"That's it?" Jimmy asked.

"When they've blown enough stuff up, we'll get to play cops and robbers," Harper said. "Bosnia style." He must have meant peacekeeping, Jimmy realized.

The Humvee crept past a charred sedan. It looked like a civilian vehicle, but it could have been used in one of the guerrilla attacks intel had warned about. True or not, blown-out tanks didn't bother Jimmy like a scorched station wagon did. The signs of action only made Ramos more jealous of the units up front.

"We can get you a defensive weapon," Ramos continued.

"Like a shield?" Jimmy said.

"No, a handgun. A pistol. Like the docs carry."

"That's defensive?" Jimmy asked.

"Yeah," Ramos said.

"I'd rather have a shield," Jimmy said. Ramos looked unconvinced. He was not the first Marine to try to slip Jimmy a gun. An unarmed man in a war zone to them was like a guy in a bar without a drink, strange and even a little suspicious. "Really, I'm fine."

A few Iraqi soldiers had straggled past, so skinny and hunched they looked like they could hardly bear the weight of their uniforms. Ramos wasn't allowed to shoot them. The Marines had strict rules of engagement, to shoot only when threatened. These disarmed soldiers offered no apparent threat, except perhaps to collapse in front of a vehicle. They smiled pathetically, approached the vehicles cautiously, as if hoping for something.

"They want to surrender," Martinez said. "Get a hot meal."

"Yeah, whatever you do, don't anybody accept a surrender," Harper said. "We'd have to feed them. Give them water. Find somebody to take them off our hands. Pain in the ass."

"Couldn't get me out here without a gun," Ramos continued.

"You guys all have them," Jimmy said, exasperated. "I trust you to keep me safe."

"What'd I tell you guys?" Harper said. "U.S. Marine Corps babysitting service."

"I'm really not supposed to have one. They said so at the hotel."

"Who? The bellboy?" Harper asked.

"No, the military. The headquarters or whatever. Our great and powerful Coalition Forces Land Component Command. Once I have a gun, I'm no longer a noncombatant."

"You tell that to the Iraqis. They kill you just the same for being American," Martinez lectured.

"I've heard that several times already," Jimmy said.

"I've seen *We Were Soldiers*, with Mel Gibson," Martinez continued. "That reporter said the same thing. When the time came, he started popping like his name was Dirty Harry." A civilian stateside might feel inadequate for imagining war in terms of movies. After he lived with a Marine rifle company, that feeling would vanish. Everything was related in terms of movies, *Braveheart* and *Gladiator*, *Saving Private Ryan* and *Full Metal Jacket*, and, with the reverence reserved for canonical texts, *Black Hawk Down*. It said a lot for the movie that Marines would hold a film about Army Rangers in such high regard. If a reporter had shot people in *We Were Soldiers*, by the Marine logic, it must be so.

"He shot that shit up?" Ramos asked Martinez.

"Oh, yeah," the driver answered.

"You'll do it up, right, Jimmy?" the private said.

"No," Jimmy said. "I'm not doing—I'm not shooting any-body."

"Sure." Ramos smiled and tagged him on the shoulder with a playful punch. "I hear you."

Their repaired oracle, the hissing radio, told them it was time to stop again. The company pulled off the road. In keeping with protocol, they came out guns at the ready, first Ramos, then Harper, and finally Martinez. A perimeter was established, but it was not their turn to keep watch. Instead they leaned against the Humvee, in the shade it cast on the desert floor.

"When I get home," Ramos said, "I'm going to have like three, four bitches in a hot tub full of champagne, man. We're going to kick it like we was freak superstars."

"Oh, yeah?" Harper asked. "What are you going to do with those girls, ringmaster?"

"Two for show—they get it on with each other while I watch—and one for the blow, baby, and an extra to get me a drink with an umbrella in it," Ramos said. "Maybe rub my shoulders during the show-and-blow."

When he was Ramos's age, a daydream for Jimmy involved the girl a row in front of him in English class. Even in his own imagination, the best-case scenario was the kind of fumbling, un-dergraduate sex in the dark that was all he had performed up to that point. Hearing this choreographed combination of synchro-nized swimming and pornographic professionalism, Jimmy was disappointed in his younger self. In your own adolescent fantasies, he thought, you ought to be able to let loose as Ramos did. What the young Marine described sounded unfeasible but fun to imag-ine. It was the feasibility on which the sergeant chose to dwell.

"Let's turn the map around," Harper said. It was a Marine term for stepping back and looking at a situation from the enemy's perspective. "She's got her head underwater—correction, under champagne—and is...pleasuring you orally at the same time. Doesn't she drown?"

"Yeah, man, I don't approve of this kind of stuff as a Christian or whatever," Martinez said, "but she needs a snorkel or something."

"Well, not a snorkel, Tino," Harper said. "As planned, she has to breathe through her nose."

"Old men," Ramos said. "Anyway, Jimmy, the last one should come around—"

"Plus it's kind of expensive," Martinez said.

"Sticky," Harper added.

"They don't have the ghetto entrepreneur mentality," Ramos said. "This is what America's all about."

"Orgy entrepreneurialism?" Jimmy asked.

"Let's see. You don't have a hot tub," Harper said.

"You got one woman," Martinez added.

"And you aren't old enough to buy champagne," Harper concluded.

"Why they always hating on a man?" Ramos said.

"Boy," his elders said in unison. Instead of arguing, Ramos cracked up.

"So at the bottom of the hot tub there's this oxygen tank," he began again.

"Private Ramos," Harper said, no doubt hoping for silence, "get us some more MREs."

"Jimmy can do it," Ramos said. "Let the water boy do his job, while the players rest up a little."

"Where are they?" Jimmy asked.

"You don't have to," Harper said.

"He doesn't have to shoot anybody. Just grab a box." Ramos had his long-stemmed brush out and was in the middle of clearing sand from the barrel of his rifle. He took the best care of his weapon of anyone in the platoon, as far as Jimmy could tell. "Sergeant, I want to borrow some oil from Lance Corporal Dabrowski, Sergeant Harper."

"I've got some," Martinez said, standing up to look in the Humvee.

"I'd like to borrow some from Lance Corporal Dabrowski, Sergeant Harper," Ramos said.

"Go play with your friends. We aren't going anywhere."

"There's smoke up ahead," Martinez said. "I don't think we can pass."

"All right, then," Jimmy said, standing up and brushing off the seat of his chem suit. "I'll grab the rations."

"No Charms," Martinez said, referring to the generic Lifesavers that came with some MREs. The Marines had a quasi-mystical approach to their prepackaged meals. Thus the Country Captain's Chicken was not only the worst-tasting MRE, it was reputed to make its eater gay. Charms occupied the most dubious rank on the superstition hierarchy. The candies were bad luck—black-cat bad luck, broken-mirror bad luck.

"I know. I know." Jimmy wandered off in search of one of the trucks carrying their food and water. The smoke in the distance grew thicker. Several funnels joined together into a black cloud a few miles down the road. He saw Lieutenant Katzenbach lumbering away from a group of chastised Marines and stopped him.

"What's going on up there?" he asked the lieutenant.

"My understanding is that a preplanned target was engaged using precision ordnance to destroy a known enemy cache site," Katzenbach said distractedly.

"That's a lot of smoke," Jimmy said.

"You've developed weapons expertise at an alarmingly fast

rate for a civilian, haven't you, Mr. Stephens?" he snapped. Jimmy was surprised by his tone.

"No. I don't mean—" he said.

"There are some tactical issues you aren't supposed to report even if you know about them," Katzenbach said. "Check your ground rules."

"Well, I ... okay, Lieutenant," Jimmy said. The lieutenant stalked off. Doug the NBC cameraman had been loitering a polite distance away with his back to their conversation. But the moment Katzenbach was gone, he turned and engaged Jimmy.

"Talking to Lieutenant Hand Job, are you? That's about all we can get out of him, fucking hand job. Waste of time talking to him."

"Yeah," Jimmy said.

"He's probably the only nonpress officer in the entire fucking military who's actually read those damn ground rules. We lost the draw."

"He's okay," Jimmy said noncommittally. Doug sided with the enlisted men across the board, even sounded like one, but Jimmy couldn't bring himself to savage Katzenbach.

"Hey, have you heard this one? How's Katzenbach's wife like a doorknob?" Doug asked, eyes flicking back and forth in case the lieutenant returned.

"Come on, Doug," Jimmy protested.

"Everybody gets a turn. Oh, yes, old weapon, new target. All the grunts say it's true. She's a grade-A ho behind his back."

"That would make it even less funny," Jimmy said.

"How is Lieutenant K like Pamela Anderson?" Doug asked. Jimmy shook his head. "Huh?" Doug asked, gesturing toward his chest, nodding. "Huh?"

"They both have big jugs," Jimmy said at last.

"Diversionary tactic," Doug yelled. "Neither of them will ever command a Marine company." He laughed. "Yo, Martin! Trick or treat, man?" he called out to a passing Marine.

"Yo, Doug. Treat," the Marine shouted back. Doug flipped him a tin of dip.

"What are you doing?" Jimmy asked, relieved to be off the topic of Lieutenant Katzenbach.

"Building morale. For every can of dip, I have a friend for life. Then I don't need Lieutenant Pussycat. It's easy. Two packs of cigarettes for a radio operator, and we know what's happening up front. Woody's happy, the Marines are happy, and I'm happy."

"Oh." Jimmy left it at that. Doug wasn't satisfied.

"Don't you want to know?" Doug asked. "Smoke? Fire? War?"

"We're competitors, aren't we?" Jimmy said.

"I sent it along already. You won't have a paper for another twenty-four hours. What do I care?" He slapped the side of Jimmy's helmet. It rocked his head much harder than he must have intended, because he said, "Oh, sorry, man."

"It's heavy," Jimmy said. He righted the helmet and tightened the strap under his chin.

"Snipers, fighting. All is fucked up in the town of Nasiriyah. Which is funny, because they're supposed to be welcoming us with open arms."

"Right, the flowers and stuff. Victory parade to Baghdad," Jimmy said. "So that was all a lie?"

"You can't have a war machine and never use it," Doug said.

"I thought you had it so you didn't have to use it," Jimmy said.

"You buy into the system a little too easily, my friend," Doug said. "Every couple years we find an excuse to invade one of these banana republics, and we barely remember why afterward, like the morning after a drunken one-night stand. Panama, Somalia, Grenada. I mean, Afghanistan I get, but Iraq? This military costs close to a trillion a year. We have to justify that expense."

"I know this theater," Jimmy said. "Off Broadway. They bought a smoke machine for one of their shows, I think it was an updating of *The Tempest*. Anyway, it was a third of their set and tech budget. Now suddenly there's smoke in all of their shows, even if it's a domestic drama, comedy, you name it."

"You learn fast, Stephens," Doug said. "Now the hajjis have their own little smoke show working. We can't cross the river if they're shooting mortars at the bridge."

"Well, it's sunny. Pleasant. I'm going to get some food and work on my tan," Jimmy said.

"Or you could file a story," Doug said. Jimmy just laughed. "It's your work ethic that I admire, dog."

Jimmy found the food truck with relative ease. It was unattended, and he climbed into the covered cargo hold to scrounge for better MREs. He didn't want to bring back any Charms, but had no idea which packages contained the cursed candy. He took out the pocket knife he'd bought in Kuwait and slit open the top of a Thai Chicken. It was Charmed. He split a Meat Loaf and found Charms again. He wondered if it was okay to bring them back with the bad part excised or if he was supposed to find ones that never had been infected to begin with. It occurred to him that instead of fretting about candy for other people, he could just take what he wanted from different meals for himself. He hunted out oatmeal cookies and Tootsie Rolls and peanut butter with the crackers instead of the squeezable cheese.

"We can rebuild it," he said to himself. "We have the technology. We have the capability to make the world's first bionic meal. Spaghetti and cheese tortellini with—oh, score—spicy pound cake. Better than it was before. Better . . . stronger . . . faster . . . shit." The truck bucked twice as it started, shaking as it accelerated over the hump back onto the road to Baghdad. "Whoa! Hey! Jimmy's not going with you."

He crawled toward the front of the truck, but there was no window through to the cab. He banged and shouted to no effect. "Stop the truck! Stop the truck! I'm not going with you! Please stop the truck." Jimmy could barely hear himself over the growling and groaning of the engine and the noise on the highway of bouncing artillery pieces and combusting diesel. Jimmy moved toward the rear. He opened the canvas flap of the truck and found that it was indeed back on the highway. For once they were going fast. Looking down at the pavement, he could see it was too dangerous to jump. Even if he didn't break every bone from metacarpal to maxillary on impact, the miles-long convoy coming up behind would do the job a hundred times over.

Jimmy sat down on the floor of the truck, placing a Bean Burrito MRE under his rear as a pillow. He tore into the oatmeal cookies, devoured the peanut butter and crackers, and even ate some of the cheese. He ripped open another box and pulled out a bottle of water.

It dawned on him that this was not such a bad respite. There was no bitching, no insults. He could eat whatever he pleased. He picked up a packet of the square generic Lifesavers. It was ludicrous that the government would knowingly curse its own troops with evil candy. The Marines had rules and customs and ideas that were so senseless, yet Jimmy had to follow every one of them. Only now that he was alone did the frustration of days of agreeing, of keeping his opinions to himself, pop like a cyst in him, flooding his body with rancor. He didn't need to be told how to take a shit. There was nothing wrong with being a sissy-ass civilian reporter. In fact, there was a lot more right about it than anything else he'd seen in the desert.

He slowly tore through the Charms wrapper, eyes squeezed shut as if it were a grenade. Nothing happened. He ate a purple one. It tasted like any generic candy you'd get from a bulk bin at the grocery store. Orange was a little better than the rest. Most important, nothing terrible had befallen him.

The popping sound started as he bit into the green one. It was no louder than firecrackers in a neighbor's backyard. He would have thought little of it if the truck hadn't screeched to a halt. Jimmy fell into a stack of chow boxes. They tumbled down onto him. Then the return fire started. He crawled out from under the MRE cases and looked out the flap. The Marines had opened up with everything they had. The 50-caliber machine gun on the jeep behind him thumped like an aggressive bass drum, writhing in the Marine's hands with each shot. Every Marine in the convoy was firing, drivers and passengers alike. Some had crawled forward and were shooting from a prone position at the side of the road. He couldn't get out and run. That would make him a target. Instead he lay flat in the bed of the truck, where the sides were metal instead of fabric.

Jimmy was rigid. He considered moving and realized he couldn't or wouldn't. He tried to stay calm, to exhale at regular intervals, but felt his heart rearing in his chest. His vision blurred, then became hyperfocused as it settled on his spent cookie wrapper. The wrinkled foil was fascinating for a long instant. It was agonizing. Either he was thinking very slowly or else so quickly that translating thought into movement felt interminable. If he had to run, it would feel like the dreams where your feet are lead. He knew without even trying.

He was still deciding if staring at the wrapper was senseless or not, rapidly scanning the ingredients from high-fructose corn syrup to oats, when the holes appeared. They materialized silently in the din around him, perforations in the canvas two feet above his body. Matching points of light on both sides shone like stars in a night sky. Rays caught the hovering and drifting specks of dust kicked up by the fight, making each particle in the bullets' paths sparkle. He kept staring at the holes until the gunfire died down and the shouts of "All clear" were discernible. Nothing would ever slow his heart down. He could hear booted feet scraping the sandy road outside.

Jimmy didn't know he was climbing out until he already had. Spent shells were scattered everywhere, as if a piñata had split open or the clouds had rained hollow metal casings. He saw two smoldering pickup trucks a hundred feet away. He heard someone screaming at him, but the shock felt like a dream, and he couldn't answer. A Marine he didn't recognize pushed him to the ground. Jimmy tried to lift his head but felt a boot on the back of his neck. It was hardly a perfect showing for his first exposure to combat, but he realized that through it all, he hadn't thrown up once. He smiled as they bound his hands behind his back.

CHAPTER 16

"CAN I GO?" JIMMY ASKED THE GUARD.

"Sir, we're getting you squared away," he answered.

"I'm with the Marines. Can't I go back to my squad?"

"Sir, I'm just supposed to watch you while they get you squared away."

Jimmy sat on the side of the road with four Iraqi men. They were thrift-store stylish in old blue jeans and shirts straight out of the 1980s. The one next to him wore a vest by Christian Dior that looked to Jimmy like it had been designed for a woman. Unlike Jimmy, who was allowed to watch as the Marines milled about, the other prisoners wore empty sandbags over their heads. Duct tape was wound around the middle, where their eyes must have been. The man in the vest was whispering in Arabic into the ear of his comrade, then turned and began whispering to Jimmy as well.

"I don't understand," Jimmy said. There was more unintelligible whispering from the man. "I really don't understand," Jimmy said much louder.

"English?" the man said.

"American." The sandbag turned toward him, but he doubted the man could see out of it. "Reporter."

He didn't know the protocol for chatting with a hooded and bound member of a foreign army. There was no manual of manners that went from salad fork to surrendered foe. They all looked the worse for wear, dirty and tattered, skinny enough for the runway. Their pants were too short and the boniness of their ankles was frightening, making him glad they still had their shirts on.

"Army?" he asked.

"Journalist," Jimmy answered. "Civilian."

"Why is American prisoner?"

"I'm not a soldier. They don't—they're just confused probably." He stopped. But the man wasn't Jimmy's enemy, exactly. Jimmy was a noncombatant. And it seemed rude not to talk to the person tied up next to you. Yet he was an Iraqi soldier.

"You are writing truth. That Iraqi people are attacked. So you are prisoner."

"I think they're just confused. I know I'm confused." The man was silent. There were three other Iraqis in the row with him. The Marine lieutenant at the next vehicle seemed much more interested in the Iraqi prisoners than in Jimmy. He'd been pleasant enough about asking Jimmy to wait. More pleasant than the Marine who announced he'd almost shot him when he fell out of the truck.

"Americans attack Iraqi people. Unprovoked aggression. We will fight for our country." It was like saying hello to the person next to you on an airplane, then realizing half an hour later that he was a straining dam of opinions, ready to crash over the first person who bumped him. "We will defend ourselves."

"Well, you seem to be doing a fine job of that, or had been or . . . whatever," Jimmy said politely. He regretted saying anything in the first place. His experience taught him that talking to some soldiers was often like listening to a skipping record. It was a brotherhood of boring conversation.

"We will fight," the man repeated.

"Go ahead." Jimmy stared down at the man's handcuffs. "Don't let me stop you."

The POW turned his head, but all Jimmy saw was the blank gray of the bag and the silver duct tape. The bagged head shook back and forth with what Jimmy guessed was rueful fatalism.

"Go home, American," he said. "We don't want you here."

"I'd love to, but I'm tied up. Like you." The Marine guard wandered over to Jimmy and tapped him on the shoulder with the butt of his rifle.

"No talking to the prisoners." Jimmy was about to agree and ask to be moved, but he took issue with the Marine's tone.

"Why?"

"Reporters are not allowed to interview EPWs."

"What's an EPW?" Jimmy jerked his head toward the Iraqi. "Is he an EPW?" Jimmy thought for a moment. "Am I an EPW?"

"Enemy prisoner of war. You aren't allowed to talk to him. That's the rule." The guard was one of the younger Marines, probably a year or two out of high school. In that time he'd been absorbed completely into their culture and grown fluent in their language.

"POW wasn't simple enough," Jimmy said.

"Sir?"

"Everybody figured POW out, so you had to start calling them EPWs to confuse us."

"Sir, I can't say. But reporters can't interview EPWs."

"Does this look like an interview? Actually, I'm prepping him for Connie Chung. She'll be out any second now."

"Reporters can't interview EPWs."

"I'm not a reporter," Jimmy said.

"Sir, you said you were a reporter."

"As long as I'm tied up, I'm not reporting. So I'm just shooting the shit with my fellow EPW here." All Jimmy wanted was for the kid to break. If he talked to him like a normal person, he wouldn't insist on chatting with the Iraqi broken record.

"Sir . . ."

"If you want to untie me," Jimmy suggested, "I'll stop talking to him."

"I can't untie you, sir."

"I'm from Jersey. I know all the words to 'Born in the U.S.A.' How fricking dangerous could I be? What do you think I'm going to do?"

"I can't untie you, sir," the guard repeated.

"Then as long as you have me hog-tied on the ground, I'm going to talk to my friend here."

"You're not supposed to—"

"Shoo," Jimmy said.

"Sir—"

"Shoo."

"Jesus Christ." The Marine leaned down and with a pleading look said, "Just keep it down. I don't want to get in trouble here." Jimmy had won on both counts. He'd forced the Marine to act normal for a moment, and he got to talk to the dusty, half-starved prisoner of war who agreed with him that he shouldn't be in Iraq.

"Sir, yes, sir," Jimmy said. The Marine rolled his eyes and walked back to a Humvee and leaned against the grille.

"If the Americans insist on—" As the captured soldier launched back into the invading-army script, Jimmy interrupted him.

"What's your name?" Jimmy said. He was starting to feel at home with the assertive thing.

"Mohamed."

"Mohamed, I don't want to talk about it."

"The unprovoked American aggression?"

"Exactly," Jimmy said.

"They cannot—"

"I'm done," he said. Mohamed couldn't see that Jimmy had turned away, his only option since he couldn't cross his arms or stand up.

"But—"

"Why are you talking to me, anyway? There are three perfectly nice guys from your own army, also protecting the country from unprovoked American aggression, who you can talk to over there." The Iraqi soldier mumbled something under his breath. It was so quiet Jimmy couldn't even tell what language he was speaking. The bag muffled his words, made it harder to understand him. The tape around the eyes made the bottom of the bag jut out, away from his mouth. "What's that?"

"I am very, very sick and tired of these men," the Iraqi said. "We have been sitting in this big hole together for a month. I have nothing left to say to them. On and on and on. 'My wife, I want to see my wife.' 'I would die fighting the Americans for just one bite of chicken.' "

"I get the picture," Jimmy said.

" 'My children. I need to see my children.' Or, or, 'We should go to Basra and get drunk.' "

"I got it," Jimmy said. "Bitching or moaning or crying or whining. The Marines are great at it too."

"My English is so terrible now."

"No," Jimmy said. "It's really very good."

"Thirteen years I haven't spoken English," Mohamed said. "I studied in America."

"Oh." Jimmy pictured a grown Iraqi man in a Christian Dior vest struggling to open a locker in the hall of a high school somewhere in Idaho. He must have been younger as an exchange student, of course, and better dressed. Unless, that is, his host family was filled with sadists.

"I played basketball for Wichita State University. This was a long time ago. When Iraq and America were friends. My English is very bad now." Jimmy felt like he had moved to fishing for compliments.

"Like I said, your English is very good."

"I don't know. My basketball is very bad, too. I should be in Olympics. Play Michael Jordan. We don't have team now."

"I'm sorry." He hadn't noticed how tall the man was. The prisoner's long legs were knotted up half-Indian style. He looked even less comfortable than his smaller cohorts, if you could call them comfortable.

"I think I am too old," Mohamed added.

"I don't—I can't tell, with the—you know—with the bag. How old—"

"Thirty-five years. Too old, I think. But this Michael Jordan. He plays with forty."

"If you play like that, you'll be okay." The sky was blemish-free, and the unobstructed sun was having its way with them. Jimmy was sweating hard and felt like he was getting sunburned, but wondered how much worse it was under the bag. One of Mohamed's compatriots was swaying and leaning against the man next to him, like he was about to pass out.

"I don't think I play like that. But okay." He swiveled his head around a bit, as though he were trying to get his bearings again. "More than ten years since last time you attack us. All my good years." The bag shook back and forth again, deeply disappointed. "How can Americans know nothing and still do everything? You sound like nice guy. But so stupid."

"People tell me that a lot," Jimmy said.

"Not you. Americans."

"It's okay. I'm not offended."

"No," Mohamed said. "You're very smart guy."

"I don't know about that. I'm sitting on a desert road in the middle of nowhere tied up by my own army."

"You just don't care about Iraq. Not the same thing as stupid," Mohamed insisted. "In eighties, Daddy Bush love Saddam. Saddam fights Iran, he's Daddy Bush's friend. Saddam take Kuwait, and everything is bad."

"I remember that," Jimmy said.

"Maybe Baby Bush builds basketball courts all over Iraq when you rule us. This would not be so bad."

"I could suggest it," Jimmy said.

"You're not stupid. I like Americans."

"You like Americans? I thought you wanted to kill us."

"Fedayeen makes us attack. Here are truly crazy people. They take our uniforms. Say they wish to die against you. They shoot our captain when he does not want to attack."

"So you didn't want to fight?" Jimmy asked.

"Yes, I did," Mohamed answered. "You are invading my country. You invade. I must fight. But I like Americans. So friendly."

"Are we?"

"I like diners," Mohamed said. "Roadside, twenty-four hours, hash browns." Jimmy guessed the prisoner salivated at the thought, as that was the effect the soldier's words had on him. His lips tasted salty, probably from lying facedown in the sand. No matter how much he licked them, they were dry. It was a dry heat, an oven heat, radiating from the sun above and the ground below.

"Me too."

"So much food, and the waitress is always calling you honey and asking you where you are from."

"Not in New York," Jimmy said, though he assumed it was that way in the Midwest.

"And they keep bringing coffee, but you only pay once."

"I haven't had a real cup of coffee in ages," Jimmy said. Mohamed began to laugh, which Jimmy thought showed a pretty resilient character, given the circumstances.

"We sound like we are in the big ditch again. Doing the bitching. Coffee. Women. America."

"Yeah," Jimmy said. "We do."

"This, this Michael Jordan, is he now as good with forty as he was before?"

"He's the greatest ever," Jimmy declared.

"But right now is he as good?" The EPW's English sounded better and better, like his mind had found the groove at last and shifted back into the unused gear. He sounded less like a B-movie dictator and more like an immigrant Jimmy might meet in New York.

"He's like, good, but not as good. He's, I don't know, great, but not the best." Jimmy's English, on the other hand, was fading under the hot sun.

"For Jordan this is not so good, I don't think." Mohamed paused.

"Mr. Reporter," the guard said, "they want to talk to you."

"Hold on a minute," Jimmy said.

"They didn't say in a minute. They said now," the guard said.

"I'm just trying to talk to—"

"You want to keep a Marine waiting to talk to a hajji?" The guard jerked Jimmy up by one arm and led him away from the other prisoners.

"Thirty-five's not so old," Jimmy called back. "Be nice to that guy," Jimmy said to the guard. "He plays basketball. Went to school in America."

"I give a shit?"

"Just be nice to him."

"He'd kill you if he wasn't tied up. No shit."

"Yeah," Jimmy said. It was easier to be a Marine if you believed that. And it was probably true.

CHAPTER 17

IT WAS HARDER TO WALK WITH HIS HANDS CUFFED BEHIND HIS back than Jimmy expected, a miniature lesson in balance and stabilization. The guard led him to a small cluster of officers, one of whom was talking to his rival and onetime assailant Matt McNulty. Jimmy was safe, he thought, because no one with any self-respect would slug a man with his hands tied behind his back. McNulty was laughing and joking with the officer, who turned out to be a major. Jimmy and the guard waited a few steps away—the respectful distance you gave someone using an ATM—for them to finish.

"Sometimes the enemy has a say. In when the battle starts. In how. In where. But you see, Mr. McNulty, they have no say in how it finishes," the major said. He was the picture of a Marine officer, tall and ramrod straight, weathered face framed by short black hair with streaks of white at the temple that bespoke experience. "You could end the piece with that," he suggested, pointing at McNulty's notebook. "But you know your job far better than I do."

"Thank you, Major Gardner. You are right though, it's a great kicker," McNulty said, closing his notebook. His eyes tightened when he saw Jimmy, but only for a moment. When he realized the younger reporter was under arrest, he could not suppress a grin.

"Oo-rah, Private," Major Gardner said. "Who do you have for me there?"

"Sir." The guard thrust Jimmy toward the major, but didn't elaborate on who he was. That kind of explanation must have been above his pay grade.

"James Stephens, sir, *New York Daily Herald*."

"He doesn't have his ID, sir," the guard said.

"I'd like to apologize for all this, Mr. Stephens, but you aren't supposed to be with our particular merry band, and, of course, given your lack of credentials at the moment, we must take certain precautions," the major said. He had a megawatt smile. Even bruised and handcuffed, Jimmy felt at ease around Major Gardner.

"It's quite all right," Jimmy said. "Procedures, protocols. I understand." McNulty poked at pebbles with the toe of his boot, a look of mental constipation on his face. He turned to the major.

"That guy's only a danger to himself. You can cut him loose, no problem."

"You know this man?" Major Gardner asked. "You can vouch for him professionally?"

"I guess," McNulty sighed. "I know he's a reporter for the *Daily Herald*."

"Brilliant. We're in business," the major said, rubbing his hands together with apparent satisfaction. He turned back to Jimmy. "We have a lot of reporters running around who aren't embedded, not following the rules. A war zone is no place for that. Why, we almost shot you, Mr. Stephens," the major said cheerfully. He was the kind of man who remembered your name right off the bat, Jimmy noted.

"I'm grateful that you didn't," Jimmy said.

"So how'd you get here?" the major asked.

"Sir," Jimmy replied. "I was with my Humvee. My guys. And, I was with the—in the truck. You know, getting MREs—"

"You were eating the Charms," the guard said under his breath.

"No. I wasn't . . . I swear."

"There were wrappers everywhere," the guard accused.

"Private," the major said. "We've spoken about decorum before."

"Sorry, sir," the guard answered. He recited, as though he had repeated it many times, "A decorous Marine will be a decorated Marine."

"A credit to his company and a credit to his country," the major said, in what sounded like a conclusion to the guard's refrain. "Continue," he said to Jimmy.

"The truck started up, and I couldn't get out. Until after the fight."

"Do you have any credentials at all? Passport?"

"The military one is in the Humvee, but, um . . ." Jimmy lifted and wiggled his right leg, nodding his head to indicate that his documents were in the right side pocket of his chem-bio trousers. Major Gardner reached into the pocket and pulled out his papers.

"American citizen at least. Very good. Cut him loose, Private. This is war. People get lost. Shuffled around. If you were with the Army, this might be a problem, right, Private?"

"Oo-rah, sir," the guard said.

"But Marines roll with the punches. Marines can improvise. I said cut him loose, Private. We'll find you a Humvee you can ride in. You can ride with me if you like."

"Thank you, sir. If I could find my own, that would, that would be even better. My gear, my Marines." He'd called them his Marines. It was a little too precious. But he did feel like he would rather be back in familiar surroundings after all that had happened. And somehow the major's eagerness was becoming a bit off-putting.

"Private, see if you can find his squad. But listen up, Stephens. You get lost again, and you're probably going to die. Step on a mine. Get captured. Lose your way and starve to death. We cannot have that. No, we cannot."

"Yes, sir," Jimmy said.

"We need you out here, Stephens. We need every last one of our psy-ops allies," Major Gardner said.

"Sir?" Jimmy asked.

"By God, we have to lead the way in quality content production. Osama has streaming video over the Internet. We will not lose the PR war again. It's not just about holding a press conference anymore, knowing your good side." He turned his head and pointed to his left cheek. "They do not call this the theater of operations for nothing."

"All the world's a staging area," Jimmy said quietly.

"We're the land of Hollywood," Gardner continued, "of the Great White Way. We should not be dogging it on programming. Why, we will need the media to convince Saddam that he's lost. He'll be sitting in some bunker, safe and sound. Only when he sees tanks in Baghdad on CNN will he realize it's over."

Hustling toward the front of the line of vehicles was the person Jimmy least wanted to see. "Stephens," Katzenbach said with surprise. "Major," he addressed the superior officer. He was flanked by a lower-ranking second lieutenant—Larson, Jimmy recalled—one step behind him.

"Is he with your unit?" Gardner asked.

"Yes, sir. I'm sorry if he's causing trouble, sir," Katzenbach replied. "He's been a little uncooperative with the mission."

"Just a little lost," the major said. "Lieutenant ... Katzenbach, isn't it?" Gardner then asked in a pointed way.

"Yes, sir," Katzenbach said.

"Controlled information is out of style. There are so many

producers out there, CNN, Al Jazeera, Viacom, Hezbollah." Gardner nodded with a superior smile. McNulty looked on from the major's side, in full agreement. "If we want to get our message out there, the true story of course, our allies in the news media, like Mr. Stephens here, need credibility, the chance to roam, the chance to make mistakes. We have to establish our credibility as hosts, as news facilitators. It serves the greater good."

"Yes, sir." Katzenbach nodded.

"A commander has the confidence"—Major Gardner emphasized the last word—"is self-assured enough to allow a little improvisation without losing his head."

"Yes, sir," Katzenbach said again. He looked tired. They all did. But the circles under the lieutenant's eyes were more pronounced, his eyes twice as bloodshot. The major walked off with two junior officers who had been waiting for him. The guard cut Jimmy's cuffs apart and walked back toward the other prisoners.

"Let's go," Katzenbach said.

"Lieutenant, if I might have a moment of your time?" McNulty asked.

"Sure, Matt," Katzenbach replied. So it was Matt now between them? Jimmy looked on as McNulty began speaking to the lieutenant in a very low voice. "Larson, accompany Stephens back to Sergeant Harper's Humvee," Katzenbach called. "It's about fifty vehicles back."

"Yes, sir," Larson said. They walked back down the line of vehicles.

"Rough morning," Larson said, with a friendly smile.

"Yeah," Jimmy agreed. He thought better of asking about the major's comments to Katzenbach. It was clear that Gardner shared the general low opinion of Katzenbach's fitness as an officer. The Marines could be an unforgiving group, Jimmy thought.

"I didn't think we were going to see any action, stuck in the middle and all. The Air Force seems to be doing most of the work again. Nothing left for us grunts." Larson seemed like a nice guy, a straight-backed, please-ma'am-thanks kid. Fair-skinned and blond, with deep blue eyes, he looked far too nice for the Corps and far too young to command an entire platoon of Marines. He had been commissioned right out of the University of Oklahoma ROTC program. But the Marines seemed to respect him.

"You a real 'get some' guy, Lieutenant?" Jimmy asked.

"When I have to be," the lieutenant answered. "We got to shut down those poison factories. That's for sure. That guy's got some nasty shit stewing in his kitchen, and we can't have it showing up in New York or Chicago one of these days."

"Nip it in the bud?" Jimmy asked.

"There it is. Can't have some Arab Adolf running around with smallpox and VX and uranium."

"Can you fight without a good reason?" Jimmy asked. "Without the weapons and all that?"

"Orders are orders," Larson said, "but it's a whole lot easier to face if you feel like you might be saving your mama or your baby sister's life."

"What about the Iraqis?" Jimmy asked.

"Well"—Larson smiled—"I can't imagine we'd like it much in their shoes. I just hope they give us a chance to show them how much we have to offer."

"Sure," Jimmy said and thanked Larson for walking him back to the platoon. He found Doug and Woody there, where two trucks, presumably attack vehicles, sat burning. Woody had stooped down and scooped a little dirt and sand into his hand. "What are you doing?" Jimmy asked. Larson waved good-bye and headed toward the front.

"Oh, hey, Jimmy," Woody said, friendly as ever. He gestured with a thumb over his shoulder at the flaming trucks. Doug looked like he was trying to frame the shot so that the trucks were in the background, clearly a battlefield live shot. "Got to hit this before they stop burning."

"You could always throw some gasoline on them," Jimmy suggested.

"Yeah," Woody agreed, looking back at the trucks, "but it's better if you don't. We're going more vérité here." Woody began dabbing his finger in the sand, then running it across his forehead. It wasn't sticking.

"Just a little help?" Jimmy asked.

"I washed my face, barely an hour ago," Woody said, shaking his head at the folly of making himself clean and presentable when he needed to go live from the highway. "Scrubbed it with a wet wipe, even a few Oxy pads, and now this." He looked down at the grit cupped in his hand and gave up, letting it pour from his hand back onto the road.

"Hold on," Jimmy insisted. He checked beneath the nearest amphibious assault vehicle for a puddle of oil, and returned victorious with a greasy, darkened fingertip. "This is the stuff," Jimmy said, smearing the lightest amount possible onto one of Woody's temples, more like a shadow than a proper streak. "Hold still. Almost . . . a little . . ." Then he added a dab on the correspondent's right cheek. "Perfect."

"That it?" Woody asked.

"Wait," he added, and mussed Woody's hair a little with his hand. "There's such a thing as too good out here."

"Jimmy," Woody said, and trailed off, as if no words could express his gratitude for this favor. He glanced back at his cameraman, who gave him the thumbs-up.

"Back to work," Jimmy said, shucking a two-finger salute in Woody and Doug's direction and continuing past. He wiped the remaining oil on his chem-suit trousers, humming to himself. He stopped at another slick spot in the road, this one more than a foot wide in diameter. At first he took it for more oil. Looking down at the rubber piece of his boot that had touched the edge of the circle, Jimmy realized it was deep red, almost dried up in the hot sun, but still discernible as blood. He rubbed the toe of his boot in the sand by the side of the road to try to get it off, but it only smeared the stain wider around the edge of the rubber sole.

No one had said anything about an American casualty, but the Iraqis were all well off the road during the skirmish, from what Jimmy could tell. It was almost certainly American blood. The man was probably alive—a fatality would have been big news— but one of the Marines had been shot during the ambush. He was relieved to find his Humvee mates unscathed.

Ramos was unusually quiet while Harper quizzed Jimmy about his absence. As Jimmy told them about the EPW, a story started to take shape in his head. Publishing an interview with a prisoner was against the ground rules, but some of what Mohamed said seemed valuable—the fedayeen part in particular, but Mohamed's views in general too. Jimmy didn't know what people at home thought about Iraqi soldiers, but if he was surprised by what the man had to say, then readers might be, too. He began typing the story before they even rolled out.

Many times Jimmy had wished for a pause in the deluge of words from Ramos as they drove. Now his sudden silence felt strange. Ramos was looking at the gun in his lap with a peculiar look. Several minutes passed before Jimmy heard him mumble to himself, "I dropped him. I really fucking dropped him." Jimmy waited for him to continue, but he did not. It was an hour before the private spoke again.

CHAPTER 18

ELLISON CROSSED THE AISLE THAT DEMARCATED THE END OF NEWS and the beginning of Arts & Lifestyle. This was terra incognita. He never set foot in this part of the floor, only summoned Tim Suskind to his office on occasion. There were framed movie posters and photos of partying It Girls with ballpoint graffiti scrawled across them. The same white cubicle walls stood above the same gray carpet, but it was more colorful and frivolous, with art calendars and publicity stills to liven it up.

Suskind's cubicle was a model of organization. It was free of clutter, aside from a red gift bag and a bottle of champagne. He had tacked a large map of Iraq to his bulletin board, but pictures poked out from underneath in which the editor wore tuxedos, mugged with beautiful young people and surgically augmented women with orange tans and expensive dresses. There were extra pairs of shoes in four colors tucked beneath his desk, two sports jackets and what looked like a tuxedo and shirt hanging from the cubicle divider, like some kind of dilettante James Bond.

"That's a ten-four, good buddy," Tim Suskind said into the phone. "I am reading you loud and clear. But you have to read me too. There is a larger picture, and you have to play smart to stay in the game." He took off his tortoiseshell glasses and set them on the desk. He looked up at Ellison, grinned, and pointed at the phone. "The story was fine," he said into the phone again. "We just couldn't ... No, it could get you bounced, and that isn't what we ... I know it's interesting, but we need you to stay with the Marines."

"Is that Stephens?" Ellison asked. He hadn't spoken to the gossip columnist since he'd left for Kuwait.

"One second, Mr. Ellison," Suskind said, holding up a finger to wait but nodding encouragingly to his superior.

"Let me talk to him." Ellison resisted the urge to reach across and wrestle the phone away from him.

"Uh, Jimmy? Mr. Ellison wants to talk to you. Hold on." He held out the phone for his boss. He wore the expression of a cringing dog that has just spotted the rolled-up newspaper. Ellison felt firmly back in control.

"Stephens? Ellison. What are you thinking? That story was a blatant attempt to get yourself thrown out of the embed program. If you think we are going to aid and abet you in that ... that sabotage, you're mistaken. Interviewing a POW indeed. I want five files a day, or you're fired, and ... Hello? Hello?"

"What happened?" Suskind asked.

"He said"—Ellison had to restrain himself from fracturing the receiver into little plastic shards on Suskind's desk—" 'Fire me' and hung up."

"You might want to ease off a little," Suskind said meekly, head down and avoiding eye contact. "I don't think Jimmy's trying to get kicked out of—"

"I'm not sure that I'm following you. Why don't you tell me a little more clearly what I'm doing wrong?" Ellison asked him quietly but harshly. The Lifestyle editor withered before his eyes.

"Nothing," Suskind said.

"No, I'm very curious. How would you like me to run the reporters in the field? Any other suggestions? How about the Washington bureau? Have I directed them well? Maybe you could just take over the entire operation. Would you like that?"

"No, Mr. Ellison, I just thought—"

"You get a decent article out of that nitwit each day. Beyond that, no thinking is required or even desired from you. Any questions?"

"No, sir," Suskind said. "I read you loud and clear. I'm quite impressed with the way you've run everything, and if I might say—"

"You might say a lot of things," Ellison told him, turning on his heel and heading back toward his office. "But you'd be better off if you didn't say anything at all."

CHAPTER 19

THE LANDSCAPE WAS CHANGING AS THEY PUSHED NORTH. EMPTY desert was giving way to greenery. It was neither lush nor tropical, but there were fields and even trees popping up along the way. Iraqis came out and waved to them, which was heartening until Harper explained that this was more to keep the Marines from bursting into their homes looking for guns and ammunition than from friendliness.

"Or just shooting them," he said.

Feelings toward the Iraqis had turned bitter as they entered their second week since the invasion. The guerrilla tactics of the fedayeen, including fake surrenders and attacks in ambulances, made even civilians dangerous in the troops' eyes. Talk of saving the country and protecting the people was over. It was now just about getting the job done.

Jimmy's own attitude wasn't much better. His chat with Ellison made him want to give up trying to file at all. Part of the problem for Jimmy was physical. Pain and discomfort were driving him as much as emotion. His feet stung with infection—trench foot, the doc called it. He had forgotten to change his socks daily, as Becky had admonished. They slept in their clothes, never showered, rarely even took their boots off. When he finally did, he found his toes were red and suppurated.

His lips were sunburned, which sounded minor, but a solid crust had formed over them, and the nettlesome sensation that came with the ever-present taste of salt had made the feeling somehow worse than the one in his feet. There were even simpler things, any one of which would have prompted a concerned visit to the doctor at home, like weight loss, perpetual dehydration, and complete exhaustion. By the standards of the field, they were subtle enough to overlook most of the time.

Ramos's mood changed by the mile. He had been tripping manically since killing an Iraqi in the ambush, euphoric and depressed, giggly and cranky. "Cleanest shot I ever took," he said once. "He might've made it. People actually survive head shots more than you think," he added not five minutes later. If he was boasting, the private would have been exclusively fist pumps and chest thumps. He did plenty of that. But he was also slipping into uncharacteristic moments of melancholy, and his temper in between was short.

"Hey, I don't have a problem with fucking Mexicans," Ramos said, in an escalating argument with Martinez.

"Then why you calling us 'fucking Mexicans,' man?"

"I don't have a problem with Mexicans, brother, but I'm just saying, my family's from Puerto Rico and Colombia, and everybody's like, that guy's a Mexican."

"You're American," Martinez said.

"I'm half Boriqua and half Colombiano."

"Where were you born?" Martinez asked.

"Makes no difference."

"Makes you an American," Martinez said. "Saves you a lot of bullshit."

"Yeah, Jimmy, José Aztec up there will trip about how lucky

you are to be in America. I'm like, the land of racism and inequality? Thank you very fucking much." They bounced out of their seats, striking an enormous pothole. Jimmy thought Martinez may have hit it on purpose.

"You're as white as Jimmy, back there, man," Martinez said.

"That's pretty white," Jimmy conceded, noting that Ramos had the light skin and European features of a Spaniard, not the rough-hewn ones of a Mayan warrior.

"Fuck that, *vato*," Ramos said. "Just 'cause I ain't had to run across no border don't make me white and shit."

"I'm starting a movement," Martinez said. "Everyone takes the test."

"What test?" Harper said.

"The citizenship test. Man, my English is better than his. He certainly doesn't have good moral character, and I bet he couldn't even pass the civics exam. Yo, Ramos. Who was the third president of the United States?"

"Yo, who the fuck cares?" Ramos answered. "Self-hating Mexican racist."

"No offense, Sergeant," Martinez continued. "But I think everybody ought to have to take the test. That kid back there is a waste of a perfectly good blue passport."

"You're a fucking mercenary, man. Yo, Jimmy, he joined the Corps for his green card. Sergeant, we got a mercenary Marine driving this Humvee."

"You are an ignorant little kid, man," Martinez said.

"Jefferson, motherfucker," Ramos said. "The third president of the United fucking racist States was Thomas slave-owning-motherfucking Jefferson." He peered out the window. Though the young Marine's head was turned, Jimmy thought he could see a smile curling the side of his mouth.

"He's right," Jimmy said.

"I know he's right," Martinez said. "Unlike you three, I actually had to take the test."

"Racists right here, too, man. You don't want to be a black man in this Marine Corps," Ramos said to Jimmy. "The brothers don't want to be wearing tight jeans and cowboy hats and going to barbecues where they play country music all the time. It's all good in the Army. Colin Powell and shit."

"So why are you in the Corps?" Jimmy asked.

"You kidding? Corps kicks ass," Ramos said. Up front the sergeant and the driver each grunted an "Oo-rah."

"At least that's settled," Jimmy said.

"What I want to know—" Ramos began to say.

"Gentlemen," Harper said. "I think we've had enough of the Mexican Civil War for one day."

"I'm not Mexican!" Ramos shouted. From the seat behind him, Jimmy could see Harper's shoulders shaking as he stifled a laugh. Then he diplomatically changed the subject.

"Man, I gotta say, that's the first time I ever got shot at," Harper said.

"Me too," Martinez said.

"And me as well," Jimmy said.

"I thought you'd lived through the gunfight at the OK Corral," Harper said. Jimmy realized he had made a mistake. He was about to cover it up with a quick lie but couldn't think of what to say.

"Yeah, I thought you were Mr. Somalia 1993 himself," Martinez said. "Mr. War Correspondent." Jimmy decided to come clean. He couldn't fake it, confusing a machine gun with an automatic rifle, mortars with rocket-propelled grenades.

"I was graduating from high school in 1993," Jimmy said. "I am neither a Mexican nor a war correspondent," he said, imitating Ramos's whiny yell. "And I've never been to Somalia."

"But—" Harper began.

"Woody said that, not me. I'm not even supposed to be here," Jimmy said. Harper already thought he was babysitting. What would he say when he knew that Jimmy was a clueless phony? What would he do? "I write about gossip. Models and actresses and what you might call 'homo' fashion designers and rich people's vacation houses. For a living." He waited for the avalanche of mockery to begin.

"In a way," Martinez said, "that's not the biggest surprise in the world."

"You get to go to, like, film premieres and meet all the women we jerk off to at night?" Ramos asked.

"Uh, yeah," Jimmy said.

"That is fantastic," the private said. "He lives the life," he added, perhaps imagining Jimmy in that champagne hot tub he'd conjured up for himself. Harper had yet to respond to the news. He hadn't so much as shifted in his seat.

"Don't you ... don't you worry about having an amateur in the Humvee? Aren't I going to get us all killed or something?" Jimmy had been prepared for many reactions, but jealousy was nowhere on the list.

"We've had an amateur in the Humvee for a while already," Martinez said. "Guess we'd gotten used to it."

"Didn't you write something about the chef back at Triumph?" Harper asked him.

"Yeah," Jimmy answered.

"So maybe it would have been, I don't know, almost insulting, us going to war and you wanting to write an article about the cook. I can't speak for every man here, but it sent a signal that you didn't take this seriously. And it sure didn't feel like a joke to me."

"But I—" Jimmy began.

"Well, let's just say it seems now like that's what you know," Harper said.

"I wasn't trying to—"

"I get that," Harper said.

"So you seriously aren't mad?" The Marines offered equivocal grunts and shrugs in response. "I mean, I lied to you."

"Not much," Ramos said. "Wanted to sound like you knew what you was doing. I'd have done that."

"I don't see how I could come out here with no preparation and not crap myself," Harper said. "Seriously, I would have shit my pants if I were you."

"I'm a puker," Jimmy said.

"A what?"

"A puker." He decided to go all the way now that he'd started. His admission of inexperience wasn't enough to convince them of his failure and inadequacy. "My first crime scene, I puked everywhere when I saw the body. Ruined evidence. Got pulled off the beat. I spent a year looking for commas and misspelled words before they let me try gossip and arts."

"You puked on a dead body?"

"In front of the cops?"

"In front of the cops, yeah, but not *on* the body. It was pretty far from the body, but there were some shells and footprints and stuff where I puked. It was kind of a fiasco."

"Was it the chunky-dinner kind of puke or more like the projectile-liquid kind?" Ramos asked. It was not what he was expecting, but to a Marine, Jimmy realized, it was the most obvious first question.

"The latter," Jimmy said.

"And you never got another shot at the cop reporting?" Harper asked.

"Never again." Anyone who couldn't handle a crime scene shouldn't be welcome in a war zone. They seemed dismayed, were shaking their heads. This, at last, was what Jimmy had been expecting.

"That's bullshit," Harper said. "Grade-A bullshit."

"You should have got another shot," Martinez said.

"What? No, I embarrassed the paper." They still weren't getting it. "The editors could see I wasn't cut out for anything serious. Just like here."

"Every Marine pukes during basic," Harper said. He explained how a recruit usually threw up a dozen times before leaving boot camp at Parris Island. It transpired that many Marines had already puked in the field, including several in their gas masks during the round of Scud attacks at the start of the war. This had not been a well-publicized fact at the time. "They're still Marines," Harper said. "They don't have to wear dresses and work as secretaries at the Pentagon just 'cause they threw up."

"Wow," Jimmy said. He had never considered that the Corps could be a more forgiving environment than a newsroom. Thinking of all the teenagers, all the raw recruits, that went through boot camp, the different backgrounds they brought to the Corps, he could see that it all made sense. And everyone in the Humvee was a screwup in some way, they'd said so themselves.

"But why would they send you here?" Harper asked. "I mean, no offense."

"We had a real correspondent. This war jockey, military expert named James Stephens. Well, James E. Stephens."

"Yeah?" Martinez said.

"And he got ... was ... he was hit by a delivery truck," Jimmy said.

"Hit by a truck," Martinez repeated.

"After Somalia and Bosnia and wherever—" Jimmy began.

"He still didn't look both ways before crossing the street,"

Martinez concluded. "So they sent you in his place. They must be insane."

"No," Jimmy said. "I think the Pentagon's more to blame. Once they'd done all the background checks, vetted everybody, there were no substitutions."

"No substitutions," Harper said.

"The Marines would only accept James Stephens for this gig," Jimmy said. "So you got him." They all laughed. From there, the subject turned to Jimmy's exposure to attractive women, or shit-hot women, as the Marines called them. Had he met Ashley Judd, Charlize Theron, and Britney Spears? Yes, yes, and yes. Had he slept with any of them? No, across the board. Had he slept with any models? Yes, several. Anyone they'd heard of? Not by a long shot. This wasn't as disappointing as he thought it would be. A fling with a Sears catalog model earned him enormous respect in the vehicle. He felt as if his virtual rank had risen from subprivate to corporal in no time.

They talked their way through the celebrity spectrum, about who was uglier in real life, who had gained weight recently, and who was gay. Speculating on male homosexuality was the most popular subject. The only actors they didn't seem to consider closet cases were Mel Gibson, Bruce Willis, and Harrison Ford. Han Solo could not be gay, the majority ruled. Brad Pitt and Ben Affleck, on the other hand, were two candelabra shy of Liberace. Right or wrong, this was a conversation where he could hold his own, and he felt a kind of relief he hadn't known in days.

CHAPTER 20

JIMMY'S GOOD MOOD LASTED WELL INTO THE NEXT TACTICAL PAUSE, and he celebrated by writing a horrifically detailed story about his physical afflictions and those of the Marines around him. He took great pride in his realistic descriptions of scabbing, oozing, and burning. They were the easiest interviews he'd done yet. Marines would roll up sleeves, take off boots, and open their mouths with great pride to demonstrate what kinds of pain they were enduring. "Play through the pain," more than one said, almost every one of them relating it back to high school sports. It wasn't the most complicated story in the world, but he researched, wrote, and sent it in a couple of hours. Once again, however, that would leave him without a hole in the ground to call his own. He was always last when it came to entrenching.

Or so he thought. He'd written the story in the shade of the NBC van, where one box served as a chair and two as a desk. Doug had a generator, which meant Jimmy wouldn't have to hook up the inverter. He stepped back into the sun, laptop snug and recharged in its cushioned case, prepared to get friendly with the soil that was less sandy every time they moved north. When he found the boys, they were at rest in their fighting holes. Ramos had even taken his shirt off and shaded his eyes with a floppy desert hat.

"Okay, Sergeant, how much?" Martinez asked.

"Bee cam dee," Harper said with a hint of uncertainty. Martinez nodded, and the lesson continued.

"Yes?" Martinez asked.

"Ah," Harper tried.

"No?"

"La-ah," Harper said.

"Thank you?"

"Shokran." Harper bowed his head with his hands pressed together like a kung fu master.

"Don't you have translators?" Jimmy asked.

"A few. But almost none. Half of them barely speak Arabic anyway." Harper held up a laminated sheet with simple illustrations of guns and missiles and little soldiers. "Everything will be fine," Harper said with exaggerated credulity, "because we have the picture card."

"Are those comics?" Jimmy asked, taking the card. There were cartoon faces lined up in rows for identification, one bald and clean-shaven, another with hair and a beard and every combination in between. In another illustration a mustachioed man with black caterpillar eyebrows and a Saddam Hussein mustache held bright red Looney Tunes dynamite. The transportation hierarchy flowed from bicycle to motorcycle, from donkey cart to hatchback.

"Officially, no," Harper said. "Unofficially, yes. Garfield is our primary means of communication with the people of Iraq. See, you point at a picture, and then the Iraqi points at another picture to answer you."

"Except when the Iraqi is wearing zip cuffs and has a sandbag over his head," Jimmy said.

"That is one of the small hitches," Harper agreed. "And we're going to be here for a while."

"Nah, man, we're out in a month," Ramos said from under the hat. "We're halfway there already."

"Why worry all the time about shit you can't control? It's so civilian," Martinez said. Jimmy noticed that there were four fighting holes rather than three. He stood over the empty one until Martinez said, "Yeah, that's yours. Happy birthday."

"Thanks. I was—" Jimmy began to say.

"You were working. We know," Harper said.

"It's more painful watching you dig than actually digging it ourselves," Martinez said, brushing off the gesture.

"Don't go getting all weepy or anything. You'll have to dig a new one in an hour anyway," Harper said. The sergeant looked at Martinez. "Give me another word."

"Water?" Martinez asked.

"May-ya," Harper said.

"Food?"

"La, shit. Ma ... no. Ah ..."

"Akl."

"I was going to get it."

"Of course, Sergeant," Martinez said. Harper would get it because he cared, Jimmy thought. He unzipped his chem suit and, as happened more easily with each day he spent in the field, quickly began to nap, the back-and-forth of the Arabic quiz his lullaby.

In total darkness his computer screen generated a powerful glow. Jimmy tried to block it. Light discipline meant not giving enemy snipers a target, similar to the Chechen cigarette problem. He buried himself under both his and Ramos's sleeping bags and set up walls with their foam sleeping mats.

"He jerking off under there?" Harper asked.

"You can hear it. Man, he's beating that thing," Ramos said.

"I'm the only guy here who doesn't start whacking it the second the sun goes down," Jimmy replied.

"Not our fault if you're shy," Harper said. "Not a lot of entertainment out here."

"I'm trying to maintain light discipline. Ramos, can you see me?"

"I still see you," Ramos said.

"How about now?" Craned forward over the computer, Jimmy spread his fleece jacket over his head and laptop as a second layer. Other than overheating and suffocating, he thought it would be fine.

"Well," Ramos said, "I guess so. I see a little light, but it's by your foot. Do you need both feet?"

"I could get by with one," Jimmy said.

"Then go for it."

He typed for half an hour, then took a calculated risk that the green display of his satellite phone would not draw fire. The sleeping bags broke up the signal too much for him to file from inside the makeshift hut. The Marines burrowed down in their fighting holes and wished him luck, which took the form of asking every few seconds if he'd been shot.

"Not yet," Jimmy said for the fifth time.

"How about now?"

"Still here," Jimmy said.

"Did they shoot you?"

"Yeah," Jimmy said at last, "right in the face."

"You poor bastard."

"Not much of a face to begin with," Harper noted.

The job done, Jimmy settled into the first decent fighting hole of his entire campaign. All was still. The stars were out. He wasn't comfortable and wouldn't sleep, but at least he felt safe. That was before the thunder started and well before he realized the thunder was Iraqi artillery. It rumbled his chest like a thousand car-trunk woofers on Flatbush Avenue.

The sky turned bright. Not on the horizon, like the first night of the war—it was right over them. The flashes were eerie green. It grew louder, so loud that there was no other sound, so loud that sound became feeling instead of noise. Shell shock, the antiquated term that had lost its force to the blandness of post-traumatic stress disorder, had meant something. It was a complete, physical shock, from the vibrating eardrums to the sensation that his intestines were quivering. He felt his bowels loosen and realized that, curled and tangled in a fetal knot as he was, all of his effort was focused on holding in his body's waste, so that he could die cleanly if he had to die.

It was death knocking, three football fields away. Not poetic death, in black robes like the Iraqi women wore, riding a sickly horse like the half-starved farm animals they passed every day, but death as geometry. The scythe was the invisible arc of each projectile, calculated against prevailing winds by whoever was charting the square of metal hail. The mathematician shouted orders to men who raised and lowered the barrels of absurdly large guns. It would end when they planted a blossom of shrapnel and earth in his fighting hole.

Jimmy could have been home, safe and sound, having lox and cream cheese in the morning, flirting with women at cocktail parties in the evening, in no danger of dying horribly. His fists were clenched, and he could feel the nails biting into his palms. He realized that he had to get out, get home, by whatever means were available. There was no reason to stay in the field and die.

The assault slackened. The sound receded enough that he could hear the ringing it had left in his ears. He uncurled slightly and reached out for his sat phone. He dialed the news desk in New York to demand his recall. Jimmy was getting the hell out of there if Ellison had to borrow Action News Channel 2's helicopter and send it into Iraq for him. He heard the automated voice mail system. "You have reached the news desk of the *New York Daily Herald*." There was a host of options: "Press three for letters to the editor." There was no button to press for a run-in with mortality.

"Don't die. Don't die. Don't die," he repeated, fumbling in the pocket of his chem pants for the notebook Becky had given him with the phone numbers. The booming of artillery cannons continued to reverberate around him. He selected an alternate number and tried it. This one went straight through to a human being. "I got to get out of here," he said as a woman's voice answered the phone. He could barely hold the phone.

"It's Jimmy Stephens. I'm in Iraq." She asked who he was with. "Who am I with? I'm with the *Daily Herald*. I'm with the Marines. I don't know." She told him to calm down and wait his turn. "Wait my turn? I'm in the middle of fricking Iraq and there's bombs going off all around me. I'm not waiting my turn." She said it sounded exciting and promised to put him through right away. Exciting for her maybe. He cursed the unknown receptionist but kept the antenna aboveground. Jimmy was not going to lose this call.

CHAPTER 21

ELLISON WAS EATING CEREAL IN HIS KITCHEN. HE WAS GOING INTO work later each day. The stares and glares at the office were shaking his confidence. It was like a zombie movie. One after another his docile employees turned into vicious monsters, out to eat him alive. He suspected someone was fomenting open revolt, but he had no allies of his own to call in for help. He was isolated.

He watched Chris Turner and Carol Richards recap the events of the day on CNN as he ate. They had the television anchor's ability to stay cheerful while reciting death tolls, but it didn't bother Ellison. They had their job to do.

"Hold on a second, Chris. We have a very important call from one of the embedded reporters in the field, Mr. Jim Stephens of the *New York Daily Herald*." Ellison's eyes widened, and the spoon stopped an inch from his mouth as a picture of Jimmy Stephens appeared, superimposed on a map of Iraq. It was his publicity shot, the one from his column where he grinned like an idiot and pointed his fingers at the camera.

"Jim's with the Marine Expeditionary Force. Jim, what do you see?"

"Get me out of here! Get me out of here! Oh, my God, I'm

going to die. You have to get me out of here," Jimmy begged the managing editor through the small white television on his kitchen counter. Milk ran off Ellison's spoon and onto the table.

"Whoa, what's going on there, Jimmy?"

"There's, there's explosions and implosions and blasts—and, and lights and fire. I want to come home. Are you going to bring me home or not?"

"I don't think we can bring you home, Jimmy"—Carol chuckled—"but we are bringing you into the homes of millions of Americans."

"What are you talking about? I—I can't hear you very well. I want to get out of here. The deal is off, you hear me? I am not going to die just to cover this. Oh, my God. I'm about to piss myself. Give me Ellison, goddamnit!" He had Ellison's undivided attention, of that there could be no doubt. In fact, the managing editor's concentration was so extreme that he didn't realize that his spoon and dozens of grains of granola were now on his kitchen floor.

"Careful with the language, Jimmy. This is a family news channel. Kids are probably watching at school," Chris chastised him.

"I can't do it. I can't do it. This is crazy. We're trying to get some sleep, then someone starts trying to kill us with some missiles and ... what? What are you talking about, Harper? Fine, Harper says they're trying to kill us with *artillery*. Iraqi artillery, American artillery, I don't care. I just want to come home. Now."

"Well, Jimmy, thanks for calling in to CNN. A chilling report from the field," Carol said, looking into the camera and making a very serious face. Viewers would be sure to appreciate the gravity of the situation, thus tipped off. Ellison found it grave. He found it very grave indeed.

"CNN? What are you talking about?" Jimmy's voice said as he was cut off.

"You really get a sense of the danger and the suffering of the troops," Carol said, turning to Chris in the studio.

"And you might say, a good sense of the danger Jim Stephens is in. Did he say he was going to, ahem, wet himself?"

"I think he did, Doug. And I hope he doesn't, because I hear there are no showers in the desert."

"Ha-ha. Right you are, Carol. Those Marines are suffering enough without that. Now a report from our own Rick Gorman in Kuwait City. Rick?" The scene shifted to the roof of a hotel in downtown Kuwait.

In the age of communication technology, there was no such thing as out of touch. Ellison could bark commands from a mountaintop, edit stories from a yacht, and fire people in the middle of a tour of the Great Wall of China. In those cases, the rapid advances worked in his favor. Now, as his home phone and cell phone both rang, as a tiny digital voice from his study announced incoming mail on his personal computer and his BlackBerry buzzed itself right off the kitchen counter, it was a sinister force.

The BlackBerry vibrated across the tile, an inexorable migration toward the spilled granola. The television was still on, but it was hawking laundry detergent to stay-at-home mothers. Ellison was upstairs, huddled in bed. Nowhere was safe for him now.

CHAPTER 22

WHAT JIMMY LIKED MOST ABOUT HIS COVER STORY AS HE PREPARED to sneak away from his squad and find a way back to Kuwait was its elegant simplicity. Rather than some transparently elaborate lie, he'd told them he was going "to get something" from "over there." Leaving his stuff behind probably had thrown them off his trail. Waiting till morning also had been a good idea, if only because he could see where he was going.

He thought he had covered nicely for his meltdown on national television. When Ramos asked him if he'd "made himself sound like a little punk" in front of his boss, he not only left out the part about dialing the world's twenty-four-hour news channel by mistake, but replied simply that he had not gotten through to the newspaper. Again, the explanation was deviously simple: a bad connection. What he had avoided, Ramos explained, was "embarrassing as hell" and "the kind of shit you can't live down." Jimmy was vehement in his agreement. It would have taken years to live down such a pathetic outburst.

The Marines ignored him, and he began to walk toward the road, then southeast on it toward the Hilton and the airport. It was far, a couple hundred miles maybe, but he hoped perhaps to find supply trucks in the rear that were driving back. At that instant, Jimmy thought he would be willing to walk the whole thing if that was the only way home.

There had been a lot of time to think the night before. He dwelled on the sound of artillery shells. Did the one destined for you whistle like in a movie as it fell, or was it the one you couldn't hear? At one point around four in the morning a strange sense of calm settled over him. He felt sure he had figured out his entire life, from how he should hang his clothes in his closet to how he ought to settle down, marry, and move back to New Jersey. But his plans dissolved with first light. All he felt was the urge to walk down the road in the opposite direction from the artillery and hope for a ride.

He hustled down the shoulder of the highway, taking another moment to ponder the state of his mental health. A point in his favor was that he was getting as far away from the war as possible. There could be little that was saner than that. A point against him was that he was singing to himself somewhat loudly.

"If I go there will be trouble. And if I stay it will be double." He paused to acknowledge the puzzled Marines he saw along the way. "Thank you. Good to see you too. I'll be performing at the Kuwait Hilton all next week." He began to sing again.

"You're going the wrong way," Harper said, falling in beside him.

"False," Jimmy said.

"I said you're going the wrong way." The reporter stopped singing and looked at the sergeant.

"Entirely a matter of opinion," Jimmy said.

"There's fedayeen and mines and all kinds of stuff between here and Kuwait," Harper said. "You'll never make it."

"There's fedayeen and mines and all kinds of stuff between here and Baghdad."

"Jimmy, the thing is—"

"Is this where you give me a big speech, maybe about responsibility?"

"Nope. Not from me," Harper insisted, as if he didn't have a tendency to sermonize. He looked backward as if to emphasize how far they were from their camp. They were still with the company but would soon be hitting the open road. There was a hint of nervousness in the way Harper shifted the weight of the M16 hung over his left shoulder. Suddenly he stuck his foot in Jimmy's stride and tripped him straight to the ground. Jimmy broke his fall with his hands and felt a jolt of pain in his wrists and elbows as he hit. He hadn't seen anyone tripped since high school and had forgotten how easy it was to bring someone down.

"You coming voluntarily?" Harper barked. The Marine bent down and grabbed the heels of Jimmy's boots. "Or should I just drag you?"

"Back to the car?" Jimmy asked, examining the new set of abrasions on his palms to add to his growing list of pains and discomforts.

"To Baghdad," Harper said.

"No way," Jimmy said. "I'll find a truck back. Someone's heading back. Maybe they forgot to turn the stove off, whatever. I'm catching a ride with them."

"Right now this is a one-way road, Jimmy. We're traveling light for speed. Very little resupply at the moment."

"Hail me a fucking Iraqi cab if that's all you can do, but I'm out of here. This whole thing was pointless." Go to Iraq, become a real reporter, gain respect. Now he was humiliated, his CNN performance probably a video file forwarded around offices, a laughingstock.

"What are they going to say when you get back? After you chickened out and ran?" Harper asked. Jimmy didn't know. Move in with his parents and hope the world could forget? Maybe if he stayed and wrote, he could earn back a modicum of respect, at least enough to keep his job. In the light of day, with the sound of artillery an echo in his memory, it no longer seemed impossible to stay. Jimmy had grown accustomed to the road, the regimen, and his companions. "You're closer to the finish now than the start. You're already in it."

It was simple and practical. Harper was right. Jimmy was lying in Iraqi dust on an Iraqi highway built by an Iraqi dictator. He was there, and it would be harder to backtrack than to get the job done. He stood up and straightened his chem-bio suit. "Can I drive part of the way?" Jimmy asked.

"No," Harper said.

"Oh, come on."

"No."

"Can I at least sit in the front?" Jimmy tried.

"No," the Marine said.

"Way to sweeten the pot."

"Just shut up and walk. That way." The rising sun was to Harper's right. He pointed roughly north.

Harper went to check in with the first sergeant. He left Jimmy at the vehicle to stow his gear and maybe get a quick shave. Standing behind the Humvee, he heard a sound and turned to see Ramos stealthily approaching from behind.

"What—uh—what you need there?" Jimmy asked him. Ramos came nearer, knife drawn. If the private had finally flipped, this was a pretty good way to show it. Ramos looked at Jimmy, looked down at the blade, and then looked up at the reporter again.

"Give you a bayonet if I can use your phone."

"What?" Jimmy asked.

"I'll give you this Iraqi bayonet for one phone call." What Ramos saw as an offer of barter, Jimmy saw as a knife thrust repeatedly toward him. "It's cool, man. Everybody needs a war trophy. This is, like, badass, but easy to carry."

"I can't take your knife."

"It's okay. I have three already. You want a Republican Guard insignia maybe? I got a couple of those too." Jimmy had watched the Marines pick through the abandoned gear of the surrendering Iraqis. Military memorabilia did not inspire him particularly.

"You just go ahead and make the call." Jimmy handed him the phone. "You have to dial, no—you have to hit zero-zero-one, then the area code and number, then send."

"This is huge, man. Thank you so much." He shoved the knife toward him again as he finished dialing, but Jimmy held his hands up and refused to take it. "Hey, is Marissa there? Yeah," Ramos said. "I'm in Iraq. That's crazy, right? Like, 'Hi, I'm in Iraq. Is Marissa there?' This cool reporter guy we roll with let me use his phone. Let me talk to her. Uh-huh. Yeah. Of course." There was a long pause. He offered Jimmy the knife again, handle first this time. Jimmy decided that it would be easier just to take it. "Hey, baby. How're you doing? Everything okay? You ain't had the baby yet? But everything's okay, right? Everything's fine? Well, why you still working? You don't have to— Don't let him give you a hard time."

Jimmy tried to back away, but Ramos inched closer again, as if he didn't want the reporter to think he would walk off with the phone. It didn't seem like a conversation Jimmy should be listening in on, but he remembered that the Marines had no sense of privacy. Sooner or later, everyone knew your personal business.

"I miss you. I love you. You've seen it on TV, right? It'll all be over real soon. We go in first but we come back first too. Won't be too long. No, I'm fine. Everything is ... I did something, though. There was this guy ..." He shook his head, face contorting in what looked like a fight against tears. It had to be the kill, Jimmy thought. Ramos pinched the bridge of his nose with his free hand, took a deep breath, and got past it. "No," he said. "Never mind. Maybe we'll talk about that when I get back. I can't talk too much more. This guy with us from the *New York Daily Herald*, this is his phone and I don't want to get him in trouble. I should go."

"It's okay," Jimmy said. Ramos shook his head.

"I miss you a lot," he told his girlfriend, formally and almost dispassionately now. "I think about you and the baby all the time. Love you. Love you too. You know that. Bye, babe."

"It wasn't—you didn't have to hurry so much," Jimmy said.

"That's okay. Made me kind of sad talking to her or whatever. Maybe it don't mix, home and the field. But it's been like a month, and it was driving me crazy. Not knowing about the baby."

"When's the due date?" Jimmy asked.

"Like, now. Couple days ago."

"The first one is late sometimes, right?" Jimmy said.

"No doubt," Ramos said. "Yo, you hungry?" he asked.

"I don't want macaroni and cheese right now," Jimmy said. There were no breakfast MREs, so he normally didn't eat until lunch. That might have explained all the weight he'd lost. "A little, maybe."

"Yo, I'm going to get you back for that favor. I got something special," Ramos said as they walked back to their fighting holes. Martinez and Harper were nowhere in sight. "I've been saving up some Ranger pudding, man. Let's have some." Ramos took a pound cake, a cocoa packet, and some water and mashed it up. For once there was no Marine joke about what it looked like. "Try it, man. It's good." Jimmy took the plastic spoon Ramos offered and dug into the brown slush. He took a bite.

"It actually is," Jimmy said. "It's actually the best thing I've had out here."

Ramos looked proud to have done something right. It wasn't often that he got a compliment in the field. They sat together, relishing the sweet mush, eating as slowly as they could. "You really try to run away?" Ramos asked.

"I got a little claustrophobic," Jimmy said.

"If I were a civilian, I wouldn't be out here, son," Ramos said. "I mean, somebody got to do this, but—"

"I don't know. Does anybody really have to do this?" Jimmy said.

"You ever get beat up in high school?" Ramos asked.

He thought back ten years. Traumas at the time, they hardly felt like a big deal now. "I had a few wedgies. My shoe got thrown in the toilet once."

"I mean attacked, Jimmy. Way I see it, someone attacks you, you got to stand up to them. Otherwise they keep coming at you." There was raw, recent hurt in his voice. He hadn't just joined the Marines for a job. "Even if you going to get beat up, you got to show them it ain't gonna be easy. You got to teach them that they going to hurt when it's over too."

"Uh-huh," Jimmy said noncommittally.

"We getting these al-Qaedas and shit," Ramos said. "For what they did."

"I thought we were after Saddam Hussein," Jimmy said. For once he thought he was right. Bin Laden was in Pakistan or Afghanistan or something.

"Hussein, bin Laden," Ramos grinned. "Blood brothers. Maybe even the same guy."

"Like Doctor Evil and Austin Powers?" Jimmy asked.

"Something like that," Ramos said. "Brothers from another mother."

"Harper says—" Jimmy began.

"Man, you don't have to listen to everything he says," Ramos said. "He may read, but he's got his own set of problems."

"Like how?" Jimmy said.

"He's all squared away as a Marine. It's just his other shit he's not so good at," Ramos said. "He made it to officers' candidate school. Could have been a lieutenant. Ended up with four days of UA in Las Vegas."

"UA?" Jimmy asked.

"Unaccounted absence, man. He didn't come back. They threw him out the school. Knocked him down a stripe. He left all his money on the craps tables. That's how he lost his truck and ended up stuck for good with us broke-ass, no-account enlisted bitches."

"I can't believe he did that," Jimmy said.

"Way I hear it, he had three and a half years of college. There's something... I don't know," Ramos said.

"He's holding himself back?" Jimmy said.

"A lot of guys need the Corps more than the Corps needs them," the private said. "It makes them right. Tells them what to do. When to do it. I think Sergeant would be like a homeless guy if he didn't have to do exactly what they said."

"Crazy," Jimmy said, pondering the distant sergeant. "But at least he looks out for us. If not himself."

"No doubt," Ramos said again. "Absolutely no doubt."

They ate the rest of the Ranger pudding in silence. "You're closer to the finish now than the start," Harper had told him. Had he heard that from a college counselor as he walked out with a semester to go? It sounded like Harper knew how it felt to sit in a hotel room, penniless, his career in tatters, shades drawn to keep out the bright desert light. Vegas or Kuwait City, it made no difference. What mattered was getting back on the road.

CHAPTER 23

THE EBAY ONLINE STORE FELT LIKE A STRANGE PLACE TO BE, EVEN virtually, while sitting in a self-dug hole in Iraq. The bright, multi-colored logo seemed out of place amid the dull green foliage and dry brown earth, a reminder for Jimmy of where they weren't. But Ramos had a plan involving the Web site, one hatched in the laboratory of his overheated brain. He needed extra money for the baby and came up with a simple equation for success.

As Ramos explained it to Jimmy, a career counselor once told him to find a job that involved something he liked doing. The skinny teenager liked shooting guns, so he became a Marine. He loved hunting for memorabilia on eBay, spending hours trolling its pages for the perfect Korn poster or hard-to-find Japanese horror film—maybe there was a way to make some cash off of that too. Collectors paid top dollar for the rare and unusual. Ramos realized that someone would pay good money for the Iraqi military souvenirs he was collecting, the kind of people who bought Nazi army helmets and Japanese kamikaze headbands.

To test the profitability of his plan, he convinced Jimmy to let him use his computer to put one of his three bayonets up for auction. The bidding started at $100, and he had six bids within minutes. Getting kicked out of the Corps for breaking the rules wouldn't help much with the bills at home, Jimmy pointed out. Ramos explained that there were rules and then there were rules. The brass knew the rule about trophy hunting would be broken, and they were happy to overlook it. It was on the books just to show that they frowned upon it in principle.

"You need quality, not quantity, in your souvenirs," Ramos explained to Jimmy that evening, a little too loudly.

"Souvenirs?" Harper asked, head snapping around to look suspiciously at the young private.

"If the civilian wanted to take something to remember the country by," Ramos said. "For instance."

"You aren't supposed to pick up that shit, Ramos. You know that," Harper said. "If you do it, don't let me find out about it."

"If I'm going to get shot by some Iraqi, the least I should get is to keep the bullet, right?" He put the bayonet away before the sergeant could ask him to give it up.

"You can keep any bullet that hits you, Private," Harper said.

"Thank you, Sergeant."

"Don't mention it," Harper said.

"So what you getting for this?" Ramos asked Jimmy. "Being out here with us?"

"Getting?" Jimmy said.

"Yeah, like what are they paying you for this?"

"Same as they always do, I guess," Jimmy said.

"You ain't getting anything extra, man? You're tax-free at least, right?" Ramos looked stunned, far more surprised than by Jimmy's revelation that he was a gossip columnist.

"Oh, man," Martinez joined in. "You are getting royally screwed, hombre."

"You guys don't have to pay taxes?" Jimmy said.

"Not while we're out here," Harper answered, a hand gesturing toward the drab highway vista. They were making a killing, relatively speaking. Every penny they earned in the war zone was tax-free. There were bonuses, hostile-fire and imminent-danger pay, and something called save pay that he didn't understand. For men with wives and children, there were funds for family separation.

"I don't think I'm even getting overtime," Jimmy said.

"Plus we aren't spending anything," Harper pointed out.

"That's 'cause you ain't got a girl in your house, Sergeant Harper. If you had a wife or a girlfriend, you'd come home and find like a new living room set and an empty bank account," Ramos said.

"Either way, I'm going to have a fat chunk when I get home," Harper said. "Enough to get my truck back." Harper had been rummaging around in his stuff and handed Jimmy a creased photograph of a big white pickup truck with gleaming wheels.

"She's—" Jimmy didn't know what to say. It was as if it was a picture of his wife or baby, which in a sense it was. But it was still a picture of a truck. "She's beautiful," he said.

"She is a beauty," Harper said, putting the picture away. "A real beauty."

The world looked different through night-vision goggles, beyond the facts that you could see in the dark and that everything was green. It wasn't as grainy as Jimmy had expected, but everything seemed flattened. There was little perspective. The cumulative effect was otherworldly. Without them, he could see next to nothing. With them, he could see a hundred yards down the road to an abandoned, half-built highway overpass. The Iraqis had driven several thick piles into the ground to support a throughway that they never built. It was a vanishing regime's Stonehenge.

"It's kind of peaceful," Jimmy said.

"Yeah, I guess," Ramos said. He was down again. Either he

was manic about his souvenirs or he looked tired and depressed. He had no gear in between. But at least he was honest with Jimmy now. Ramos had given up on his earlier Satanic babbling and his invented criminal background. He talked about school, being the smallest kid on the football team, the unfashionable hand-me-downs he had to wear, and how he'd dreamed of being hard, like the baddest kids in town. He talked about death, and mostly one death in particular. "You know how I know I really killed that guy?"

"No," Jimmy said.

"It wasn't like he just fell," Ramos said. "His head exploded. I could see it in my scope."

"Maybe it was just blood," Jimmy said. "You nicked him and a lot of blood came out."

"I don't think it was wrong or anything. But part of me wishes I hadn't done it. Or had to do it."

"You're a Marine," Jimmy said, as if that cloaked him in emotional Kevlar. "It's your job."

"Yeah, yeah. I know," Ramos said. "But it still feels weird. I dream about him. Or the guy I pretend he might have been. This is stupid, but I mean . . . A guy who lives in one of these houses we search. A guy with a baby. I don't want to dream about him."

The president kept saying America's quarrel was with Saddam and his sons, not the Iraqi people. Where did that leave Ramos? He wasn't taught to hate the Iraqis. He wasn't fighting to defend his home and family. The American military was expected to win easily and convincingly, but somehow inflict as little damage as possible. The whole campaign left them little to celebrate other than a job completed. The Yankees wouldn't hoot and holler after mopping up a team of Little Leaguers. They would just feel big and brutal and a little uncomfortable in their coats of muscle and sinew.

Jimmy thought they needed a new name for whatever it was they were doing in Iraq. War just didn't cover it. War was worldwide violence like the two biggest mistakes of the last century, mechanical death by the thousands at the Somme or shorelines stained red along the chain of Pacific islands. It was Europe in flames or America cleaved in half over slavery, not a march on a wheezing country's capital. It needed a different name, something without the phoniness of liberation or the taint of pacification. Anything to help Ramos sleep.

Overhead a kestrel wheeled in the clear blue sky. Jimmy found himself charmed at the sight of the little hawk hovering overhead, its checkerboard wings holding it up in a headwind. He was still staring up at it when he stumbled. He lost his balance, felt the lurch in his stomach, the jerk of fear that comes from losing control, even for a moment.

The guffaws were right beside him. Looking around, he saw three Marines, one with his legs outstretched and a sly smile on his face. "See-vilian," the Marine, a lance corporal, said. "One of them medias walking around." Jimmy said nothing. He stared at the Marine, at his comrades. He was no longer afraid of the haircuts or the muscles or the guns. It was no longer exotic. He didn't need the ribbing. Jimmy was pissed. "Aren't you one of those reporters?"

"Ree-porter," said the tripping Marine's buddy. "What kind of reporter are you?"

Jimmy stared down at the ground, seeing only the desert combat boot on the foot that had tripped him. They weren't from his company. At least he was pretty sure he would have recognized them. "Boot," Jimmy said. "Bill Boot. *National Geographic.*"

"*National Geographic,*" the first Marine said, laughing harder than ever. "With the droopy brown African titties."

"That is what we are best known for. Our area of expertise," Jimmy said.

"What the fuck is the *National Gee* doing here? Shouldn't you be taking a picture of a penguin or some shit?" This must have been a successful joke by their standards, because the Marine who said it received a high five.

"You've hit the general area of my interest, *id est,* the animal kingdom, but of a different class," Jimmy said. "You must hear about it. Perhaps I might even persuade you to join me in my hunt."

"I like hunting," one of the Marines said. "What are we hunting?"

"Scorpions," Jimmy announced. "Very rare scorpions."

"I've killed me a few scorpions already, that's for sure."

"These are no ordinary scorpions," Jimmy began. "The lobstrous scorpion"—it was the best he could do, picturing the scorpion's little claws—"was merely speculated upon until we received a few samples from a colleague at the Baghdad Museum of Natural History. He had been nearing an end to his research when we ceased to hear from him. We feared the worst, but the waiting, the waiting to prove the existence of a new species . . . well . . . that was particularly excruciating."

"Is there a reward?" one Marine asked.

"I suppose some reward, some small amount . . ." Jimmy said.

"How much?" his friend pressed him.

"Perhaps five hundred dollars," Jimmy suggested.

"Fuck yeah, Bill. We'll find your bug," one of them said.

"Well, what do they look like?" said another.

"They are very hard to see, just a quarter of an inch long fully grown, with brown and black markings on their backs. The stinger is yellow," Jimmy said.

"Yellow," the Marine repeated.

"The poison of the Iraqi miniature scorpion is roughly three hundred times more potent than that of a normal scorpion," Jimmy said, wondering if there was such a thing as a normal scorpion.

"Three hundred times more deadly?" the quietest of the three Marines asked.

"More potent," Jimmy corrected. "Deadliness is determined by a range of factors, children and the elderly being most susceptible."

"Oh, so we're okay."

"From a normal scorpion, of course," Jimmy agreed, looking away as if he had something to hide.

"And a lobster?"

"Unusually potent," Jimmy said. "Rather strange, in fact. The tests, the tests run back in our laboratories"—he marveled that they hadn't noticed his steady progression from writer to scientist—"suggest that unlike an average scorpion, even a small dose of this poison would kill a large Arabian horse or a smallish hippopotamus." He watched their eyes widen. It was all he could do not to laugh. He wished he had brought a tape recorder. "A smallish normal hippopotamus, as opposed to a pygmy hippo." Jimmy had loved the zoo as a child, and rarely had it stood him in better stead.

"And a human?"

"No question," Jimmy said. "No question. Any human. With just the littlest prick," he said, clawing the air with a curled finger, pointing at his initial tormentor. The Marines leaned back several inches as if his fingernail were the stinger in question. "Or several pricks," he added, looking at the Marines philosophically.

"Are you sure?"

"No, no," Jimmy laughed. "A great deal is required to establish certainty in science. I can be sure of hardly anything. The poison was so powerful, and so deadly and so . . . so magnificent that I wondered if it was perhaps a synthesized practical joke on the part of my colleague." They nodded vigorously, a practical joke. "Yet it seems unlikely that the regime would silence a scientist in the process of tricking American scientists. Your military intelligence suggests the only reason to do that would be if work were under way to weaponize the poison."

"Weaponize?" a Marine repeated. They were all looking warily at the ground.

"That's just a pet hypothesis of my own," Jimmy said. "Very unlikely. I'm sure you're perfectly safe."

"Where would we want to be looking for these things?" the Marine who had tripped him asked.

"The normal places," Jimmy said. "Bedrolls, boots. They like warm, dark places. If you're sitting or lying down, they might crawl up a pant leg," Jimmy said, "or into a T-shirt. Most fatalities, the stings originated in the armpit or the groin area." He observed unconscious tugging or scratching of the crotch by all three Marines. "But they are so small that I don't think you would feel them on you. There's little hope that you'll see one. It's more likely I'd find one after . . ."

"After what?"

"Nothing," Jimmy said. "I meant—"

"After they kill us? Don't you mean?"

"No," Jimmy said. "Of course not. Absolutely—think nothing of it. I meant after the war, when I can set up a proper study. That's all. Nothing at all to worry about."

"Nothing—" one said.

"—to worry about," concluded another.

"Nothing at all," Jimmy said, a rotten grin beginning to tug at his face. "I wish you gentlemen a pleasant day. I have work to do if I'm going to be ready to collect samples as we get closer to Baghdad. Toodle-oo." He stomped and stumbled away, staring, bending down to poke at rocks, all along aware that the Marines were watching, frightened by the biggest cream puff in the field. He felt a little evil, a little sadistic, and kind of good.

CHAPTER 24

THREE GRUNTS GATHERED AROUND JIMMY'S LAPTOP. THE SAT-PHONE connection was painfully slow on most normal Web pages, such as the Yahoo! e-mail account Jimmy had set up for Marine mail, but it greased the skids for some of his tougher interviews. The recon Marines would not have sat still even for this brief interview without the promise of sending e-mails home.

"What I'm trying to get out of you," he told the group, "is a better idea of what it's like to be in the lead element. I'm in the back most of the time. What's it like up front?"

"Is it sending?" one of the Marines asked.

"It's a little slow, Todd," Jimmy reminded him. "We're in the desert, not an Internet café. So tell me. You guys are the point of the battalion. At any given moment, you could get shot at. What's it like?"

"It's cool, I guess," said another Marine.

"I need a little better than cool, guys. This is costing like four bucks a minute," Jimmy said, with no idea what it cost but with absolute certainty that he wasn't paying for it. "A deal's a deal. You give me a good story, and I hook you up with some messages home."

"Okay, well, like, we do live-fire exercises all the time at

Twentynine Palms. But in the back of your mind, you always know that it's fake. Here, even when you think you can relax, you're so hyped up and so ready for something to explode that you're on, like, adrenaline burnout. You're just always on."

"Yeah, I mean, every time a dog crosses the road, my heart skips twice," added the one who had remained quiet and hadn't even sent an e-mail. "First I freak out because I see something move, but it's just a dog. Then I freak out that maybe the dog got spooked by an ambush or somebody hiding up ahead."

"Does that make you trigger-happy?" Jimmy asked.

"Marines aren't trigger-happy. We're just prepared."

"Look, man," another said. "A lot of times when we return fire, there are civilians around. I don't want to shoot a kid, but I don't want to die because I'm being stupid and worrying about someone else either. At first our rules of engagement were crazy. Let guys go by with guns because maybe they'd capitulated. Then they light you up when your back's turned? What the fuck pencil-dick civilian motherfucker came up with that?"

"Yeah, or down the line they set up an ambush. You let 'em go and another Marine dies," said the one waiting for his message to go through. The other two nodded solemnly.

"Is that your worst fear?" Jimmy asked.

"No, man. Green on green."

"Fratricide."

"Your message sent," Jimmy said. "And Zucker got one back from his mom. You want to read it?"

"Shit, yeah," Zucker said, his grin indicating that thoughts of fratricide and rules of engagement had vanished as he opened his first message from home in weeks.

It was Tim's idea to set up the Marine e-mail account, and it had paid off. He was even more useful when it came to helping Jimmy shape a story out of hours of disorder. Unlike Ellison, who seemed to take it for granted that Jimmy understood the kinds of articles he should have been writing, Tim related—translated almost—Jimmy's past experience to what he needed to report from Iraq. Jimmy patterned a maintenance piece after a five-year-old story he had written on the gaffers and best boys behind the scenes on a film set. Then he explained the backstage importance of logistics in the war machine.

He spent a day in an amphibious assault vehicle, crafting "One More Sardine in the Can," his opus on overlapping legs and cramped shoulders for the fifteen men in the back. This was based on an article about spending an entire night on the wrong side of the velvet rope. Jimmy also realized that it really had been a privilege to ride in a Humvee with his own seat. What he thought was a reeking container designed to catch every smell he and his three companions could generate became a source of nostalgia as he steeped in the juices of the Marines in the AAV.

At a suspicious factory that turned out to be an overlooked military installation, he took notes as the Jarheads stormed it in formation, and again as they walked out, carrying flags and AK-47s and other looted items. Jimmy also recorded it for posterity when the lieutenant colonel in charge of the battalion made them pile up all the goods in a stack and leave them. He didn't specifically write down how Ramos had winked at him and flashed the butt of an Iraqi pistol stuffed in his pants. He thought an oblique reference to the fact that some souvenirs weren't found by the officers was sufficient for his article.

"After the CNN debacle," Tim wrote in an e-mail, "I'm not sure your job can be saved. But if you keep writing decent articles, you might at least be able to find a new one." It was the closest he had come to a compliment on Jimmy's work since before he left the office to perform surveillance at Nobu. Not exactly an inspiration, but it kept him working.

Jimmy walked through the rows and rows of sleeping Marines, their fighting holes arrayed like an open-air graveyard. Jimmy had spent the night out at the wire, the roadblock set up at the front, guarded by the big M1 tanks and infantry sentries to protect against head-on assaults. It was chilling to hear the men talk about shooting civilians at the checkpoint. They fired warning shots, of course, but the Marines expressed real doubts that a sudden burst of gunfire on a dark highway would encourage anyone to stop. They thought it had the opposite effect, encouraging them to drive faster. The Marines were unable to differentiate between suicide bombers and families on their way home, so both got strafed if they came too close.

Lieutenant Katzenbach sat alone, as usual, in the empty no-man's-land between two infantry companies. He had an AK-47 in his hands. He stared down the barrel into the distance for a good minute before finally noticing that Jimmy was there.

"You're up early," the lieutenant said, lowering the rifle.

"Late," Jimmy answered, seeing the white line of dawn reaching up to turn the night into day. "I was with the wire sentries all night."

"Late, then." Katzenbach placed the gun back in his lap. He seemed exhausted but wired. They had all lost weight, but Katzenbach more than the others. Instead of looking fit, he appeared gaunt, sucked dry. He seemed sad and empty. However lonely he normally was, it must have been far worse in the field. Jimmy thought he might cheer him up.

"How about calling your wife?" Jimmy said, reaching for the phone in one of the big pouches on his chem suit.

"What's that?" Katzenbach asked.

"I thought you might want to give your wife a call," Jimmy said, pulling the phone free and handing it to Katzenbach.

"What are you implying?" he said, slapping the phone. It fell from Jimmy's hand and landed on the ground. His look was savage.

"Nothing, I—sometimes the guys like to call home," Jimmy said, bending down to pick up the phone. The wife, the rumors of infidelity, it came back to him too late. "I didn't mean—"

"It's—it's against the rules," Katzenbach said quietly, as if he could barely control himself. He looked down at the rifle in his hands. First Jimmy watched him slide back the bolt. Then Katzenbach removed the clip and whacked it against his knee. He wasn't stroking the weapon lasciviously. His movements were mechanical and automatic. "The men can't call home. Don't you respect any of our rules? Rules I'm charged with enforcing?"

"I do. I try to. So where'd you get the AK-47?" Jimmy asked, pointing at the gun, looking for any way to change the subject.

"I have an Israeli version at home, but it's not the same as a real one," Katzenbach continued in the quiet, distant voice. "It's not really a 47. There aren't very many AK-47s. Most of the guns we call 47s are really AKMs. They're modernized versions of the original. It's the most produced weapon in history. Maybe a hundred million of these things in Afghanistan, China, Angola." He thrust the rifle butt into its braced position against his shoulder with drill-instructor crispness. It was pointed over Jimmy's right shoulder, but close enough that it made him nervous.

"Wow," Jimmy said. He knew it was a Russian design, but the curved clip had the cruel bow of Arabian swords and daggers, dangerous like a sick grin. Katzenbach wore a sick grin.

"These have been hunting American soldiers and Marines for decades," Katzenbach said. "It's on the flag in Mozambique. The flag. Did you know there are kids running around there named Kalash? Named after the gun."

"You're kidding, right?" Jimmy asked. He didn't think it was a very good imitation of engaged conversation, but felt like he had to say something.

"No, I read it somewhere," Katzenbach said, raising his head up a couple of inches from the sights and letting the barrel drop a little. He sounded like a diner patron making easy conversation with his neighbor at the counter now. The queer suddenness of his dissociation was a shock. "Schoolkids in the Soviet Union could break them down blindfolded. All of them. Every schoolkid."

"Yeah," Jimmy agreed. Katzenbach seemed a little unbalanced. He didn't want to test him.

"One of the truly great inventions. One of the few things that works. We all know almost nothing ever fucking works." The trembling anger in his voice could not have been directed at broken appliances or crashing computer software. "It's like Eli Whitney and the cotton gin. Standardized, interchangeable parts. Almost impossible to break. Cotton gins are exactly the same today as a couple centuries ago, and the AK has hardly changed in fifty years."

"That's amazing," Jimmy mumbled.

"You know," Katzenbach continued, "Whitney ended up making guns at the end of his life." He laughed bitterly. "This fucking thing is like the bastard stepchild of Whitney and Henry Ford." He spat the word "bastard" in a way that Jimmy couldn't miss. The stories about his wife might not have been the cruel jokes that the reporter thought they were. He nodded to the lieutenant slowly and reassuringly. "Yet," Katzenbach said in a way that seemed intended to show that he had regained his composure, had switched roles again, "Mr. Kalashnikov didn't make a penny. What if Kalashnikov had worked for Henry Ford? He'd be a millionaire."

"Mm," Jimmy said. His pity wouldn't make it better. In fact, it would probably make it worse. Sorry they all know about it. Sorry she's cheating whenever you're deployed and sometimes when you're there. That might get him shot. No pity, no fear, and he'd hope the sad lieutenant hadn't lost his mind.

"He would," Katzenbach said. "He'd be a millionaire."

"Well," Jimmy said, trying a different tactic, "I'm sure he does all right in Siberian pickup bars."

"What?" Katzenbach asked.

"It's a great line. I invented the gun that's killed more people than anything since the spear," Jimmy said.

"Always kidding," Katzenbach muttered. "What the fuck? What the fuck is wrong with you?"

"Give me a break," Jimmy said, pointing at the barrel of the AK-47, which was barely two feet from his knee. "I get nervous around those things." There was a funny silence. Jimmy half expected Katzenbach to point the gun at him, to test him. He even wondered if the lieutenant was capable of killing him, a thought Jimmy brushed off as paranoid.

"Why are you even here?" Katzenbach asked, sounding exhausted.

"Didn't want to lose my job," Jimmy said.

"That's a shitty reason. McNulty at least wants to win the Pulitzer Prize again. Write his name in the history books."

"Why are you here, then?" Jimmy countered.

"I'm a Marine," Katzenbach answered. "It's my job."

"Then why are you a Marine?" Jimmy continued through a tight jaw.

"My dad was a Marine," Katzenbach said. His eyes narrowed, and Jimmy guessed that his father was another delicate subject. He would never ask if the man had been abusive or strict, killed in Vietnam or a decorated hero his son couldn't live up to. Enough was expressed through the explosive crack of air in the first *d* of the word *dad*.

"Your dad," Jimmy repeated.

"Drag it through the mud. Shoot it. Don't even have to clean it first." Katzenbach was talking about the AK-47 again, droning on in a monotone. "They roll and roll around the world. This one might've killed people in Rwanda or Chechnya. Might have been in Cambodia. I don't know exactly what it is, so many knockoffs, Bulgarian, South African, Indian." He couldn't mask his pain with this litany of facts, explanations, or even acting out. "It's been around the block, and it's still there. Bag of rice here, bag of corn there. A couple twenty-dollar bills at a black market in Syria, and it's on the road again. It travels and kills. Kills and travels."

"Good night, Lieutenant Katzenbach," Jimmy said.

"Some countries have more of these than they've got phones," Katzenbach said to himself as Jimmy shuffled past him. "This is the enemy. The idiot gun. No training necessary. We have the big guns, but it takes nothing to bring a couple of these out, kill my men as they walk the streets, keep the peace."

"Or good morning," Jimmy added. He walked back toward his crew, scooted beneath the Humvee, and tried to go to sleep, expecting no more than a half hour of rest before he was woken up and pushed back into the car. It suddenly seemed like a luxury not having a girlfriend or wife back home. The exhaustion, the irritation, the stress, the fear, the loneliness, and the rage made them all more sensitive. It must have been so much harder to wonder what was happening there in your house, imagining a faithless wife whether it was true or not.

Jimmy didn't have to torment himself. His home was frozen and inanimate, the only changes a slight gathering of dust and the dead strands of the spider plant, growing more brittle as the brown desiccation chased the last remnants of green up the stems and toward the roots.

CHAPTER 25

IT GAVE THEM PAUSE WHEN THEY SAW THE ARM. FIGURATIVELY, IN the sense that it was something to really think about, but literally it gave them pause in that each vehicle in the convoy slowed down as it passed the arm.

The drivers let up on their accelerators as they stared, and every passenger turned around to watch it recede. Dead bodies were not unusual, but the arm was something else. It was less repulsive than the dogs, which chewed away at corpses along the highway to Baghdad. They were common enough, and the unofficial rule appeared to be that it was open season on any dog mangling a dead Iraqi. The sound of a single rifle crack usually meant that a Marine had picked off a stray.

A few Marines had seen the dog, its head buried deep inside the otherwise intact cow with its legs sticking straight up like the four points of an upturned bar stool at closing time. It dove through the cow's asshole, as no Marine tired of telling, to eat out its intestines. All swore it was a story so disgusting it would never be repeated at home, but it was told with such zest that it seemed impossible that unwitting acquaintances wouldn't be treated to the story of that dog for years to come.

The arm inspired a quieter, far less grotesque reaction. Jimmy heard the simple question "Did you see the arm?" over and over again. There was no body nearby, no pool of blood, no sign of where it had come from. Perhaps it had been dragged to the side of the road by one of the dogs, which, shot by a Marine at the front of the convoy, had limped away to die. But what was left was an arm, sleeveless, slightly crooked, severed high above the elbow, reddish flesh and a disc of bone still visible.

Somehow the arm inspired more thought than a clothed, dead man lying on the street, gave its owner more life as Jimmy imagined the hand grasping the top on a jar of honey or the whole thing sneaking around a girl's shoulder in a movie theater. He thought often about the arm and its owner and the fact that he would never forget it no matter how far he drove or flew from it.

They passed many signs of finished violence while participating in few skirmishes themselves, which was fine with Jimmy. Life in the middle felt dull to the Marines who actually wanted to "get some," shooting and being shot at with greater frequency. Like Ramos before his first kill, they believed they had the right to a little action and excitement, and the war wasn't providing enough for their liking. That some of their colleagues up front would have preferred a little less didn't enter into their thinking.

The middle of the pack carried a second-string feel. The glory hounds, as their comrades saw them, could be seen on the maps in little pins and stickers and felt-tip markings, right up front, getting the most action. There were more medals to earn that way, and maybe a fast-track promotion in the process. But Jimmy suspected it was barroom pecking order that they wanted the most, respect from their peers. So Jimmy tried not to give them the look that said, "You've lost your mind," when an interview would turn to the subject of insufficient enemy fire.

Their big chance came through the magic of blocking maneuvers, where the first groups through would fan out to set up a line perpendicular to the route of attack, allowing teams in the rear to leapfrog forward. When it all clicked and their regimental combat team was the farthest forward of any non-recon unit, they were rewarded with nothing less than a presidential palace. It was thirty miles outside Baghdad, and they were the first Marines on the scene. The other palaces they had visited were long since picked over by other Marines. Something about arriving a few days late removed most of the luster. Jimmy was ready to crank out a story when Katzenbach interceded.

"No reporters," he said, with a hand on Jimmy's chest. His fearful recoil seemed to please Katzenbach. There was a cruel twist to his smile. He had shown no sign of a cruel streak when Jimmy met him.

"Lieutenant, this is grade-A material. This is why I'm here," Jimmy said. The redecorating process was already under way. The epic painting of Saddam with a rifle raised in the air above him featured breasts and panties in a more representational style than the hyperrealist intent of the original artist. How they had managed to climb up there and deface it so quickly was beyond him, but they had. Who saved spray paint for two months in the desert just to feminize a picture of a dictator? He knew the answer was Marines.

"We're searching the facility and you can't go in. Sergeant," Katzenbach said to the highest-ranking of the three guards at the entrance, "remember him." Katzenbach grabbed Jimmy roughly by the jacket of his one-of-a-kind tan chem suit. "If I see that he's gotten in, I'm holding you accountable."

"Yes, sir," the guard said, looking Jimmy up and down. The reporter stood there for a minute before slinking back to his squad.

"What's wrong, Cronkite?" Harper asked. "Thought you were sniffing out a scoop."

"Katzenbach won't let me in. He ordered the guards to shoot me if I so much as try to set foot in there."

"Jimmy, if you could get in, would you go?" Harper asked.

"Of course," Jimmy said. There was something mischievous about the way Harper asked him, but it wasn't clear. "If they let me."

"How about if you could get in," Harper said slowly, over-enunciating each word, "but they wouldn't let you?"

"Sergeant Harper," Martinez said. "Sergeant, you wanted to stay out of trouble."

"I don't want to cause a problem, you know?" Jimmy said, thinking back to Harper's weekend in Las Vegas and his demotion. Another serious infraction might get him booted from the Corps.

"Saddam's secret palace, on the front page, man," Harper said.

"I may not be very good at this," Jimmy said slowly, tempted despite what it could mean for Harper if they were caught, "but I know they'd want a story about that."

"Excellent," Harper said, and began to poke around with his K-bar in the dirt, cutting Xs and Os for them to follow like a football coach. When ordered, Ramos stripped off his pants with equal enthusiasm.

Harper and Martinez moseyed to different ends of the perimeter and screamed, "Gas! Gas! Gas!" In no time, as their training dictated, every Marine within earshot was screaming it too. The instigators sailed anonymously back to their Humvee in a sea of gas masks. No one took it very seriously, as there were false alarms all the time, but it usually took twenty minutes to sound the all-clear.

The guards didn't look like they were making much of an effort to protect the entrance as Marines streamed in and out. If they'd been paying close attention, they would have noticed that Ramos's green trousers didn't reach the tops of Jimmy's rubber galoshes, or even that his galoshes were a different model from the ones all the Marines were wearing. Since they were looking for a civilian in a tan chem suit amid the sea of green, they didn't even glance up at Jimmy as he strolled by with Harper and Martinez.

"Wow," Jimmy said as they walked through the twenty-foot-tall doorway and into the marble hall. The pillars in the entryway were as big around as oak trees. He'd left his notebook behind but was trying hard to remember every detail. There were no lights in the palace, but gaping holes from the aerial bombardment poured harsh sunlight into the corridors. Shattered chandeliers had crashed down from ornate ceilings while oil landscapes in heavy wooden frames somehow managed to cling to the walls. Gold faucets in the bathroom were obvious vulgar touches, but the gilded bases of the toilet, where hair and stray drops of urine usually gathered, were stubbornly decadent.

"They've already pulled the bodies out," Harper said. "You missed that."

"I think I'll be okay without them," Jimmy assured him. He'd seen bodies, but either moving past and at a distance or the burned-out corpses that had met a sudden end from a Cobra or high-flying jet. They didn't seem human with their skin like kindled black newspaper in a fireplace, ready to float away with the slightest gust of wind. Those little Pompeiis were terrible enough. He would certainly prefer to avoid the fresh ones that still looked alive. The memory of the arm alone was more than he needed, he thought.

In silence they paced the interior of the complex. There was a storage room filled with hundreds of primitive chem-bio suits and the atropine kits that were supposed to save the Iraqis that used them from nerve-gas exposure. Jimmy picked up one of the kits. It was tin, like an old box of bandages, with Arabic script down the side. He thought Ramos might like to have one for his enterprise and held on to it. In another room they found giant fifty-gallon stainless steel vats on a range.

"Anthrax?" he gasped. The three of them peered inside.

"Lunch," Harper said, as they looked at a cold stew, red with lumps that might have been potatoes.

They found cells, some completely unfurnished, others with single chairs. Sometimes they were metal, but other times they were made out of wood stained nearly black. "Torture," Harper said. "For shock treatments."

In the central courtyard, a bright blue swimming pool was surrounded by AK-47s, shrapnel in black-licorice twists, artillery casings, and broken glass. There were half-dug fighting holes in the center, where the palace walls wouldn't collapse on them. Martinez couldn't resist pointing out that they were just about Jimmy's depth. Then he drew the line on their visit.

"You got what you need. I don't want to be a private again when we leave this base, or him either." He jerked his head toward Harper, who laughed. "Let's get going."

"Yeah. This'll be fine," Jimmy said, knowing Harper was the one who needed convincing, not him. The sergeant reluctantly followed them toward the exit.

"Just a goddamned minute," Jimmy heard. The voice was muffled by a gas mask, but it was Katzenbach. They kept walking. Jimmy wanted to go faster but knew that would give them away. "Just a goddamned minute."

He felt a hand on his shoulder. Spinning around, he was staring right through the lenses of the lieutenant's mask.

"What have you got there?" Jimmy looked down at the Iraqi atropine kit. He had picked it up and never set it down again. All it took was one stupid move to unravel three or more careers.

"Sir, I don't know, sir," Jimmy found himself shouting. He'd never stood up so straight in his life.

"You don't know?" Katzenbach said. "You just happened to be holding it?" His mask was so close to Jimmy's they almost touched. "What's the rule about souvenirs?"

"No souvenirs, sir. Leave everything for the Iraqi people, sir," Jimmy shouted, surprised at just how Marine his voice could get.

"That's right." A glimmer of hope extinguished as Jimmy heard the all-clear sounding outside. Once the masks were off, they were busted. "This is the last time I'm warning anyone. What's your name, son?"

"Private Jones, sir," Jimmy said, hoping there were several in the company.

"Jones, if I see you pick a flower ..." He let the threat trail off. "Is that understood?"

"Sir, yes, sir. No souvenirs, sir. No flowers, sir."

Katzenbach was so worked up he didn't bother to take his mask off or even take the kit from Jimmy's hand, but stomped over to the three Marines at the gate. The slippage in his self-control that one morning at dawn was now bleeding into his work hours. "Stop anyone carrying anything out of this compound, is that clear?" Katzenbach was shrill, angry.

"Yes, sir," the sergeant answered for all three of them. Katzenbach walked out of the palace in a hurry. He must have been fuming. Jimmy, Martinez, and Harper walked out too, but in the opposite direction, Jimmy still holding the tin container that had caused this outburst. As they were leaving, the sergeant called out, "Hey, you can take the masks off."

"Yeah?" Harper said, stalling as Jimmy kept walking.

"Yeah. All clear. False alarm."

"Oh. Thanks." He pulled his mask off and fell in behind his partners. Martinez began removing his. Jimmy gave it another minute.

CHAPTER 26

"HE'LL BE FINE," HARPER SAID. "HE CAUGHT IT IN THE SHOULDER. He should be okay." The group's toughness looked more fragile, and by extension more aggressive, than usual. It was an incongruous mixture of grimness and grins that suggested serious emotion behind a very thin exterior. Someone they knew, a Marine called Dawkins, had been shot.

"Lucky bastard," Ramos said.

"Oh, shut the fuck up," Martinez said.

"Bullshit," Ramos shot back. "He's on the *Comfort* by now," the young private said, referring to the Marine's hospital ship floating in the Gulf. "No more hajjis. No more sweating his balls off. No more MREs. Anybody ask if he did the war, he's got a scar and be all like, 'Yeah, I was there,'" Ramos said, pointing at his shoulder like he was talking about the coolest tattoo in the world.

"You're an idiot," Harper said, silencing Ramos. "That's too close." Jimmy had to agree, even if he didn't say so out loud. The shoulder is six inches from his heart and even closer to his neck. That was way too close.

They were busier and busier every day. The wired boredom of pushing through southern Iraq was past. Now there were house-to-house searches and demolitions of weapons caches as they solidified positions just a few miles outside Baghdad. There was disagreement among the officers over how to deal with the guerrilla attacks. Most wanted to push ahead into Baghdad, but others wanted to secure the terrain around their latest staging area before making the push into the capital.

They drove along through wheat fields and past huts made of dung, mud, and straw. When the lieutenant ordered them in, they broke down doors and tore through every possession under the Iraqi villagers' woven roofs. They rustled up farmers in black robes wearing black and white checked keffiyehs. The men lay facedown in the dusty road, bound with the uncomfortable zip cuffs Jimmy knew too well. Women in black abayas watched, sometimes weeping. It made him feel sad when he looked at them, and slightly ashamed.

"Be careful," Harper told them. "You never know who's hiding in there." They entered a house, Martinez and Ramos commando style, Jimmy at a stroll once they called all-clear. It was bare and neat, with simple wooden furniture.

"It's in here somewhere," Martinez shouted.

"What?" Jimmy asked. There was nothing in the house but the kind of bare furnishings a poor rural family could afford. "What?"

"Look under the mattress, Macho," Martinez ordered. He was knocking over objects and tossing them around in a sudden fury.

"For what, *Playboys*?" Ramos asked.

"Private," Martinez said, huffing loudly, "we have got to find that oil."

"For real?" Ramos asked.

"If we find the oil, they'll let us go home. We have to find it," Martinez shouted.

"Shit, come on. For real, Tino?" Ramos said again, beginning

LAST ONE IN 213

to search more vigorously. Martinez laughed loudly at the little private.

"Yeah, *muchacho*, there's oil everywhere. Fifty barrels secures you a week-long leave. One thousand barrels earns you a ticket home." He laughed some more and sat down on a wooden chair that looked ready to snap in two under the weight of the stocky Marine in his bulletproof vest and field gear. "Ten million barrels, and we'll liberate your skinny ass, too."

"Knock, knock," Harper said, appearing at the door frame. Martinez stood up abruptly. "No WMDs?" he asked.

"No, Sergeant Harper," Martinez said, standing up at attention.

"How many guns?" he asked.

"Not so much as a hunting rifle, Sergeant."

"That always makes me more nervous," Harper said, glancing around the room. Drawers were emptied onto the floor, pans knocked askew. "This place is a wreck. Clean it up a little," he added.

"Sergeant?" Ramos asked.

"Clean it up. We're supposed to be liberators, not invaders. I, for one, would like to salvage a little goodwill from the Iraqi people," Harper announced. They began putting clothes back. Ramos began to arrange the thin blankets on the bed.

"Join the Marines," he said. "Travel to foreign lands and make the hajjis' beds."

"The little maid. Now you're getting in touch with your Latino roots," Martinez said.

"Fuck you, man."

"Look at the little Mexican," Martinez teased. "Your mom work in a Ramada, Macho?"

"I said, fuck you."

They left the hut and joined the rest of the company on the

outskirts of the village. It was the blazing hour of afternoon when stores back in Kuwait City closed for their midday break. As they moved close to Baghdad, the eucalyptus trees and mud huts gave way to apartment buildings, mixed with industrial parks. Jimmy wished he spoke Arabic as he called out questions to weeping women holding pictures of husbands, sons, and fathers, shoes and robes dusty from walking the streets looking for them.

He bent down to fiddle with the dog tag threaded through the laces on one of his boots. He saw Ramos stuffing something into his rucksack. "What you got there, private?" Jimmy asked.

"Sh. Quiet, man. It's silver from the mayor's house. See, it's got crazy lions on it and shit," Ramos said.

"Wow."

"There were stone lions outside and this giant picture of Saddam, man. They'd be worth a ton, but I couldn't get them back to the States. No way."

"Put the silver away before the lieutenant makes you take it back," Jimmy told him. Ramos had a newborn daughter at home now, and he calculated over and over again what he could buy for her with his haul. If the private got caught, it wouldn't be good news for Jimmy either, considering he had half of the kid's stash in his own bags. How he'd become complicit was a step-by-step process of "hold this" and "just put this away for a second." Politeness turned quickly into aiding and abetting. Jimmy didn't know how to say no, and now his bags were full of evidence.

Iraqis came out to watch the Marines destroy an antiaircraft installation next to the local school. They offered tea to Jimmy and the Marines, who had set up their command post inside. Outside there was a pile of AK-47s waiting for disposal.

It should have been relaxing, a peaceful moment, but there was a growing certainty among the grunts that a bloody fight awaited them in Baghdad. A few of them dissected *Black Hawk Down* scenarios in hoarse whispers. It was bad form to sound too frightened, but whenever the subject of Iraqi resistance came up, everyone seemed to be thinking the same thing. The Iraqis hadn't put up much of a fight. They must have pulled back to the capital, planning to use urban guerrilla combat to bloody their invaders until they gave up.

Open terrain was one thing, but driving in that unarmored Humvee through a hostile city bristling with rifle barrels at every window seemed close to suicidal. Jimmy was less scared than he expected. He was habituated to the routine, mounting up when the Marines mounted up, pushing ahead because that was what they did, not questioning why. But if he let himself dwell on the prospect of street-to-street fighting, he could feel an edge of the old panic encroaching again.

A group of Marines placed thermites around an antiaircraft cannon hidden under the shade of a tree down the block. They lit the fuse and ran. Orange flames and a thunderous explosion marked the destruction of the heavy gun. Marines hooted. A few Iraqis applauded. A Humvee with speakers attached to the roof rolled by, spouting what Jimmy thought was meant to be soothing Arabic. "What are they saying?" he asked.

"Give us your beer and your women, and you will not be harmed," Ramos interpreted.

"They're telling them that we aren't leaving until it's safe," Harper said. "They won't help if they think we're going to abandon them like last time."

"Hajjis! You are all safe!" Ramos shouted far louder than Jimmy expected. "Your beds are made! Return to your homes!"

"Private?" Lieutenant Katzenbach said. The Marines stiffened noticeably with the executive officer's arrival.

"Sorry, Lieutenant," Ramos said.

"He gets a little excited if we give him too much sugar, sir," Martinez said.

"No, I think it's great that you guys are at least trying to show a little respect for the Iraqis," Katzenbach mused. He sat down beside Ramos, trying on his old friendly smile, ghastly on his now hollow, sunken face.

"How's that, sir?" Ramos asked nervously.

"Well, you could be calling them towel-heads or sand niggers, and instead you use the respectful 'Hajji.' "

"How's that respectful, sir?" Ramos asked again, with wide-eyed shock.

"Hajji, like the hajj. The pilgrimage to Mecca that all Muslims are supposed to make before they die," Katzenbach said. The private's response was silence. "You don't really know about the hajj, do you, Private?"

"Well, not really, sir," Ramos admitted. "But you're saying it's a nice thing to call someone, sir? Like 'sir,' sir?"

"Yes," Katzenbach said, head turning away from Ramos, a strange look of concentration on his face suddenly. "Something like that," he muttered. "Did you hear that?" Katzenbach asked Jimmy.

"Hear what?" Jimmy asked.

"Someone meowing," Katzenbach said.

"I don't think so," Jimmy said. There were dozens of Marines inside the perimeter at the schoolhouse. One of them might have punctuated an insulting story about the lieutenant with a meow, but Jimmy had not heard it.

"I did," Katzenbach said. "Who said that?" Katzenbach growled, looking around.

"Wow, sir," Ramos interrupted, trying to distract him. "God

bless those hajji bastards. God bless 'em, every one. Tell me more about this hajj."

"Who said that?" Katzenbach asked again, rising up and moving toward the schoolhouse wall, where a group of Marines lay in the shadow. He picked out one who couldn't suppress a smirk. "I'm writing you up, you hear me?"

"Sir, I...I haven't...," the Marine, a lance corporal, stuttered.

"Don't sir me," Katzenbach said, kicking dirt and pebbles onto the lance corporal's uniform like an angry baseball manager. "Be a fucking man. Say what you really think. Call me Boob Job. Or Pussy. Or whatever the fuck you say behind my back. Are you a man?"

"Sir, yes, sir," the Marine said, standing up. "Of course, sir. I—" Katzenbach shoved him against the wall before he could make it all the way up. The Marine fell back down to the ground.

"You afraid to fight like a man? Gossip and slur behind a man's back instead? You're not a man, Lance Corporal. You aren't fit to be a Marine," Katzenbach seethed. No one in the schoolyard moved, including the Marine cringing at his feet. His earlier gentleness gone, it was now apparent how big Katzenbach really was, bigger than anyone out there. Covered with grit and stubble, his upper body heaving with every breath, Katzenbach looked like the most dangerous man in the schoolyard, probably for the first time in his life. Sergeant Harper approached him slowly from behind.

"Lieutenant Katzenbach," Harper said. "Lieutenant Katzenbach, there's...you're needed in the command center, sir." He waited. Jimmy could see the lieutenant's breathing slow. "Sir?" Harper asked again.

"Sergeant?" Katzenbach said quietly.

"Command, uh, the captain," Harper said, though he had been sitting with Jimmy all along. "They're asking for you. You're supposed to come with me." Katzenbach turned and faced them. There was a look of relief in his eyes, as though he had passed through a long ordeal that was over now. He did not seem crazy or spoiling for a fight. He looked like he was ready to go to sleep.

"Lead the way," he said calmly to Harper. "Lead the way."

CHAPTER 27

AS PROMISED, THE IRAQIS HAD SET MORE OIL FIRES. THE FIRES obscured Baghdad in a curtain of black smoke, but the Marines continued to advance. Armored columns had faced heavy organized resistance, but Army tanks had smashed through to the government complexes and held the city center. The lead Marine units had entered the city from the opposite side, taking heavy fire. Jimmy's regimental combat team drove in cautiously behind them, guns at the ready, but with something of the tourist's awe nibbling at the edges of their professionalism. The resistance had slackened for the time being. They began to wonder if the war might be ending just a few weeks after it had begun.

Jimmy's eyes did not search for open vistas, captivated as he was by the scene on the other side of the highway, where a steady stream of looters went past them, some waving, some completely ignoring the invading Army a median away. A donkey cart pulled a load of computers. One man pushed a large basket on wheels with nothing but office phones inside. Two women in traditional clothing carried armloads of yellow insulating foam. Jimmy wondered what you could do with chunks of foam, but figured the order of business was to grab now, think it over later. More successful

Iraqis pushed generators and refrigerators past them on dollies. Was the dolly, Jimmy wondered, part of the loot, or one of the luckiest possessions for a Baghdadi to own on this day? The price of a wheelbarrow must have been astronomical.

"For rent," Harper said. "Palace. Unfurnished. Tigris view."

"We should buy a fridge, man," Ramos said.

"Power's out, Private," Harper reminded him.

"Man, Dawkins is sucking on ice cubes right now," Ramos continued.

"Not if he's in Pittsburgh. It's probably snowing there," Harper said. There was a pause. It was early April, less than a month since they had set out.

"Below freezing," Ramos repeated, the way a prospector said "gold" with a faraway look in his eyes. It had never sounded as good as it did just then, with the temperature up over a hundred degrees and all of them weeks past their most recent showers. "Below freezing" sounded so good, no one could say anything after that. They watched the looters' procession on the other side in silence.

Four men rolled gigantic tires, fit for bulldozers, down the street. They were the only ones smiling among the masses, unable to escape the game, the natural race that unfolded when each of them had the same ridiculous tire to move. Childlike smiles played under thick black mustaches. The Iraqis did not seem to want the green polyester Army uniforms that littered the roadsides. Black military berets polka-dotted the landscape in clusters around empty foxholes.

"The king," Martinez said, pointing out the window at a man with white hair poking from beneath his cap, white stubble on his chin. His black tuxedo clashed with the brown cap. He wore the tux, it appeared, so he would not have to carry it, because behind him he dragged an enormous red velvet curtain. It might have been one of the curtains for the state theater or the opera house, it was so large, far too large to carry. He had slung a corner over his shoulder and pulled it instead. It looked like a cape that was twenty feet long. There were no servants holding up the ends, so it scraped along over the sand and the dirt and the dust. A boy, his son or grandson perhaps, walked beside him, a brass light fixture in each hand, trailing his own little train of cords and wires, with bits of plaster still clinging to the ends. Jimmy pictured the boy in a newly sewn red-velvet suit, entering a small house with a red velvet sofa, red velvet shades, and red velvet bedspreads, poor except for the sea of red and the burnished brass light fixtures burning bright. Grandpa sat on the sofa in a tuxedo, watching soap operas on an old black-and-white television.

"Hail to the king," Harper said softly.

"Hail," Jimmy said.

"You forgot a brick," they could hear someone in the convoy yelling at the Iraqis. "Hey, you left a brick behind, you dumb fucking hajjis," the voice screamed.

"That better not be one of mine," Harper said, and no one answered. Jimmy did not recognize the voice and was not about to ask if the others did.

As they neared the city center, it became clear to him that Baghdad had little to do with the exotic Arabian Nights that the name evoked. There were few plants, some scattered date trees, and the buildings were mostly concrete slabs. The mosques they passed looked like models built from boxes, lacking the lightness of inspiration. The Marines had molted out of their chem suits and into their battle-dress uniforms, spring birds in tan shedding their winter coats of green. Blue and white signs pointed the way to the "City Centre" in British English as well as Arabic, except for when the burning oil in the trenches threw up too much black smoke to see them. The facades of important buildings were bedizened with bullet holes, messages scrawled in inside-out braille, reminding them that the fight was barely over and could start again.

They approached the downtown, and people began to fill the streets. There was yelling. Jimmy couldn't understand the words, but he felt it was unfocused, the noise of people who had been forced into silence, experimenting with volumes they had never attempted. A boy handed Ramos a plastic flower through the open window of the Humvee. "We are the champions," Ramos began to sing, and Jimmy didn't have the heart to tell him that unlike Metallica, Freddie Mercury really was gay. "No time for losers," Ramos shouted at the Iraqis as they drove past them, " 'cause we are the champions," he sang, "of the world." Harper turned like he was about to say something, saw the beaming look on the private's face, and stifled whatever comment had been brewing.

"Yo, we freed 'em," Ramos said. "They ain't even wearing masks or nothing."

"What masks?" Martinez asked.

"The ladies, Tino. The ladies ain't wearing their masks no more."

"That's Afghanistan, Private," Harper said.

"What?" Ramos asked.

"Afghanistan," Harper said. "They never wore burkas, I mean masks, here."

"Okay," Ramos said, nodding approvingly. "Okay. And that's good, right?"

"Sure, Ramos. That's good."

There was chanting and cheering, but it was isolated. The streets weren't full like they were during a ticker-tape parade after the Yankees won another Series. There were clusters of people, and it took Jimmy a second to understand where those clusters formed: at the television cameras. It was as if the Iraqis implicitly understood their roles as extras in the hit film *Iraq War II*. Off camera many milled around almost listlessly, like office workers set free on a sunny afternoon by a fire drill, going nowhere in particular.

"Thank you, Mr. Bush," a man in the crowd called.

"They love us," Ramos said.

"The Catholic women in Northern Ireland served tea and cookies to the British soldiers when they first got there," Harper said.

"He hates seeing people happy," Martinez said.

"So what now?" Ramos asked. "We going home?"

"The real fighting starts," Harper said.

"They don't look like they want to fight us," Ramos said.

"Fighting each other," Harper answered.

"The Sandies and the, uh? Sergeant?"

"The Sunnis and the Shiites, Private."

"Yeah, whatever. Well, if any ladies would like to personally thank Ramos," the private yelled, leaning out the window, "please form an orderly line. There is plenty of Ramos to go around."

"Private Ramos, hands and feet inside the vehicle," Harper shouted. It was the sharpest Jimmy had ever heard him. "This is a war. Act like it."

"This is a parade," Ramos said. For once, Jimmy wanted to side with the private. It was over.

The city opened up along the muddy Tigris River. Something like the National Mall, with a full complement of ministries and monuments, rose up before them. The only Iraqis in sight were dead. There were no people living there to drag the corpses away for burial as they did in the residential neighborhoods. At a bend in the river they followed the rest of their combat team onto the grounds of a government ministry building. Jimmy had never seen the Pentagon up close, but this was the scale he imagined, a stone box eight stories high and easily two blocks wide.

Once they passed the Abrams tanks that guarded the entrance, it came alive with American activity. The buzz of a U.S. military base overlaid the monumental vision of Saddam incongruously. They were told they could relax for a job well done, safe behind a high, thick wall. It was a destination, but a contingent one that lent Jimmy no sense of ease.

As the sun set, they could hear gunfire beginning beyond the walls. "Why ain't we fighting?" Ramos asked as he cut open an MRE with his K-bar.

"Let 'em kill each other," Martinez said. "Less work for us." Jimmy heated up a meal but ate only the peanut butter crackers. He had expected a thrilling feeling, a sense of elation at completing the journey. Instead he felt a hollow sense of uncertainty, like the Iraqis milling around in the streets. He would have to do something. Things had changed.

Jimmy established a new routine. They had a headquarters, slept in the same spots every night. Troops clustered in Hussein's palaces and ministries, taking the old regime's positions of strength and turning them into places to relax, meeting points. The lucky ones had swimming pools and stashes of contraband, like expensive Scotch. Jimmy's particular ministry just had files. Many of the same faces from Kuwait patrolled the area with notepads and cameras out.

The more Jimmy talked with his colleagues, the more he realized there were other green correspondents like him. There were kids younger than he was out there who also had never heard gunshots before they embedded. Even the older ones talked freely now about their fears. Jimmy moved easily among his colleagues, safely recognizable in the tribal mask of the combat caravan's dirt, grime, oil, and sand.

Lieutenant Katzenbach was relieved of his command for striking a subordinate. In and of itself, the shove may not have been enough to get him removed. But Matt McNulty's Sunday magazine feature about the insecure officer's journey through Iraq— the mockery he endured, his depression, his disaffection, and finally his bullying of lower-ranking Marines—did the trick. The reporter detailed the lieutenant's growing sense of anger at his own Marines and his intimate revelations of distaste for the people he was liberating.

Jimmy was glad he didn't see Katzenbach before he left. He reminded himself that this had begun long before his arrival. His effect on Katzenbach's life must have been small. But he couldn't help wondering if he might have been kinder, might have given the man the ounce of support he needed to make it through. It had been a petty decision to avoid Katzenbach, out of a desire to avoid the stench of his desperation.

He heard about it the way other people heard about it, as he dropped his helmet and peeled off his flak jacket at the end of a hot day roaming the Iraqi capital. Handcuffs weren't even involved, just a hand on Katzenbach's shoulder, a convoy ride to Baghdad International Airport—formerly Saddam International—and a flight back to Kuwait. Jimmy read about it online in McNulty's story and was left with no doubt: Matt McNulty, now living in the Palestine Hotel, was a hell of a reporter.

Doug and Woody joined their network colleagues in an office at the Palestine Hotel too, disembedding, they called it. Jimmy had the address. "Drop by the NBC Empire's world domination headquarters," Doug had said. "Always a spot on the floor for you."

But Jimmy couldn't picture leaving Harper and Ramos and Martinez to investigate the city without him. He stayed with his unit, unsure what else to do besides make the daily rounds with them. The squad's patrol route led them through blocks and blocks of rectangular apartment buildings, a triumph of function over form that drew ugliness to new heights. Children skittered over the rubble, the remains of their homes or someone else's it wasn't clear, but all rubble belonged to all children in a way.

Jimmy learned to read the signs of destruction like a naturalist on a morning constitutional. Tin roofs ripped apart by bombs looked like the jagged points of maple leaves. A hole busted cleanly through concrete left the metal support bars behind, twisted downward like the abandoned roots of a disintegrated tree. Where the bunker busters had fallen, it looked like the aftermath of a mudslide, churning masses of cookie-dough earth burbling up from where they had exploded underground.

The Marines patrolled by day but stayed inside at night. Intermittent policing meant that scores from the previous regime were settled violently at night. Neighborhood groups had begun to set up their own barricades, crude compared to what the Americans could build, just furniture, debris, and rocks, to block anyone trying to enter. The local men glared at them with Kalashnikovs in hand. The Marines in his squad waited for a game plan from their superiors, but none was forthcoming.

CHAPTER 28

"FIRST COME, FIRST SERVED," RAMOS SAID. HE WAS CATALOGING HIS collection and deciding whether scrutiny from the officers necessitated burying some of his plunder. What had begun with a few enemy shells and bayonets for fun was now beginning to look like the seeds of a proper retail outlet. Jimmy was impressed, first and foremost, with the level of organization. Posters with Saddam's face and emblazoned with Arabic script were rolled into a single tube. Flags, with different patterns but all some combination of red, black, white, and green, were neatly folded together. He had medals and insignia clinking together in a metal bandage box.

"Isn't it stealing, though?" Jimmy said glumly.

"It is not stealing," Ramos insisted in his businessman's voice, which regularly supplanted his gangster tone now. Fatherhood could change a man, Jimmy thought, even if he had never seen his baby. So could war. He wondered which was a stronger pull on Ramos right now. "Much of what you see here is the result of barter. That is a long-standing tradition, trading things that I have a lot of—like MREs—for things that they have a lot of, like shit from Iraq." Jimmy had observed before that the private could bring a lawyerly logic to bear on the question of his enterprise when called upon to defend it.

"Those are the government's MREs," Jimmy pointed out.

"Damn, if you're going to be getting picky like that, Jimmy, it's going to be hard for us to, like, engage this debate and shit." Ramos looked a little wounded. "They're burning flags, tearing up signs. It's worthless to them. Back home it isn't."

"I guess," Jimmy admitted.

"They don't need all this Saddam shit in the new Iraq. They have to look to the future, J.," Ramos said optimistically. "For my little girl, it's bringing us another future, in a place I call Baby Gap."

"The promised land," Jimmy agreed.

"For the general audience at home, it needs Saddam on it. They don't know nothing about Iraq without Saddam." He held up a watch with Saddam's face on it, off center so the hands didn't sprout indelicately from his nostrils. "On the other hand." He reached into his bag. "There are real military collectors, they want real hardware. Like this shit. Mortar sights and sniper sights. I got one of each." He pulled them from a small sack. The mortar sight looked like an old sailing tool to chart the stars, the sniper one a sleek modern spyglass.

"Wow," Jimmy said.

"Soldiers are all into weapons. So like, that shitty-ass pistol I had? I traded that for some more silverware. Here." It was wrapped in a pair of his drab underwear, the softest—and Jimmy hoped the cleanest—thing he had to protect his most valuable loot. It looked to Jimmy like any fine place setting, but there was the familiar eagle stamped into the handle, marking it as Iraqi treasure. "See, even if Iraqi stuff isn't worth anything, this is real silver, so it's always gonna be worth it."

"Real silver," Jimmy repeated. He was sweating hard even in the shade. With the electrical grid out of service, there was no air-conditioning in the rising temperatures of the Iraqi spring. Jimmy could not even imagine summer. While the constant heat was oppressive, it took second place behind the swarms of large blackflies as the most unpleasant thing about Baghdad in April.

"That's my best piece," Ramos said. "But, shit, I heard about this dude got a gold-plated pistol from a presidential palace. That'd probably put my little girl through college."

"How are you going to get it back home?" Jimmy asked.

"Some things maybe don't have to go home. You can sell to the guys coming in, the ones who missed the gold rush. Other things mail home real easy in a letter—patches, insignias, things like that. Money," he said. He had a thick sheaf of banknotes with Saddam Hussein in a suit and tie on each. "It goes in the envelope home, at U.S. postage rates. Thirty-seven cents. It's bonus time."

"This is so . . . American," Jimmy said.

"Dick Cheney getting rich. Why should Halliburton make all the cash? Halliburton didn't have to kill nobody. I did."

"I could probably help you get some stuff home," Jimmy said.

"We can talk about that when it's time to ship out," Ramos said. "But don't think I don't feel the love, Jimmy Steves." He punched Jimmy affectionately in the shoulder.

"No, I mean I might be going soon," Jimmy said. "Isn't the war over?"

"Damn," Ramos said. "It's like I'm losing a brother."

"Come on, now," Jimmy said, feeling bashful.

"And gaining a smuggler." Ramos had suckered him.

"I see how it is," Jimmy said. They both laughed, but the look in the young private's eyes was genuinely sad. Jimmy took out his laptop. Ramos began carefully ordering the Iraqi bills by denomination, an inflation-wrecked fortune shuffled through a nineteen-year-old's fingers.

Jimmy stood by a decimated block of houses, interviewing residents. The men wore Western clothes, tracksuits and sneakers or slacks and button-downs. In Baghdad there was little of the traditional dress of the hinterland. While a surprising number of Baghdadis spoke English, it was usually broken and imprecise. It frustrated Jimmy that he couldn't speak Arabic.

"Ask them when it got hit," Jimmy said to the chubby, mustached man who was acting as an impromptu translator. There was an overflow of opinions raining down in their language that must have gone well beyond the date and time. Strangers bicycling past pulled up to hear the complaints to the journalist. As always, the children were the most curious.

"One week," the volunteer interpreter said at last.

"How many dead?" Jimmy said.

"Twenty-one."

"And what have they done for shelter, shelter"—he made an upside-down V with his hands, hoping it suggested roof— "since ..." He didn't finish because of the explosion—not too far away, but not close enough to present an obvious danger to them. Jimmy started to try to ask the question again but stopped. No one seemed too worried just then. There were so many explosions. But he looked over his shoulder instead of repeating himself.

It was a small trail of smoke, campfire small. It could have been a grenade or even something trivial like a car accident and a bad gas can. Already the wind was teasing the belch of black smoke apart into diffuse strands. There was no sound, just a widening smear of gray in the blue sky.

Jimmy acted nonchalant, in the mode of the new Jimmy who wasn't afraid of explosions and gunfire. He flipped a page in his reporter's notebook for fresh scribbling. He looked up again. There wasn't a trace of the fumes from the little blast to be seen, but he couldn't stop thinking about it. They had left the Humvee around the corner, past another apartment building that had been spared by the bomb that leveled its neighbor. The explosion might have come from that direction, if he wasn't imagining it. He put the top on his pen. He put the pen and the notebook in his backpack. "I think ... I think I need to go back to my guys," he told the local interpreter. "I'm really sorry. I'll come back."

Instead the man followed a few steps behind Jimmy, and the people crowded after them, maybe because they were telling their story and they didn't want to stop or just because they were inquisitive. Jimmy broke into a run as he went back up the street. He stumbled on a loose paving stone but kept going without looking down. When he found his crew, there would be mockery to come. The new Jimmy was still yellow, still spooked by a little pop in the distance, one of the smallest explosions he'd heard. He turned the corner.

"Oh, no. Oh, no. No, no, no," he said. He wanted to sit and he wanted to run, so he stood still. He wanted to close his eyes, but he stared.

The Humvee's windshield was broken out and the passenger's side charred. Harper was slumped against the half-open door, his clothes and body nearly black, not like the Iraqis killed by air strikes but like a body, cooked, still full of flesh. Martinez sat on the ground a few steps away, blood streaming from a wound to the side of his head. Harper's entire body looked like Martinez's back.

"What happened?" Jimmy asked, inching closer to Martinez. "What happened? Are they still here? Jesus, what happened?"

"Macho. He found something. I don't know what. Might have been a grenade. Or a fragment bomb. Sergeant said put it down. Put it down. They're dead. Shit, man, they're dead." Jimmy touched Martinez's back. There were sharp things sticking out, windshield or metal or whatever hits a person when they're standing far enough away not to die with their friends but still too close.

He hadn't seen Ramos, and when he went around the side of the Humvee, he realized there wasn't much to see. It had blown up in his hand, and that hand and that arm and a lot of other things were gone. And Harper must have been sitting in the front passenger seat looking bored and surly and telling his nineteen-year-old private to stop being an asshole when it happened.

They were dead, and they looked so small. Ramos was the size of a boy, and Harper, so imposing alive, was in reality hardly bigger than Jimmy, stripped now of his air of command, his personality, his life. They were small, small and dead.

Jimmy sat down next to Martinez and folded himself up, put his head on his knees and waited. He wondered why he didn't take his shirt off and cover Martinez's back. There was no question that he should have gone looking for help. The crowd had stopped a few paces behind him. No one moved to do anything, so they waited, suspended. Jimmy didn't even know what they were waiting for.

They were waiting for Dabrowski, who had gone back to his Humvee to radio for a medevac because he was the best Marine they knew and was always doing the right thing. Then there were more Marines than they even needed and they were rough with the crowd and angry, guns drawn. They were pushing and threatening the locals. Jimmy saw one Iraqi push back and take a rifle butt to the head. He did nothing.

There was gauze and there were compresses and three docs plugging up Martinez. But he was talking to Jimmy, saying, "I was taking a leak. At the back of the truck. Harper said put it down. It isn't fair. Harper's dead and stupid little Macho's dead."

"I know," Jimmy said.

"Isn't fair," Martinez tried to continue but stopped, tears in his eyes. "Little Macho. You stupid little fucker."

"I'm sorry," Jimmy said. "I'm sorry. I'm sorry." He turned toward the Humvee, then turned quickly again and started walking away, walking past the wet spot on the road that explained why one of them was alive while the other two were dead. What was Jimmy's excuse?

If he'd known they were going to fly Martinez out, he would have waited. They took him away, and he could have been on the USNS *Comfort* in the Gulf or at Ramstein or wherever serious casualties ended up. In some hospital ward, Martinez would lie under a dripping bag of saline, trying to figure out where to draw the line between lucky and unlucky. In his daze Jimmy missed his chance to say good-bye to the only one of the three he could say good-bye to.

He couldn't stop thinking about them, not as he'd last seen them, but alive and laughing in the Humvee or lying back in the fading red desert light, talking about the first thing each of them would do when he got home. Their faces wouldn't leave him.

It was breathtaking that someone could spend weeks in a war zone and only worry about himself. It was egotism worth noting in a textbook somewhere, but he didn't know where. Jimmy was alone for the first time. Now he threw up, puked his guts out under the tires of a high-backed Humvee, more scared than he'd ever been. Fear for one is only so big, but fear for dozens or hundreds was too much. Doug and Woody could get hit on assignment. He needed to find out where Becky was, if she was okay. Their families back home must have been sick with worry. And his own family. He wanted to do something. He owed everyone so much, and there was only one option. So he wrote.

CHAPTER 29

BOTH OF ELLISON'S HANDS HURT. HE HAD POUNDED THE DOOR AND punched the wall. He had brought his palms down on the desk so hard that it sounded like a thunderclap echoing through his office. It was after kicking the bookshelf that he finally gave up, not because he broke it but because he didn't. Ellison expected a loud crack and a spray of hardcovers in all directions, chaotic destruction to reflect his stormy mood. It turned out to be an ineffectual blow. The shelf didn't budge, and Ellison felt weak, even a little pathetic.

His anger was spent, and he simply sat among his half-packed effects, feeling for the first time in his life entirely irrelevant. The biggest news story of the year continued, and he had no role to play in it.

There was a timid knock at the door, and Tim Suskind eased his head into the office. It would almost be fun to throw something at him, Ellison mused cruelly, but even if he had wanted to, his whole body felt drained after the tantrum. "I guess you heard," Suskind said.

"Yes, I did," Ellison said gamely, feeling the moment was right to play the noble, defeated general rather than the crazy old Lear.

Suskind was too fragile for Sturm und Drang. His former subordinate took a seat. Ellison noted approvingly that he was wearing a traditional blue suit, Brooks Brothers by the look of it. Perhaps it was Ellison's impending departure, but at last he felt a welling of affection for the man. Suskind may have been anxious and indecisive, but he had put himself on the side of right when the big story broke.

"Hardly seems fair," Suskind offered. "You've only had three months. No one could turn a paper around in that amount of time. But you're taking it well."

"Thanks. Our dear publisher said the experiment had failed. Circulation was down. The same man who wanted to reinvent his newspaper went yellow exactly when he needed the strength to ride it out. He said, 'A tabloid needs to be a tabloid.' "

"You still deserved better," Suskind said.

"It's no time for tears," Ellison said. "We fought the good fight and lost. Nature of the beast. I thought I might take my severance package and head upstate. Find a small paper that will let me train young reporters. Terrorize a corrupt city council. Get back to what the business really ought to be about." The very thought of some upstate cow town turned his stomach, but he had to find something. He knew the *Times* wouldn't take him back. He had swallowed his pride and asked.

"That sounds like a great idea," Suskind agreed. "After this mess."

"I'll tell you what I feel pretty good about," Ellison said, picking up three folders full of clips and dropping them in front of Suskind. He flipped through Jimmy's clips from the war. "He wrote something pretty incredible today about those boys that died," Ellison said. "I'm glad he wrote it. That was worth forty years of his old job's 'who fucked who and guess who's wearing Versace to the party.' "

"I found it deeply moving," Suskind said admiringly.

"What about you?" Ellison asked. "Back to Arts & Lifestyle, I presume."

"No," Suskind said hesitantly, his eyes cast downward. Ellison felt his temper flaring again, this time nobly, in defense of his loyal second.

"Don't tell me you've gotten mixed up in this? Christ. That chicken-shit bastard said I had to go, not that he was going to purge every decent man in the newsroom. Tim—"

"That's not exactly—" Suskind broke off. He tried again. "I still have a job at the *Herald*."

"Where have they stuck you? The copy desk? Made you a deputy in your own department?" Ellison was pleased to find that he still had a little spirit when he saw that a wrong had been committed. One last fight before he bowed out.

"Actually, right here," Suskind said.

"Where here?" Ellison asked.

"Here, here," Suskind said, pointing down with both forefingers. Ellison's brain resisted computing the gesture.

"My office?" he asked in disbelief.

"Well, *my* office." Suskind laughed awkwardly. "But take as much time as you need. I feel terrible about this, everything that's happened."

"Your office?" Ellison said.

"They wanted an internal candidate, someone with experience all over the paper."

"Metro, Arts," Ellison said. "War."

"I guess." Suskind shrugged innocently. He was just the obsequious sort that got behind you with the knife, Ellison realized.

"You should go," Ellison said.

"I just wanted you to know that—"

"You should go right now," Ellison said, picking up a glass

award statuette from the Press Club off his desk. He felt the strength coming back to his throwing arm.

"Just have Cheryl give me a call when you're out," Suskind said as he headed for the door. Ellison looked at the award in his hand. It said, "Outstanding Beat Reporting, 1982," and he realized it was more than twenty years old, and he was turning sixty himself in a year. Ellison slumped down in his chair. Where the hell was he going to go? Then he looked at Jimmy Stephens's clips spread out on the desk and took heart. If he could make a reporter out of that lightweight, Ellison thought, he ought to be able to make something of himself again, whatever that turned out to be.

CHAPTER 30

"CONGRATULATIONS, CORPORAL DABROWSKI," JIMMY SAID. "THAT new stripe looks good."

"Oh, thanks, man," Dabrowski said. He was sitting alone among the squad's sleeping bags. "Haven't seen much of you lately," the newly promoted corporal said as Jimmy sat down beside him.

"I've been hanging out at the power station, watching them try to get it going again."

"So they're actually doing something up there?" Dabrowski asked. "You can't fucking tell."

"They're trying," Jimmy said. "Not getting much done, but trying."

"Sounds pretty much like everybody these days." Dabrowski dug a clump of dip out of a fresh can. The support group had managed to set up a PX at the Oil Ministry, which was one of the easier ways to keep the Marines happy. He offered the can to Jimmy, who took a clump of his own. He stuck it under his lip expertly, thinking that if he grouped smoking and dipping together under the heading of nicotine, he'd picked up only one bad habit during the war.

"Everything's fucked up," Jimmy said, opening up the knapsack with his reporter's notebooks. He pulled them all out and began paging through them to find his most recent interviews, rubbing his fingers over the smooth, discolored surface of the once-manila covers that had been treated over the course of weeks by the oil on his hands. The previously stiff notebooks were pliable like the leather of an old bomber jacket now. His notes ran haphazardly from one pad to another as he forgot where he'd jotted down his last thought. One subject would start in the front, another in the back, then they would cross in barely legible pages where he'd written in ink on both sides.

"Shit," Dabrowski said, spitting tobacco juice away from where Jimmy sat. "What do you do if you run out?" He was holding one of Jimmy's notebooks, one that was at full capacity, with both sides of every page filled in.

"How do you say 'stationery store' in Arabic?" the reporter asked.

"Fuck if I know," Dabrowski answered. He kept looking through the notebook, and Jimmy realized it was an old one from the drive through central Iraq, filled with comments by "H," "R," and "M," which Dabrowski wouldn't need much help to figure out. "Shit," the Marine said again, shaking his head.

"Sorry, man," Jimmy said.

"No. It's cool, Jimmy. I just try not to think about them very much." Dabrowski looked down at the new stripe on the shoulder of his uniform.

"It pisses me off," Jimmy said.

"What does?"

"That stone-face shit. How the senior noncoms told you guys not to get upset, not to show any emotion about it. Fucking pisses me off. How are you supposed to keep yourself from getting emotional about your friends—about your friends dying? How can they order you how to feel?" Jimmy could tell he was choking up a little and set his face in a hard grimace that was supposed to hold back the tears. It did for the moment.

"They don't order you how to feel. They can't do that. They just tell you how to act," Dabrowski said. In the days since the explosion, Jimmy had burrowed deeper and deeper into his work, which was a busy, safe place. This was the kind of conversation he'd been trying to avoid. "A lot of things about doing this job wouldn't make sense to you. You can't do patrols if you're crying about your buddies. It sounds fucked up and fascist, but we got to wait till we get home to mourn this. We got to."

"Yeah," Jimmy said, not because it was what he felt but because it was the shortest thing he could say.

"I like what you wrote about the guys, though," Dabrowski added. "I thought it was really good. Everybody liked it."

"Mm," Jimmy grunted, his nose and cheeks twitching, a teary blur beginning to form in his eyes.

"You didn't say they were losers who blew their asses up. You didn't say they were heroes. You just said they were guys. And I thought you did them right. That's what they were like. If you'd made them sound perfect, it just would've been bullshit."

Jimmy stood up and walked away without a word. He had seen Marines do this when they needed to get it together and assumed that Dabrowski would understand. He didn't know if it was bad or good, but it was another habit he'd picked up from them. Maybe the officers were right when they told the young Marines to shut off their feelings.

He wanted to ignore the dead, but the dead defied stereotypes. One corpse would look peaceful and asleep, with hardly a scratch on it; another would twist into sick positions that announced its fatality. Nothing alive could have limbs pretzeled into such angles. Then when you had seen them all, begun to walk past them too casually, all of a sudden there were corpses that you knew. Jimmy moved quickly and purposefully toward an empty corner of the Oil Ministry's thick wall, an escaped tear already teasing his face like an itch.

The spot was right in the unobstructed glare of the sun, something they all avoided on those cloudless, hundred-degree days. Every one of them had become accomplished seekers of shade and the relative comfort it provided. The only place to be alone was out in the open where no one wanted to be. Thinking about his friends, dead and alive, Jimmy tilted his head back and let himself cry, secure in the knowledge that the harsh rays would begin to dry each tear the instant it was shed.

Jimmy tried to keep himself interested, his notes legible, as the colonel walked them through the sanitized and generalized version of the events unfolding around the country. It wasn't often that he went to the briefings, but the president's new emissary was expected in Baghdad shortly. Jimmy was curious.

That day he had dutifully begun copying the bullet points as they flashed onto the wall, Accomplishments, Operations Under Way, Goals, Planning, and The Future. Each heading came with five examples, and Jimmy had given up by Accomplishments, Bullet Number Three, "detaining suspected FREs." FRE was the latest in snappy acronyms for the people they arrested. The letters stood for Former Regime Elements. Off the record they called them dead-enders, which had a certain amount of cockiness and lacked the antiseptic residue of FRE. It couldn't have hurt that it implied the death rattle of resistance rather than the tiny wails announcing its birth.

Jimmy's eyes wandered to the thousands of tiles that had gone into the decoration of just this one room in Saddam's palace, trying to stay awake as the colonel's words swirled around him, "cordon and search operations," "destroyed enemy fighting positions," "limited air strikes." A few days earlier the president had stood on the deck of an aircraft carrier and declared the war at an end. He said "major combat operations" were now complete, though he declined to draw the line between major and minor. In an instant, however, "massive bombing campaign" fell out of fashion at the press briefings.

"Limited is the new massive," Jimmy said out loud, not meaning to, but realizing he had said it when his neighbor laughed. He tried to picture what a limited air strike looked like. Maybe it meant a small guided bomb falling from above the clouds, one that toppled only a single building. Or it might have meant merely the 4,200 rounds a minute from an A-10 Warthog's seven-barrel cannon, a few dainty Hellfire missiles from a Cobra attack helicopter. Whatever this limited air strike was, it showed a real sense of decency and restraint.

"Don't you guys go giving me a hard time," the colonel said in that joking we're-all-friends-here manner of press conferences everywhere. "There's a new sheriff coming to town tomorrow, as you're all well aware." Then he handed off the press conference to a new civilian arrival by saying, "Any questions about all of that can be addressed to Brett."

There was a rush and a clamor as the press conference ended. Reporters crowded around Brett, lobbing questions about the arriving administrator. The frenzy began to die down as they realized that Brett was not going to say anything interesting or newsworthy, that he was probably trying to break a personal record for the most ways a person can rephrase a three-sentence news release. "Did you have a question?" Brett asked Jimmy.

"Not per se," Jimmy said. "I'm just hanging out."

"I've only been here for two days, so I'm a little out of it,"

Brett said. He struck Jimmy as a friendly guy roughly his age. They shook hands, exchanged names and pleasantries.

"Where are you from?" Jimmy asked with great interest. "I mean, where did you come here from?" Brett probably didn't realize that he looked as out of place as an alien would, if aliens wore chinos, blue oxford-cloth shirts, and spanking new desert combat boots.

"I live in Washington," Brett said, "but no one's from Washington. I'm from Cincinnati originally."

"What brought you to these parts?" Jimmy asked as they passed beneath an arched entryway and into a reception area with towering ceilings and giant chandeliers three stories above them. Jimmy had seen chandeliers like that up close, on the ground in palaces that had taken hits from bunker busters. A lot of them were strung-together plastic beads instead of crystal. It was as though they were on the set of a Cecil B. DeMille dictator movie.

"I was working for Congressman Fillmore, Ohio 3, you know."

"Yeah, I know," Jimmy said, suppressing a laugh at his assumption. "Ohio 3, of course."

"And I thought, I need to earn my stripes. Get in there. This is going to look good on the résumé, as I'm sure you know."

"Mine is looking wicked sharp these days," Jimmy said.

"Anyway," Brett continued, "I'd done the campaign thing, and I've got my night law degree from GW, which is like key, you know, but I thought that rebuilding Iraq was a new challenge and a really great one."

"I'm sure the Iraqi people were thrilled to hear that you were available," Jimmy agreed, fairly sure that Brett wasn't listening. His enchantment with his own voice seemed near complete.

"So I figure, get a little seasoning before the convention."

"What convention?" Jimmy asked.

"The presidential convention," Brett said, as though it were completely self-evident. Jimmy remembered hearing the same tone in a Marine's voice when he asked about a scorpion fight.

"Isn't that ages from now, next year?" Jimmy asked.

"Yeah, I'm on the advance team," Brett said. "It takes a long time to get something like *that* up and running. A lot of moving parts to consider. The beauty of this op is that it's lean. It's good practice."

"So you're here for what—a year?" Jimmy asked.

"A year?" Brett said, rearing back. "My tour is ninety days, man, and that's going to be enough. The Iraqis don't want us here forever, which is good because we're preaching self-reliance."

"They told you that," Jimmy said. They walked through a splendid ballroom filled now with office cubicles that must have come into the city in the cargo hold of a C-130 transport plane. Uniformed support staff typed away on laptops.

The look Brett gave him said that he was at last listening to Jimmy's cutting remarks, as did the mechanical speech that began to fall from his lips. "We are assisting the people of Baghdad and Iraq. We want to provide essential services so they can lead comfortable, productive lives in a free society." Brett reached down and grabbed a liter bottle of water from one of the stacks of crates that sat in every room. "Improve, support, legitimize."

"Maybe if you got them some water too, they'd feel more legitimate," Jimmy said.

"I hear this same complaint constantly," Brett said, as if repetition invalidated it.

"For the whole twenty-four hours you've been here?" Jimmy asked. They walked through the military's expanding gym, Universal weights, treadmills, and elliptical cardio machines wedged between enormous black marble pillars.

"And back home. You guys are just so negative. We free millions of people from tyranny and oppression, and you want to bitch about the little glitches with the water and the power plants. This is all way off the record, by the way," Brett added. "I'm vulnerable. It's the jet lag."

"The water and power have been out for weeks in a lot of places. When my cable's out at home for an hour—an hour—I get mad. You must be the Buddha or something if you can live without water or electricity for two weeks and still be calm."

"It isn't the same here," Brett said. Jimmy felt dizzy. Maybe it was the pendulous motion of the soldiers' feet on the elliptical machines, but he felt like he needed to sit down.

"Who told you that?" Jimmy asked. Brett didn't answer. "I'll tell you something. Sort of like a tip, which means it's free. The natives? They're used to having power and water. Maybe you should go out and talk to a couple of them."

"We're expecting representatives to—"

"Hit the streets," Jimmy suggested. "Take the picture card. What's the cartoon drawing for democracy?" He thought for a moment. "Probably looks a bit like a mob."

"No one is claiming this is paradise yet. As the colonel said, we'll have to degrade and disrupt the anti-Iraqi forces."

"Who?" Jimmy asked.

"The anti-Iraqi forces are the real problem facing this country," Brett said, taking a hit from the water bottle.

"We are?" Jimmy said. This was a pretty radical statement; maybe Brett's jet lag was worse than either of them thought.

"They are," Brett said.

"Who?"

"The anti-Iraqi forces."

"I thought we were fighting Iraq," Jimmy said.

"We liberated Iraq," Brett corrected.

"So," Jimmy said slowly, "we're the pro-Iraqi forces, and the anti-Iraqi forces are the Iraqis."

"Exactly," Brett said. "We're mopping them up. A small group of Iraqis, loyal to Saddam Hussein, I mean." They had stopped outside, where soldiers lounged by a circular swimming pool on white deck chairs. They took turns jumping off the spring and platform diving boards. Their laughter was a good sound. It made Jimmy think of being a kid and playing Sharks and Minnows with his friends, eating terrible frozen pizza during adult swim breaks, and lifeguards whistling at them for running.

"This is going to be a spectacular place," Brett said with real conviction. "The administrator has a plan. We're going to show how an overregulated economy can become nimble, agile over-night. We are going to have a flat tax." Jimmy could not have been more stunned if Brett had slapped him with a glove and challenged him to a duel. The country was near anarchy, and Brett was work-ing on the tax code. Sanity had yielded to PowerPoint. Jimmy shut his eyes.

"Marco," he said quietly.

"What?" Brett asked.

"Marco," Jimmy said, taking a blind step backward with his hands out.

"What are you talking about?" Jimmy couldn't see him, but from the sound of his voice, Brett was confused and a little embar-rassed.

"Marco," Jimmy said sharply. "Explorer, China—"

"Polo?" Brett asked.

"Tag," Jimmy said, touching oxford cloth around the spokes-man's shoulder, "you're it."

"You've been here too long," Brett said. "Too much sun, maybe. I think you should tell your boss to get you back to the States."

Jimmy shut his eyes again. "Marco," he said. Brett didn't answer. He could hear the splashing and the joyful shouting of the soldiers in the pool. He didn't want to open them again and see the tanks and uniforms. "Marco," Jimmy repeated. He opened his eyes and saw that Brett was gone. It was time to find the driver he had hired for the day and go. He needed a drink.

CHAPTER 31

"I SAID, 'CAN YOU GET ME TO MANSOUR?' AND HE, OF COURSE, says, 'Insha'allah,' " the one with the English accent recounted, hunched over with both elbows firmly planted on the dull blue surface of the bar.

"Insha'allah," his blue-faced American companion repeated knowingly.

"What about you, mate?" he asked Jimmy. Jimmy turned to his right and looked at him. The short, round Englishman was also a soothing shade of blue. Jimmy was drunk on some kind of local gin made out of dates, a drink he seemed to take as a form of penance or medicine. He had taken it with alarming consistency for the several hours he had been there. It took him a minute to remember why the world was bathed in this dreamy blue light. He was wearing his goggles.

"Yeah, what about you?" the American followed up, tapping him on the shoulder. Hard-hitting interview, Jimmy thought. He hoped but doubted they would leave him be.

"He's mute, I tell you," the Englishman said. "Must be print. Hello, there, friend. I'm Tucker, and this is my friend Winslow."

"I'm Aquaman," Jimmy said, finding speech of greater difficulty than he had presumed before actually opening his mouth. "Leave me the fuck alone."

"Who's he supposed to be?" Tucker asked.

"Aquaman doesn't wear goggles," Winslow said.

"Doesn't he?" Tucker said.

"So what about it?" Winslow asked.

"I'd say he's a newbie who snapped," Tucker said.

"Green," Winslow agreed.

"Blue," Jimmy said. The city had overwhelmed him with its variations of yellow and brown. It was a jaundiced city. Red was the color of spilled blood. Green was the sickly wash of night-vision goggles, the dehumanizing, desensitizing color of midnight murder and stealthy porn. But this chilled-out blue, this icy blue, he could look through.

"What you need is a good story to sink your teeth into," Winslow, the one who was sitting right beside him, insisted.

"Distract you. Shake you out of that funk," his comrade agreed.

"The NIA . . . New Iraqi Army, maybe? Chalabi's folk," Winslow said.

"Portends a bright future, doesn't it?" Tucker asked. "Thought NIA stood for Not in Action."

"They're getting plenty of action," Winslow said. "They've single-handedly taken over two dozen empty mansions on the waterfront."

"You know what they said about the first missionary families that went to Hawaii," Tucker said. "They came to do good and did very well indeed."

"You talking about Halliburton or the exiles?" Winslow asked him.

"Take your pick," he said. "Why don't you write about the oil, the delicious goal of this delicious war."

"I am so tired of that," Winslow said. "If we wanted their oil, we could have bought it on the spot market."

"You're a kleptocracy, though, sort of compulsive," Tucker said.

"What you need is a can't-miss, an evergreen," Winslow suggested to Jimmy. "At home you could do Munchausen syndrome by proxy."

"Or your Angola prison rodeo," Tucker offered. "In Louisiana, not Africa."

"Well, that's not really—"

"I'm setting the stage. That's all." Winslow turned to Jimmy. "We have to have our standards. I'd say in this case you want a zoo. A zoo's a good—"

"Every war has its zoo," the Brit declared.

"Look at the old lion in Afghanistan," Winslow said in agreement.

"Ah, Massoud," Tucker sighed.

"Not him," Winslow said. "The lion in the zoo in Kabul."

"Oh," Tucker said. "He was a hungry one." Jimmy looked disdainfully at them and took a deep pull of his drink. He began standing up to leave, but fell back into his chair, uncertain whether he could manage under his own power. "You could always try the amusement park," Tucker suggested.

"You have to capture the everyday," Winslow said, "contrast the happy with the sad."

"He isn't really responding," Tucker said, referring to Jimmy. "Are you alive, boy-o?" He waved a hand in Jimmy's face, and Jimmy waved his own back, which was a weak attempt to slap it out of his sight.

"Maybe what you need to do is tackle a serious issue, to be a serious journalist," Winslow said.

"Capital *S*, capital *J*," Tucker said dismissively.

"In which case, if I were you, I would write about the Sunnis," Winslow suggested. "They are angry as hornets."

"It's true," the Brit chimed in. "I was out at al-Adhamiya, and they looked more than a tad cranky."

"I myself am a Civil War aficionado, and the scenario reminds me of the Confederacy in Reconstruction," Winslow explained. "You'll see them in pickup trucks with Republican Guard flags and 'The Baath Will Rise Again' bumper stickers. Mark my word." Jimmy heard him but was marking nothing. He stared straight ahead.

"Bartender," Tucker said, knocking on the wooden bar. "Another round."

"What are you having?" Jimmy asked.

"Local ouzo," Tucker answered.

"Arak," Winslow clarified.

"Just this once," Jimmy agreed. The bartender slid them three, straight and neat. They raised their glasses, though Jimmy's was shaking.

"To a new arak," the Brit said with a chortle.

"A new arak," they all said. They clinked glasses and threw them back.

"Well," Tucker asked Jimmy. "Are you feeling like a new man?"

"I'm a degenerate war correspondent," Jimmy said, slurring his words.

"That," Tucker replied, "is more like it." They lifted Jimmy off his stool and led him to a waiting car that sped them to the Hamra Hotel. The elevator was out, so they tramped up what felt like a dozen flights of stairs. Jimmy removed the swimming goggles and dropped them between the railings and heard the cheap plastic clatter when they reached the bottom. They burst into the hallway and came to a stop in front of a noisy door. Without so much as a knock, Tucker threw it opened and entered.

"You'll fit in fine," Winslow said. "No one here is quite right." The tobacco and marijuana hit Jimmy's nose immediately. The damp air from the packed room stroked his cheeks. The conversation roared above the music in half a dozen languages. People had paired off and were making out unabashedly on the sofa and the floor. Jimmy felt intoxicated above and beyond alcohol. He had another drink. He sang a song with Tucker and Winslow to which he did not know the words and did not care. Across the room he saw a woman with wild, curly hair and a devilish smile whose gaze did not waver when his eyes met hers, so he walked over without second-guessing himself.

"Hello. I'm Jimmy Stephens," he said, though she was in conversation with two other men at the time.

"Well, Jimmy Stephens, what can we do for you?" she asked. She had a seductively haughty English accent.

"That is a broad question," he said. "And I will reserve judgment for the time being." A man glared at him like he would have been happy to throw Jimmy out, but Jimmy could not bring himself to worry.

"So what brings you to the Hamra, Mr. Stephens?" she asked.

"I'm a low muckraker," Jimmy said. "A gossip columnist."

"How simply adorable," she said, and with the last word banished her previous two companions. "I was afraid you might try to talk to me about this dull war we've followed you into."

"No, no," Jimmy said. "Wouldn't dream of it. Is there anyone here worth gossiping about?"

"Only if your taste runs to minor television news celebrities," she answered.

"I'm used to a somewhat higher caliber of celebrity in New

York," Jimmy answered. "I'll have to find a better way to amuse myself." Somewhere in the part of his brain impervious to alcohol Jimmy knew that he was speaking shamelessly and leering at the body pressed against the moist T-shirt, the slope of her braless breasts inches from his body. He wanted her in a low and immoral way, and improbably, she seemed to be responding.

"Where would you take me in New York?" she asked him.

"A night out?"

"Precisely," she said.

"We would go to SoHo and buy you something decent to wear," he said, gesturing at her stained shirt. "Then we would wander down to TriBeCa and put ourselves in the chef's hands—*omakase* tasting menu at Nobu. And after we'd drunk hundreds of dollars of wine as if it came in screw-cap bottles, I would escort you to the nicest stall in the men's room." He thought she might slap him. Instead she asked a question.

"The nicest?" she said.

"The left one," he answered.

"Marvelous," she said and led him out of the party with an arm around his waist. She pulled him back to the stairwell, where she clutched and groped him and he responded in kind. They managed to navigate their way a few floors down, where they crashed into a door he assumed was hers. She produced a key, and they fell together into the room, past the box spring and the bed frame and onto the mattress on the floor, below any sniper's view through the window.

She climbed on top of him, put her tongue in his ear. They rolled over, and he felt her fingernails scrape his back, under his arms, and finally across his nipples. He tensed with pain, and she giggled. Her hands were licentiously indiscriminate. She had no regard for the accepted order of bases, but then again the English didn't play baseball. His thoughts were muddy and slow. He felt clumsy pawing her, but her body responded to any touch. He thought he wouldn't perform after all the liquor but found without effort that he was very wrong. She shoved him aside so she could lift herself as she pushed her pants down.

"Don't you want—" Jimmy began to ask, but she cut him off.

"Just fuck me," she said, sounding exasperated and impatient. "We can hold hands later if you want." He had played tough and ready upstairs and knew he should not disappoint by revealing himself now to be someone else. He touched her smooth thigh, and she shivered. "That's it," she said. He felt something that might have been his conscience stir and ask him to depart, but this was the first unclothed woman he had touched in months. He stayed. He ran his hand over her stomach. It felt hot. "Don't be shy," she said, pushing his hand lower. "You can do a bit better than that, can't you?"

He looked into her eyes. They were bright with a mild case of insanity. He nodded. He climbed on top of her again and fucked her more aggressively than he had any woman in his life. She yelled things like "That's it" and "Come on." But he wasn't listening closely. He was amazed at the feeling, at the doing, after all the helpless watching. He was struck by their smells in this heat, without perfume or antiperspirant. They sweated and stank in a raw, bluntly human way that said they were alive. They rubbed together in parts sticky and in parts slick. He paid attention to her volume and her motions instead of her words and knew harder was better, holding her wrists down was favored. He did not stop to analyze her inclinations as he normally would have. She got what she wanted out of it, and so did he.

They smoked harsh local cigarettes as a gray Baghdad dawn crept into the room. The mattress hid in the shadow. He stubbed his out on the carpet and reached for his pants. "There's another party tonight. Do you want to come?" she asked.

"No," he said, standing up.

"You can't. You're busy." She suggested his excuses for him. "You have to work."

"I just don't want to today," Jimmy said, pulling on his own T-shirt.

"Off to visit the lepers and the poor, are we?" she asked.

"Something like that," Jimmy said. He felt sick.

"How dull," she said, exhaling. "We could have another go first," she offered.

"No, thanks," Jimmy said.

"Right, then," she said. "Good-bye."

"Good-bye," he said, and shut the door behind him.

CHAPTER 32

JIMMY WALKED INTO THE OIL MINISTRY COMPLEX. THE GUARDS LET him through the checkpoint with a nod and no search. They knew him well. Beyond the Marines standing guard, more were resting, sleeping bags laid out all over the grounds like it was an outdoor YMCA. He headed back to his spot, not far from Dabrowski and the rest, but not that close either. He dropped his stuff and sat down. Jimmy picked up his laptop and began typing, flipping through the pages of his notebook.

"Jimmy?" said Becky, a camera hanging off each shoulder. The last he had heard, she was up in Tikrit with a helicopter squadron. He wanted to ask her what she was doing there, but his tongue felt rusted in place, stiff in his mouth. He kept typing and didn't answer her. "Jimmy, baby, I'm ringing the bell. Throwing in the towel. It's time to come out."

"We're going to be here for a long time" is all he said. It sounded stupid, dramatic. Somewhere Martinez must have felt like rolling his eyes. Jimmy wasn't doing anything ridiculous, he thought, like buying Harper's truck out of hock or trying to marry Ramos's girlfriend. He was just writing stories and talking like the sergeant.

"They tell me you aren't sleeping. Maybe it's time to stop."

"Who are they?" he asked, glancing up from the keyboard. Under the helmet and the Kevlar she looked pretty and alive. Becky moved behind him, looking down at the screen where he had been composing his latest story. She rested a hand on his shoulder.

"The war's been over for a month," she said. "The publisher wants you back."

"Still plenty to do," Jimmy said. "It's getting worse, not better."

"There are other *Herald* reporters here now," she said. Becky was using a soothing voice, as if, he thought, she worried about his stability. "You should at least take a break. A couple weeks to clear your head. I'm going back to Kuwait."

"Yeah," he said, sighing. But taking a break seemed unfair. The invasion was insulated, separate, privileged enough. The way they ate compared with the people out there. For correspondents like Jimmy there were visits to hotels for booze and even better food, and when they felt like it, a parachute back to Kuwait City. The soldiers and Marines couldn't do that, and the Iraqis certainly couldn't.

The hardest part of all would have been going home, listening to an impassioned argument about contemporary art at the L Café in Williamsburg without turning over a table and walking out as the dishes clattered on the floor. Sitting down to eat fresh vegetables every day, whenever he wanted, out of season or obscenely priced, without feeling sick about himself would have been more challenging than staying. Maybe it was stupid, self-flagellation of the lowest order, an idiotic renunciation. Hermits wore rags and lived in caves in search of meaning, people labored in leper colonies to honor their ideals. Was doing his job such a bad thing, if that was what he wanted?

Still, he knew that Becky was right. She reached over his shoulder and shut the cover to his computer. "There's nothing new to say today," she said. "They're hungry and waiting for electricity. You said that yesterday. And the same thing the day before."

"I'll say it a little different," Jimmy said, but his resistance was shaken. The hand on his shoulder felt good in a safe way. He was suddenly so drowsy. Jimmy fought it. He opened the computer and resumed typing. Two keys had stopped working, *v* and *k*. He just left the letters out and let the editors guess, typed the dead keys out of habit, and continued without notice of misspellings. He rubbed his eyes several times. The laptop battery beeped its own exhaustion, so he got up and grabbed the inverter and carried the computer over to Dabrowski's Humvee. Becky stayed where she was, watched him hook it up to the battery under the passenger seat without asking. The Marines jerked their heads in acknowledgment but had given up trying to chat with him.

"They told you to go home," Becky yelled. "The new boss is very keen on having his gossip columnist back." Dabrowski and his Marines thought that was worth a laugh. Jimmy laughed too, shaking his head.

"That isn't going to happen," Jimmy said. "I told Tim that already."

"That's up to you. I'm going home," Becky said, standing up and coming over to the vehicle. "And when I go home, that means it's really over, 'cause I don't miss shit."

"There was something I had to do," Jimmy said. He looked out past the fence at a line of Iraqis inside the compound's stone wall, waiting to talk to the occupation officials. The line was too long. They would wait all day and not get to talk to anyone. If they came back the next day, they'd be just as far back. This had become a game he was playing against himself.

"Something," he said. Jimmy looked at Becky. She looked back, nodding with a twisted smirk, encouraging and ordering him at the same time. It steadied him. He couldn't go alone, but something told him he could rest, at least for a while, if he was with her. "Maybe there wasn't."

"Come on, big guy," Becky said, putting a hand on his shoulder. "Let's go home."

"I'll take a break," he said, "but I'm coming back. I have to come back."

"You have a deal," Becky said.

It took him only a few minutes to pack. The technical equipment was all that he needed and his notebooks all that he wanted. He had lost just about everything except what was essential to the job over the last few weeks. His clothes hung loosely on his body. The khaki pants carefully tailored in Kuwait City had to be cinched around his waist with a belt he bought in a local market. Now that Becky was there, he became aware of his smell, a blend of curdled milk and moldy potatoes, for the first time in what felt like ages. She had clean clothes. She had showered in the last two months. Every swirl and line from his fingertips to his palms was distinct from the dirt ground into the skin of his hands.

There were two Huey helicopters out in the pavilion. It was sunny, and the flight crews sat in the shade of their aircraft. They wore tan jumpsuits, like astronauts or *Top Gun* pilots. There was something easygoing about their conversation, relaxed about the way they lounged around their aircraft waiting for orders.

"One time," a pilot said, "I had one coming right at me. I know it wasn't that big, but it looked enormous, seriously." They all laughed knowingly. "I've never been so scared in my entire life."

"Oh, hell," said the pilot next to him. "I had three coming at me. Didn't know which way to go." There was more laughter as the pilot opened his eyes wide in mock fear and looked around in all directions. "Thought I was finished."

"Missiles," Jimmy said. "Yeah."

"What?" the first pilot said.

"Missiles," Jimmy said again, and for lack of a more specific addition, "crazy."

"We're talking," the pilot said, "about birds."

"Birds?"

"Birds," the pilot said.

"If a big bird goes in your engine, you might as well have been hit by a missile," he heard Becky say behind him. "I'm sorry," she said, stepping beside Jimmy. "I forgot to introduce you. Guys? This is Jimmy Stephens. He's a rookie reporter with my paper. A friend of mine, but a real greenhorn." She winked at him.

"Hey, Jimmy," said the pilot who had let him know about the birds, standing up to shake his hand. "I'm Gopher. You flying with us?"

"Looks that way," Jimmy said.

"Damn, he looks beat. Don't he?" said the other pilot. "Maybe we should take him back to one of those nice hotels in Kuwait."

"That would be fine," Jimmy said. "That would be just fine." They strapped him into a seat in the back with Becky and the two door gunners, who checked the ammunition in their mounted machine guns. More and more frequently Iraqis were taking potshots at helicopters as they came and went.

The cockpit was filled with a mixture of thirty-year-old instruments and recent installations. Needles bumped and shivered on the dashboard as they had for decades, while a black-and-white monitor displayed the infrared image of the landscape and a moving map tracked their location with global positioning satellites. Once they turned up the engines, Jimmy couldn't hear over the racket of the rotor blades without his helmet's hookup to the intercom.

"Think we might see a camel?" Jimmy asked into the mouthpiece.

"How's that?" he heard the pilot ask back through his earphones.

"I been here a couple months, and I haven't seen a single goddamned camel," Jimmy said.

"We'll get you a camel," the one called Gopher said.

"Guy back there with you shot a camel," the copilot told him. Jimmy looked toward the cockpit and saw a thumb jerking at the big young guy manning one of the guns.

"Maybe I was aiming for the camel," the strapping door gunner said.

"You were aiming for the truck. The one with the big gun on the back that was shooting at us," Gopher said.

"Maybe," the young man conceded.

"We have got to stop teasing that kid," the copilot announced, " 'fore he jumps out of the aircraft." Jimmy thought of Ramos and Harper's threat about the homos in Metallica. He actually smiled. The helicopter lifted smoothly off the ground, throwing up a great billowing cloud of dust that Jimmy hoped the pilots at least could see through, since he couldn't. The aircraft hovered for an instant before skimming a few yards, then climbing a hundred feet into the sky.

"Jimmy, has that pretty little lady Becky told you about how you're a guest in the aircraft of champions, the champions I say, of the Marine Corps Spades Tournament in Pearl Harbor? She hasn't? Becky, what have you been talking to this fellow about that you forgot all the important stuff? It was last year. We had what you might call a difficult matchup in the semifinals ..."

Jimmy pulled the audio cord out of his helmet and heard nothing but the white noise of the blades beating and the gears turning overhead. He watched Baghdad recede in the distance. A few stray tracer rounds pursued them, but they were nowhere near fast enough.

ACKNOWLEDGMENTS

This book could not have been written without the unstinting assistance of Julian E. Barnes and Michael Phillips.

I would also like to thank the Marines of HMLA-267, particularly Sameer Bakhda, Josh Busby, Karl Crnkovich, Paul Gosden, and Dallas Poore. Helene Cooper, Elizabeth Farrell, Siobhan Foley, Mark Garner, Thomas Girst, Bryan Gruley, Christy Harvey, Greg Jaffe, Phil Kuntz, Brandon Lilly, Courtney Lilly, Jeff Lytle, Stephan Maus, Matty Metcalfe, Winter Miller, Arthur Phillips, Charles Ranney, David Rieff, Kit Roane, Laura Secor, Yaroslav Trofimov, Jan Wagner, and John Wilke all helped in different but significant ways.

There has been a great deal of excellent writing on the invasion of Iraq. In addition to many of those named above, the work of Tom Ricks, George Packer, and Evan Wright in particular informed and inspired my own.

I am deeply grateful for the unwavering support of my agent, Marly Rusoff. At Ecco I have been helped along by Abigail Holstein and needed all of the guidance and general brilliance that my editor, Lee Boudreaux, could offer.

From start to finish, Lauren Reynolds has been my greatest support and love.

About the author

About the book

Read on

Insights,
Interviews
& More...

Meet Nicholas Kulish

© 2007 by Sarah Shatz

Nicholas Kulish was born in Washington, D.C., in 1975 and raised in Arlington, Virginia. He graduated from Columbia College in New York with a bachelor of arts degree. He held a series of odd writing and Internet jobs in Hong Kong and New York before landing a position as a news assistant at the *Wall Street Journal*. He worked his way up to staff reporter in the paper's Washington bureau, covering everything from economics to the presidential recount in Florida following the 2000 election. In 2003, Kulish embedded with a Marine helicopter squadron during the invasion of Iraq, where he began working on *Last One In*. He left the *Journal* to take a Fulbright creative writing grant in Berlin. He now works as an editorial writer for the *New York Times*. ✒

Days of Thunder, Arabian Nights

MOST OF THE TIME BOREDOM is a mild affliction. While waiting for a war to start, it can be acutely painful, bequeathing to the mind a wide field to seed with tiny, terrible thoughts that blossom into gruesome scenarios of pain and suffering, death and dismemberment. In the run-up to the Iraq War, correspondents like me spent several weeks—in some cases months—in Kuwait City, waiting for the go-ahead to join military units. It was too much time with too little to do.

Generally the solution to this kind of boredom is near at hand, in unlimited supply and of a roughly 80-proof potency. In the Muslim emirate of Kuwait, that was decidedly not the case. Alcohol is illegal and the law is enforced well enough to stall recent arrivals (if not the wealthier Kuwaitis themselves) from enjoying a snifter or six. Black-market solutions supplied a few parties, but consistent, mind-numbing carousing was out.

One cannot overestimate the amount of time reporters will spend moaning, whining, and complaining about the absence of alcohol in a dry country. Nice dinners on expense accounts and shopping sprees for tailored desert wear do nothing to quell it. Both the quality and the quantity of complaint would be more appropriate for a lost polar expedition considering alternate sources of food as the supply of sled dogs dwindled. It was, I realized, not unlike high school. Twitchy, sober packs made up mostly of young men roved the ▶

> **One cannot overestimate the amount of time reporters will spend moaning, whining, and complaining about the absence of alcohol in a dry country.**

3

city after dark, with boundless energy and almost nowhere to direct it.

That may begin to explain why I was so excited when word of the great discovery reached me. It is hard to understand now, with New York's many diversions within easy reach, but there was definitely cheering and possibly—I have tried to block it out—jumping up and down. There was a go-kart track in Kuwait.

I learned this from my colleague Michael Phillips, the *Wall Street Journal*'s most seasoned war correspondent. He had covered conflicts in Somalia and Angola for the Associated Press before joining the Marines in Afghanistan for the *Journal*. He was so wise in the ways of warriors that I had sent a postcard back to the Washington bureau joking that he had enlisted and started sniper school.

Michael knew that the best way to cozy up to Marines was with Copenhagen dip, and he bartered his way into his own pair of night-vision goggles with it. "Want to go go-karting?" he asked as I tried them out, watching his blind eyes staring a few degrees away from where I sat in his pitch-black room at the Marriott.

"Are you kidding?" I answered, momentarily blinding myself as I flipped on the lights still wearing the goggles. "Let's go."

When we arrived there was hardly a car in the giant parking lot. My spirits fell as I assumed it must be closed, but a single kart was buzzing around the empty, tire-buffered track. Several employees rushed out to assure us that they were open for business, offering us some of the finest virgin drinks and a game of pool in their "bar" before we began to race.

"Full, every night," one of the dejected staff members explained, "until the base restriction." After a series of shootings of military personnel and contractors, trips off of U.S. military bases had been limited to necessary business, and with heavy security. I had seen a group of soldiers guarding their Humvees in the parking lot of a Kuwaiti Ace Hardware like they were in a live-fire zone. From the way they held their rifles it was clear that it could easily have become one.

The dangerous undercurrent only surfaced intermittently. At the Hilton, the hotel staff gave me an enormous room overlooking the front entrance. I was quite pleased with my luck until my friend and coworker Helene Cooper pointed out that the two-story glass windows of the lobby were right where a suicide bomber would aim his vehicle if he got past the gate. Everyone else had turned down my sweet accommodations in the name of safety. Indeed, armed Kuwaiti soldiers in black and blue camouflage, with a large-caliber mounted machine gun on their Humvee, guarded both the entrance and exit, with bomb-sniffing dogs checking every vehicle. I switched to a tiny room at the back of the hotel and was happy to get it.

But it was nothing like the unbelievable security conditions that reporters face in Iraq in 2007. They risk their lives every time they step outside to conduct an interview. In 2003, in Kuwait, you mostly felt safe. Unlike the soldiers and Marines, we could still browse records at the Virgin Megastore or eat at ▶

❝ I had seen a group of soldiers guarding their Humvees in the parking lot of a Kuwaiti Ace Hardware like they were in a live-fire zone. From the way they held their rifles it was clear that it could easily have become one. ❞

the KFC downtown with the country's South Asian guest workers.

What was stifling for the troops was a business disaster for these racing entrepreneurs and an opportunity for us. There were no lines, no waits, and no strangers to gum up our rivalries. We were free to tear up the track.

And tear it up we did. Whipping around the track in the open cars beat debating whether the anthrax vaccine would give us Gulf War Syndrome, as was rumored, or trying to install new software to make your e-mail work over a satellite-phone Internet connection. Gas drills and warnings about Scud missiles were far behind us. It was all about the thrill of the race.

During my childhood, the go-kart track was among the greatest possible birthday destinations, far ahead of Chuck E. Cheese's or the wave pool. For the impatient preteen, already lusting after car keys and the freedom they represented, go-karts felt like a brief elevation to driving sixteen-year-old, a false maturity. Those nights at the Kuwaiti race track had the opposite effect. I was experiencing a second adolescence, and had the shriveling maturity to prove it.

From the first green flag it was clear that I had a serious impediment to victory. My 230-pound body was straining the little kart's glorified lawn-mower engine. On a straightaway, pedal to the metal, Michael, a nimble marathon runner and much, much lighter, left me far behind. The employees couldn't get over the sight of me folding my six-foot-eight-inch frame into that tiny toy

> 66 The employees couldn't get over the sight of me folding my six-foot-eight-inch frame into that tiny toy car. 99

6

car. They even made me pose for pictures. They could very well be pointing at a photograph of me right now, telling stories about this singularly ridiculous sight.

I, on the other hand, wasn't laughing, and their mirth was only making me madder. As my losses mounted, it became clear that the only way to take the checkered flag was to drive more aggressively. Never before had I had a problem drawing the line between bumper cars and go-karts. The former were for ramming, the latter were not. It should have been a bad sign that lines from the Tom Cruise stock car movie *Days of Thunder* were racing through my head, specifically the words of the Robert Duvall character after Tom Cruise's car first gets hit by a competitor: "He didn't slam you. He didn't bump you. He didn't nudge you. He rubbed you. And rubbin', son, is racin'."

"Rubbin' is racin'," I thought, as I "rubbed" Michael's rear tire and sent him spinning into the rubber sidewall. I lost control for a moment but still took my first second-place finish of the night.

In the next race I floored it from the start and took the lead through brave stupidity, skidding on the edge of disaster with each reckless turn. But behind me I could hear the humming of another engine. I looked over my shoulder and confirmed what I dreaded, that Michael was charging up hard on my tail. Teeth clenched, I watched him pass me as we headed for the second-to-last turn. I took an aggressive inside line, preparing to risk it all. I was going to rub him again. Hell, I might even nudge him.

What I hadn't considered was the ▶

possibility that Michael might lose control of his kart. As I tried sneaking up beside him for a glancing side-to-side tap, he spun out and became a sitting duck, one directly in front of me that I was going way too fast to avoid.

I rammed him full speed. I lurched forward sharply but was fine, despite the sick crunch I heard, the kind of sound that tells you something's wrong. Or maybe it was the fact that the other drivers weren't whizzing past to victory but had stopped too. It was a good thing they had because Michael stumbled out of his kart and hopped two steps clutching his hip with one hand before crumpling to the skid-mark covered track.

"Jerry," I imagined having to tell our boss, "Michael can't cover the war. I, uh, you see . . . I kind of broke him." He lay very still and was obviously in a great deal of pain. I got out of my own kart and knelt down beside him. "What if he misses the war?" I wondered.

Then it dawned on me. What if he did miss the war? What if his infantry company was the one that got hit with the chemical and biological weapons that the administration had promised were waiting for us? What if he wasn't there when his squad sprung an ambush and caught waves of Iraqi bullets? Seeing Michael on the ground like that, it came home that we were all going to separate in a few days and throw our lot in with troops going into actual combat. No way to help or protect each other, no certainty that things would turn out okay. Why wouldn't I want him to miss the war?

> ❝ I rammed [Michael] full speed. I lurched forward sharply but was fine, despite the sick crunch I heard, the kind of sound that tells you something's wrong. ❞

"You . . ." Michael began to say, eyes screwed tight with pain, ". . . asshole." He smiled weakly. "You tried to kill me. Asshole."

"Hey," I said. "It's not my fault if you can't take a fast turn without spinning out." We both laughed a little, on my part mainly with relief. In that moment I was glad I hadn't seriously hurt my friend. I helped him stand up. He was still in pain, but nothing was broken.

The argument continued over Big Macs at a Kuwaiti McDonald's, just like a group of little boys after a soccer game. I boasted and joked with the rest of them, but inside, my mood was melancholy. The image of Michael falling to the ground was stuck on a loop, embellished by my imagination. The war had come to stay in my head, and no levity or entertainment could get it out. ❧

> 'You . . .' Michael began to say, eyes screwed tight with pain, '. . . asshole.' He smiled weakly. 'You tried to kill me. Asshole.'

War Through Other Eyes

THE LOCAL TELEVISION CREWS swarmed through frigid, midwinter Fort Dix, New Jersey. They were there to report on us, their miserable journalist comrades who were dodging blanks and ducking fake mortar fire on the coldest day the state had seen in five years. We were fighting frostbite to prepare for a war in the desert.

I kneeled in the snow, photographers and video cameramen orbiting around me, wondering who had done the far-too-realistic makeup for the faux thigh-bone fracture I was supposed to splint. At our tents, a *Daily Show* correspondent appeared and asked one of the local television reporters if observing the media boot camp had prepared her to cover the coverage of the war. She attempted a serious answer.

Back home, it felt almost impolite to bring up the impending conflict amid the cheerful din in a bar in Washington's Adams Morgan district. None of my friends wanted to hear about the war, and everyone grew uncomfortable when I told them how unprepared I felt to administer first aid to casualties. There was a long silence at the table until someone asked, "What happens if they start shooting at you?" I mustered up the toughest, meanest Cool-Hand-Luke face that I could and said, "I run." Everyone laughed.

I imagined what it would be like if a newspaper sent someone far less prepared than me into battle. All night we talked about films and records instead of the differences between Sunnis and Shiites. Why not send an arts and entertainment

> **We were fighting frostbite to prepare for a war in the desert.**

reporter, or even a gossip columnist? I decided to abandon the novel I was working on and start taking notes.

Soon I was sitting on a folding chair on the Kuwait Hilton's tennis courts, under palm trees tickled by the breeze off the Persian Gulf. It was a lovely day except for the fact that we were trying on our gas masks. During this exercise, one part summer camp and one part life-or-death educational seminar, each group of a dozen reporters had an army sergeant acting as mother hen, trying to remain stern and serious while also making fun of our ineptitude.

After what felt like an interminable wait, Central Command deposited each of us with our respective military units. I had a moment of pathetic clarity when I dropped my bags in a porn-strewn tent in the desert, filled with foul-mouthed Marines who looked as ready to accept me among them as gang members are enthused about initiating a kindergarten teacher.

Just before the invasion began, the Iraqis launched an unexpected missile attack. Loudspeakers shouted "Code Red" as we rushed for the bunkers, pulling on our protective gear in mid-sprint. An attractive young lady from one of the morning talk shows had been interviewing Marines, asking them to record messages for the audience back home. I witnessed a hysterical break-down for the first time in my life. In a sea of wisecracking grunts with gas masks, this poor woman was without one. She was crying and shaking and shrieking. I felt bad for her, but also thought to myself, "Jimmy Stephens, gossip columnist, reporting for duty."

As I did my level best to be professional and productive, this fictional character ▶

> **❝** I had a moment of pathetic clarity when I dropped my bags in a porn-strewn tent in the desert, filled with foul-mouthed marines who looked as ready to accept me among them as gang members are enthused about initiating a kindergarten teacher. **❞**

became an outlet as well as a filter: for my strangest and darkest thoughts, for fears I couldn't express out loud, for details that made no sense in the newspaper, and for larger questions that were above my pay grade, as they say. At each step the game was, "What would Jimmy do?"

Jimmy's experience in the war is not my own. I was embedded with Marine attack helicopters, Cobras and Hueys, flying out of a base in northern Kuwait. Jimmy's Humvee ride to Baghdad is much closer to the experience of many of my friends and colleagues who were kind enough to provide technical support in the writing of the novel. And far from being an unknown, the military was a part of my life growing up.

My father retired from the United States Army as a lieutenant colonel, after a career that ranged from commanding an armored cavalry recon platoon in Germany to defending court martial proceedings in Vietnam to government contract appeals work in Washington. His stories of war and foreign lands on the one hand and byzantine bureaucracy on the other were a constant in my youth. Growing up, I was used to calling the grocery store "the commissary" and the drug store "the PX."

I had made friends with the Marines in my squadron. Behind the cursing, swaggering Cobra helicopter pilots and oil-stained mechanics were real guys I could relate to during midnight discussions under the desert stars. I felt an understanding for all sides—Marine, ignorant outsider, serious correspondent.

> 66 My father retired from the United States Army as a lieutenant colonel. . . . His stories of war and foreign lands on the one hand and byzantine bureaucracy on the other were a constant in my youth. 99

Within days of returning to Washington
I had given notice at the *Wall Street Journal*
and begun working full-time on the book.
With reams of firsthand reporting and access
to many of the reporters who had been riding
with infantry platoons, I found an abundance
of material for what was evolving ever more
definitively into a satire. ∽

Author's Picks
Satires, War Stories, and Books on Iraq

FICTION

The Complete Works of Mark Twain

America's greatest satirist, with a keen eye for the ridiculous.

PUT OUT MORE FLAGS, SCOOP, and THE SWORD OF HONOUR TRILOGY by Evelyn Waugh

The first finds an indolent England stirring in the face of war. In *Scoop*, a nature columnist joins the company of jaded correspondents trying to cover a civil war in Africa. *The Sword of Honour* follows the misadventures of Guy Crouchback during World War II.

OUR MAN IN HAVANA and THE QUIET AMERICAN by Graham Greene

In these vintage Greene novels, a vacuum cleaner salesman in Cuba becomes a spy and idealism in Vietnam ends in disaster.

CATCH-22 by Joseph Heller

This story of World War II bomber crews could not be funnier, could not be more heartbreaking, and is as close to perfect as any novel ever written.

MORTE D'URBAN by J. F. Powers

A worldly priest, Father Urban finds himself banished by his order to a dilapidated retreat in Minnesota, in an underrated comic novel

66 [*Catch-22*] is as close to perfect as any novel ever written. 99

steeped in the pedestrian details and rivalries of men of the cloth.

NONFICTION

THE SOCCER WAR by Ryszard Kapuscinski

Kapuscinski redefines war reporting with his highly personal and utterly mesmerizing accounts of postcolonial conflicts, including a war between El Salvador and Honduras set off in part by rioting after a World Cup qualifying match.

DISPATCHES by Michael Herr

Herr relives the disjointed battleground of Vietnam as nightmare, hallucination, and confessional for the soldiers and reporters caught up in the war.

JARHEAD by Anthony Swofford

Affecting memoir of a Marine sniper who served in the Persian Gulf War.

THE ASSASSINS' GATE by George Packer

From the intellectual origins of the Iraq War to in-depth reporting on the ground after the invasion.

COBRA II by Michael R. Gordon and General Bernard E. Trainor

How the war was planned and fought, by a dogged reporter and a retired Marine Corps lieutenant general.

MAKING THE CORPS and FIASCO by Thomas E. Ricks

Follow a training platoon through boot camp on Parris Island and learn how the Marine

Author's Picks *(continued)*

Corps is a culture unto itself. A scathing history of the war from the invasion to the insurgency.